D0835789

MEANS TO AN END

John Rowan Wilson

MEANS TO AN END

DOUBLEDAY & COMPANY, INC., GARDEN CITY, NEW YORK, 1959

All of the characters in this book are fictitious, and any resemblance to actual persons, living or dead, is purely coincidental.

Copyright © 1959 by John Rowan Wilson
All Rights Reserved
Printed in the United States of America

PART I NEW YORK

PART II LONDON

PART III PARIS

PART IV NEW YORK

PART V LONDON

PART VI NEW YORK

PART I

CHAPTER I

MARSHALL GLANCED at his watch and said for the third time, "I'm afraid I have to go now." He tried to sound regretful, but the effort was wasted since in any case the girl hardly seemed to hear him. She was deeply involved in some complex and mildly slanderous theatrical anecdote of which he had long since lost the point. He wondered, as so often on similar occasions, what on earth had attracted him to her in the first place. Boredom? Loneliness? A mistaken idea that she might be interesting to talk to? In the middle of the day, fully clad, at a distance of only three or four feet, she was not even especially desirable.

He scribbled his name across the bottom of the bill and managed to move her, still talking, out of the restaurant into Fifty-third Street. There was spring in the air, fighting with the gas fumes, the grit and wastepaper, the blasts of sooty air coming up the gratings from the subways. Possibly because of the spring, possibly those two extra manhattans which had seemed justifiable under the circumstances, Marshall felt a resurgence of optimism, a vague hope that, contrary to all experience, something exciting and unusual might be waiting for him just around some corner or other. He tried to crush the feeling immediately, recognizing it as a danger sign, a prelude to some spontaneous action which he might afterward regret. It was an impulse of a similar kind which had resulted in this abominable luncheon today.

The girl looked back at him as he almost pushed her into a cab. He had been a good audience and she was sorry to lose him.

"You wouldn't like to come and watch me rehearse?"

"I'd like to very much. But I have to be somewhere——"

"Okay. Well, some other time——"

"I'll call you up," he promised. It was what you said to people you were never going to see again. He watched the taxi out of sight and began to walk the two blocks to his office.

The spring (or the manhattans) lasted him along Fifty-third Street and quite a distance down Sixth Avenue. He carried it with him, in diminished form, through the lobby of the office building, up the express elevator, past the door which said "Marshall Corporation—International Department." But as he made his way through the high-pitched voices and clattering typewriters of the outer offices, it suddenly left him, to be succeeded by a mood of thoughtful melancholy. He became conscious that he was more than usually late for the meeting.

Miss Curran, Kingham's secretary, was in her usual place, sitting on guard over the entrance to the Holy of Holies. He asked her, "Have they started?"

"They started fifteen minutes ago, Mr. Marshall." Her voice was quite devoid of expression. She was neither amused nor reproachful, she merely stated facts. She had known the company since the early days, when there was no International Department and Kingham was no more than a keen goggle-eyed salesman. She looked at Marshall with a merciless, dead-pan stare which he always found disconcerting. Was she noting the flush on his cheeks, the slightly alcoholic brightness of his eye? Was she comparing him unfavorably with his brother or his dead father? Was she sympathetic, contemptuous, envious—or perhaps simply totally uninterested? There was no means of knowing.

"I don't suppose they've really missed me," he said with an attempt at joviality. "If it's going to be anything like this morning——"

If it was going to be anything like the morning, he thought, he might as well not have turned up at all. Uneasily conscious of the discourtesy of being late, he consoled himself with the reflection that Kingham need never have called him in the first place. Occasionally, for some reason unexplainable except by sheer perversity, he would do this; men would be kept sitting, sometimes for days on end, in conferences about subjects with which they were not concerned, their presence unregarded, their opinion never asked. This morning had been taken up entirely with a report from Wilcox, the European representative, who had just flown home from London. It had been a long and complicated report and the discussion following it would be even worse. The European interests of the company were a tangled web of holding companies, distributorships, agencies, subsidiaries, and cross-licensing agreements—it was a perfect field for argument, for new angles and fresh concepts, for the throwing out of ideas. . . . The meeting might go on indefinitely.

But it was too late to go home now. Accepting the inevitable, he opened the door of the conference room and slipped into the vacant seat at the end of the table. There was not even a pause in the discussion as he entered the room; nobody so much as bothered to look around.

Now spring was no more than a memory. In the conference room there was neither time nor place nor season of the year. Poised, windowless, two hundred feet above street level, it might well have been some cavern quarried deep within the bowels of the earth. Here, night and day were one. A sickly, shadowless light was diffused through the room from a series of opaque panels on the wall. The atmosphere, ingeniously held uniform in temperature and humidity by the air-conditioning system, was curiously tasteless and soporific, a constant invitation to sleep.

On the long table there were jugs of ice water, paper cups, cigarettes, books of matches, memo pads, all discreetly labeled with the emblem of the company. Almost everybody was smoking. The voices droned on through the heavy afternoon, sometimes fluent, sometimes halting, sometimes aggressively confident, sometimes heavily deferential. Issues were raised and disposed of, problems were considered, results were analyzed, recommendations were made. Opinions rose with the cigarette smoke, to be sucked out by the fan and eventually dispersed in merciful dilution through the air of midtown Manhattan.

Marshall felt his eyelids beginning to droop. Alarmed, he wriggled in his seat, took a sip of water, and lit a cigarette. It would never do for him to fall asleep; inattention might be concealed and even under certain circumstances excused, but actual slumber . . . It had happened once before, he remembered, after a late night with some friends in the Village. He had recollections of Kingham's sharp, nasal voice making some point about the supplies of insulation material in Bolivia and then a stab of pain in his right ankle where Richardson had kicked him awake.

Kingham had said nothing. This did not mean, as Marshall well knew, that the incident had passed unnoticed or been regarded lightly. Kingham was not that kind of man. And it was well known that he took these meetings very seriously. They were his own conception, the first innovation he had made on taking over the International. "An informal get-together," he would explain, "to give the department heads a chance to kick their ideas around and really get to know each other. Nothing too formal, you understand. I head the meeting, of course, because somebody has to get the thing started. But from then on it's strictly up to the boys themselves. They can relax, bring up any subject they're interested in, shoot at each other if they want to, shoot at *me* if they want to. That particular day, nobody's the boss, and we can all take our hair down." And he would add, "It's been a most rewarding experiment."

For Kingham himself it was, perhaps, rewarding. By the others the meeting was regarded as an extra Management conference rendered more complex and tedious by the necessity of acting out an elaborate charade of informality. This had to be done with discretion; there were still vivid memories of the early days of the experiment when various individuals (no longer employed by the company), had taken Kingham's instructions a little too literally. But it was necessary to put up a show, and experienced members of the committee, those who knew how far to go, would often engage in spirited little arguments with each other, though always on a friendly, Christian-name basis. Kingham would watch these benignly, like a schoolmaster refereeing a boy's boxing match. His job, as he saw it, was to see fair play without spoiling the fun. Occasionally, but not too often, somebody started an argument with Kingham himself. For that, you had to pick your day.

Today was not one of them. It was soon plain that the men closest to Kingham had sensed that this was no occasion for departmental shadow-boxing, however good-natured. Gradually even Marshall, through a fog of smoke and boredom, became aware that events were not following their usual course. Somehow, things were not going well for Wilcox. His facts were subjected to query, his conclusions disputed. Nobody went so far as to criticize him openly; it was more a matter of an impatient wrinkling of Kingham's forehead, a testy inflection in his voice when pointing out the inadequacy of an answer. It was hard to resist the conclusion that Wilcox had briefed himself inadequately, had not given sufficient coverage to the territory, had spent his energies on nonentities while missing out on the important people altogether. A question would be asked about some point of detail—the sales figures for Sweden, the new currency restrictions recently introduced by the Portuguese Government. No doubt Mr. Wilcox would have the figures with him? Well, no, he didn't have them with him right now, he was afraid, but they were in the file, he could easily . . . No, no, it was all right. As it happened, John Richardson had got them out just before the meeting, having anticipated that the matter might be raised. Well, then, John, perhaps you'd like to tell us what your thinking is about this one. . . .

Marshall looked down at the table and began to doodle absentmindedly on his memo pad. This, he reminded himself as his pencil moved in a series of elaborate, vaguely Freudian patterns, was no concern of his. If they were out to crucify Wilcox, there was nothing he could do to stop them. He had been present at such spectacles before and knew the uselessness of intervention. It was best to preserve the attitude of the naturalist, to watch them like fish through the glass wall of a tank, fighting, rutting, making their messes in front of his eyes—so near, yet never quite near enough to touch him. Kingham, it seemed, would eat Wilcox; perhaps, with luck, someone in due time would eat Kingham. Who? he wondered. Richardson? Livera? Or more likely some larger fish altogether, from outside the International, some savage razor-toothed vice-president, some hypertensive pike in bifocals. It was possible. In this world anyone might get eaten, even Mr. Bernstein himself, if he relaxed his concentration for a moment. Nobody was immortal—except perhaps himself. Too unimportant to fear, yet too dangerous to attack, he alone carried pretensions to immunity.

Weary of whorls and rectangles, he began to draw caricatures—the easy way. That is to say, he would draw the faces first and then decide who they were meant to be. It was a pleasant and unexacting way of whiling away a dull afternoon. After a few minutes of earnest concentration he was left with a sketch of a cross-eyed old harridan with bushy eyebrows and a hatful of wax fruit. Obviously, he decided without hesitation, a lady novelist. But which one? Colette? Willa Cather? Mrs. Humphry Ward?

Unable to reach a satisfactory decision, he dropped his pencil on the table and turned his attention back to the meeting. Wilcox was taking it well, all things considered. Occasionally he would give a thin little smile and a nod of agreement, just to show that he was not the sort of man who turned sulky under criticism. He had obviously understood and accepted the process which was now going on. Perhaps he had indeed, as was continually being implied, fallen down on the job. Or it might be that this was merely a demonstration, that certain private and personal scores had to be paid off, that some policy decision had been made which required that Wilcox should, in this particular instance at least, be discredited.

If that was the case, the outlook for Wilcox would be more hopeful than it superficially appeared. There was always a good chance that some reversal of policy, some reshuffling of personalities might restore him to favor. The only thing which would be fatal to him would be a loss of self-control at the present moment, a surrender to the temptation to hit back. It seemed that Wilcox was well aware of this danger. At certain crucial points he had developed a tendency to gaze fixedly at the ceiling through half-closed eyes. His lips would move slightly, as if repeating something silently to himself.

Repeating what? Marshall wondered. Some maxim from Dale Carnegie or the *Reader's Digest,* some fragment of Kipling's *If?* More likely he was repeating figures. How much would he be earning? Fifteen thousand, probably. Not bad for a man just over thirty. More than he was worth. The old man had said: "Always pay your executives more than they are worth. That way you get loyalty."

And so you did. Because when a man was pulling down fifteen thousand a year he got into the habit of living that way, with a couple of cars and the right sort of house with the right sort of mortgage on it. He had an expensive wife and two or three kids and a country-club subscription and quite a load of insurance. And the nearer his commitments approached the amount of money he had left after taxes, the more scared he became of losing his job and the more loyal he became. . . .

On this basis everyone around the table was loyal—everyone, that is to say, except himself, doodling subversively on a piece of company paper. He could see that his behavior was annoying Kingham and could almost imagine the fatal word of condemnation forming in the other man's mind—Marshall was disloyal. With his family name and private fortune, with his minor but not insignificant shareholding and a brother on the Board, disloyalty was a luxury he could afford. If he performed no other function in the organization, he could at least be independent and unafraid. Inherited wealth, he thought as he absently added a pair of pince-nez and an incipient mustache to his portrait, was one of the few remaining defenses against the tyranny of vulgar ability.

Kingham stopped in the middle of a review of some sales figures. "Did you say something, Chris?"

Could he possibly have spoken aloud? "No," he said, "I didn't say anything."

He spoke carelessly, but the disturbing fact was that it needed a deliberate effort, he had to work to keep the respect out of his voice. Kingham regarded him impassively, the schoolmaster who is quite confident of his power to enforce discipline but prepared to be indulgent on this occasion. Then he resumed his speech. He was a slight, birdlike man. His nose was pointed, his eyes dark and bright behind the horn-rimmed spectacles, his thin hair slicked back over his scalp like the feathers of a starling. His mouth was tight and small; his chin, though slightly receding, gave no impression of vacuity or weakness. He was dressed, as always, with great care. Two triangular points of a white handkerchief, one monogrammed, peeped above the aperture of his breast pocket. As he spoke he rested his small hands, palms downward, on either side of his notes. His voice was crisp and confident. Every now and then he would glance swiftly down with a sharp pecking movement, pick up a fact from the sheet of paper in front of him, and incorporate it into his argument.

It was after five when the conference broke up. Afterward the members of the committee stood around in groups, chatting. The ash trays were crammed with the butts of half-smoked cigarettes. Marshall watched Wilcox slip unobtrusively out of the room. He was preparing to leave himself when he felt an arm on his shoulder. He looked up to see Kingham smiling down at him.

Kingham pointed down at the drawing. "Who's that supposed to be?"

"Nobody special. Have you any suggestions?"

Kingham shook his head. The smile remained, fixed and patronizing. "It shows talent," he said.

"Thank you."

"Almost professional, I'd say. But then I'm no judge." Marshall made a noncommittal noise. Was there hidden malice behind these remarks, or was it merely a heavy-handed attempt at amiability? Kingham went on, "Didn't you spend a couple of years in Paris or something? I seem to remember your father telling me——"

"Yes," said Marshall shortly. Naturally, he thought with some bitterness, his father would have told Kingham. He had told everybody. It was the sort of story that appealed to him—a victory for himself. "My father thought I was crazy. And it so happened he was right."

"He often was," said Kingham, "about a lot of things. He was a smart old man."

"I don't give him any credit in this case. He would have thought Michelangelo was crazy."

Kingham laughed. "I guess he would, at that." He lit a cigarette and said pensively, "There are a lot of things about art that I don't get at all. I mean, how did you know in the end that"—he hesitated, searching for some more delicate way of describing failure—"well, that he was right and you were wrong?"

"People tell you—people who are supposed to know. You tell yourself they don't know, that nobody really knows. And then one day you look at something you've done and you find yourself agreeing with them. After that——" He shrugged his shoulders.

Kingham wrinkled his brows. He was a man who prided himself on his interest in people. He liked, he often said, to be able to get inside another man's problems. "But if you went on working? If you really wanted to succeed badly enough——"

Marshall made a grimace. How had he been fool enough to let the conversation get as far as this? "We're talking about two different things," he said abruptly. "Don't ever let them tell you that genius is an infinite capacity for taking pains." He folded the sheet of paper into four, tore it up, and dropped the fragments into an ash tray. Perhaps Kingham would take the hint and leave him alone. But the hand remained on his shoulder.

"There was something else," said Kingham, "that I wanted to talk to you about."

Marshall looked at him with interest. What could be going on? He had not received as much attention as this in years. He was not Kingham's type of man. Kingham liked the bright boys, the keen boys, the Richardsons, the Wilcoxes, clear of eye and clean of limb, bursting with ideals. "Go right ahead," he said.

Kingham looked around the room. There were still one or two other people left. "Not here, I think."

"Is it important?"

Kingham nodded. "We might discuss it over a drink. Perhaps you could meet me at the Phoenix in about half an hour's time."

CHAPTER II

THERE WAS just time to call in at his office and sign the day's correspondence. As he walked down the corridor he was conscious once more of the world outside. Shafts of April sunlight splashed, like searchlight beams, across the main corridor, giving patchy illumination to the pale green walls, lighting up the colored maps and photographs of factories, the bronze plaque which had been affixed in honor of his father (recalling that memorable day, three years ago, when the old man had succumbed to a fatal apoplexy after failing to bribe a senator over some government contracts). The executive offices of the International opened off one side of the corridor—Sales, Technical Direction, Production, Advertising, Market Research. He opened a door labeled "Publicity Co-ordination" and went in. In the outer office there were two stenographers and Rose Bauer, his assistant.

Rose was a plump, almost pretty blonde of about his own age, married to a trombonist in the New York Philharmonic.

"Anything new?" he asked.

"Well . . ." She flipped over some papers. "There're some figures about the production potentialities of the new plant in Montreal—a picture of Mr. Bernstein receiving the Order of the Golden Fleece, third class, in some South American republic——"

"Christ."

"Some information on the use of precision instruments in guided missiles, with particular reference to our K 702——"

"That sounds good."

"We probably can't use it. There's some question of secrecy. One of our people in Japan has won a lottery——"

"How much?"

"Sixty thousand yen. So far as I can gather, that's about fifty dollars. But I've circulated it, anyway."

"That's the girl. Anything else come up?"

"Charlie Parker called. He wants a cover for the house magazine."

"Give him Mr. Bernstein and the Golden Fleece."

She looked doubtful. "Last issue we had Mr. Bernstein and the Chamber of Commerce."

"Never mind. We can't get too much of Mr. Bernstein."

He was conscious of a querulous presence at his elbow. It was his secretary, Miss Tracy.

"Mr. Marshall, your office is full of letters for signing. If you don't come in right now I shall miss the afternoon mail."

"Okay."

He walked through with her into the inner office. The letters were filed neatly on his blotter; as usual, they were monotonously accurate, without even so much as a spelling mistake to enliven them. As he read through the drab, shopworn, repetitive phrases he was filled with distaste. This sort of thing was all very well for Rose—distributing handouts, buying drinks for journalists, replying to inquiries from shareholders. She might pretend to be cynical about it, but in fact she enjoyed it. Also, the job was valuable to her—Fred Bauer was an unstable personality even for a musician. Only last week he had got drunk in Cincinnati and came in four bars too soon on the Sibelius. . . .

Yes, for Rose it made some sense. But for him—the whole outfit stank of a sinecure, a nice warm place for the old man's son, where he couldn't do much harm. He turned over the letters irritably, at increasing speed, and handed them back to Miss Tracy.

"Is that all?"

"There are these as well."

She handed him a sheaf of typed memoranda on the pale blue paper used for inter-office communications. They were the fruit of a recent burst of reorganization put through by Kingham at the instigation of a firm of management consultants. Memoranda which had once been dealt with individually by department heads were now circulated among all the members of the board of management of the International. There was a special sheet attached for comments and signatures. Most of the memoranda were quite trivial. Since they circulated in order of descending importance, it was almost unknown for anybody to disagree with the first opinion expressed.

"Hell," said Marshall, "I haven't time to read all these."

As the most junior and insignificant of the departmental heads, he was the last to receive the memoranda. He noticed that all the present collection had been approved by the others before reaching him. Without bothering to read them he scribbled "Agreed" on each one, added his signature, and handed them back to his secretary.

By New York standards, the Phoenix Hotel was something in the nature of an ancient monument. In a city where progress was king, it remained as one of the few reminders of the luxury which was fashionable in the early years of the century. Marble floors, high decorated ceilings, extravagantly wasteful in space, endowed it with a cavernous distinction. Always, even when all the rooms were occupied, it appeared to the casual visitor half empty. The bar opened like a small private chapel off the cathedral bulk of the main hall. Here the tables were spaced well apart, the waiters alert but soft-footed, the charges frequently capricious and invariably extortionate.

Marshall ordered a drink for himself and lit a cigarette. Kingham would be late. A scrupulously punctual man, it was his custom to keep his juniors waiting, as a matter of prestige. The length of time varied with the status of the person concerned—it was regarded as a useful method of gauging one's current rating in the company.

It was just on a quarter past six when Kingham entered the bar. Marshall recorded the fact with interest—up till now he had been a twenty-minute man. Could it be that by some mysterious process he had gained in favor? It seemed unlikely. He watched the sleek head turn quickly to right and left, scanning the room for acquaintances. The barman nodded respectfully, and Kingham nodded back with an assured smile which came up from deep in the recesses of his expense account. Then he walked over to the table.

"Sorry to keep you waiting, Chris," he said. "I was just getting ready to leave when Bernie called up."

"That's all right."

There was a slight pause. Marshall had the feeling that something was demanded of him. Did Kingham expect him to be impressed by his intimacy with the president of the company, this casual use of nicknames? If so, he was ready to play in, up to a point. But he could never be sure of such things. He felt his own inadequacy in this particular world. Any of the others—Richardson, Livera, Wilcox—would have known instinctively how to react.

"Had Mr. Bernstein anything special to say?" he asked finally, conscious of the stiffness of the question but unable to do anything to improve it.

"No. He just likes to toss the ball around—let us know he's alive." Kingham picked up a handful of salted nuts and swallowed them. "What's that you're drinking?"

"Scotch."

He called the waiter. "Two scotch—on the rocks." He looked round at the pillars and the palms. "You know, this place has something."

"Yes," agreed Chris. "Of course it shouldn't be in America at all. It's more like a spa hotel in Aix or Baden-Baden. You can practically see the dowagers knitting behind the potted palms."

Kingham laughed perfunctorily. After a pause he said, "How long did you say you were in Europe?"

"Four years. First at Cambridge, then in Paris."

"Do you speak French?"

"Not well." He explained, "At the art schools the foreign students used to stick together. Most of my friends were American or English."

"You liked it over there?"

"Yes." His voice was careless, noncommittal. He was not to be caught again. Even after several years the memory of this particular episode in his life had the power to raise emotions in him which he found it almost impossible to control. The way to handle it was to prevent it from getting hold, to think of something else, pretend that you were talking about a thing that had happened to some other person, someone you hardly knew.

"Would you like to go back?"

"It depends."

He was doing fine. Kingham was looking at him in a puzzled way, surprised that he was showing so little animation. Suddenly he changed the subject.

"How do you think the meeting went today?"

Marshall regarded him warily. What was he up to now? "All right. Pretty much as usual."

"What did you think of Wilcox?"

"Wilcox?"

"Yes. You know what I mean. How did you think he was measuring up to the job?"

Marshall floundered. "That's a difficult question. Unless one knows all the circumstances——"

Kingham held up a hand. "That's okay. You don't have to say any more. Maybe I shouldn't have asked." He paused. "Just the same, I wanted your reaction. My guess is that if you'd felt completely confident in him you'd have come out with considerably more enthusiasm. Right?"

"No," Marshall protested, "that's not so. I genuinely meant——"

"Forget it," Kingham cut in. "Forget I ever asked you. Whatever you think about Wilcox, I know what *I* think—and I feel badly about it. You see, Wilcox was my boy—I pushed him all the way. And what it amounts to is that I pushed him too far and too fast. If there's been a mistake," he asserted handsomely, "I take the blame for it. But we can't run a business like this successfully unless we face up to the facts. Personal feelings have to take second place. The truth is, Wilcox hasn't measured up to the job."

Awkwardly Marshall began to protest. He had the feeling of being present at an assassination, with no very clear idea as to what he ought to do about it. He had not been involved in the attack on Wilcox and he could not understand what Kingham's object was in dragging him into the matter. As a rule he was told nothing about what was happening until afterward, and sometimes not even then. Frequently the stenographers knew more about what was going on in the office than he did. He was not accustomed to confidential talks of this kind.

Kingham brushed the protests aside. In spite of disagreeable necessities he was, he conveyed, fundamentally benevolent.

"One has to remember," he said, "that Wilcox is still young. I haven't lost faith in him. I still think he's a fine guy and we're lucky to have him. He just wasn't ready for what I gave him. He was short on background." He shook his head regretfully and went on with some solemnity, "It's clear to me now that what we need is someone with a broader approach. Not just a keen boy like Wilcox who's never been out of the United States in his life. Someone more sophisticated, if you get me." He paused for a moment to let the idea make its mark and then said, "How'd you like to go to Europe for a spell, Chris?"

So *that* was what it was all about.

"In Wilcox's place?" he asked.

"Yes. I'm going to move him to another area where he'll feel more at home."

"You think," asked Marshall with a touch of irony, "that I'd be a success?"

"I wouldn't offer it otherwise."

"I haven't so very much business experience."

"I thought of that. But it doesn't matter too much. Your position would be more liaison than executive. Primarily, what we want is character and personality. You'll pick up the rest fast enough as you go along. You know," he said thoughtfully, "I've been thinking for some time that you weren't very happy in your present job. Am I right?"

"I haven't complained," said Marshall.

"No. But I just had the idea. . . . And I don't blame you. It's a department, I know. But not really a top-line one. It always seemed to me that you were a little wasted there. I've been looking for a way to use you, to build you up. And I'm convinced that this is it." He sat back. "Well, what do you say?"

Marshall hesitated. It was, on the face of it, a considerable opportunity. If nothing else, it would get him out of public relations and away from the New York office. The job sounded interesting, and he would be working in a country he had always liked. He would have some degree of independence. . . .

And yet the offer was puzzling. He could not persuade himself that Kingham liked him or had any regard for his abilities. Why then should he wish to "build him up"? There were plenty of other young men, enthusiastic, loyal young men who would jump at the opportunity. There must be *something* wrong with it.

Cautiously he said, "It sounds attractive. Could I have a couple of days to think it over?"

Kingham frowned. He was not accustomed to having his favors treated in this cavalier fashion.

"Is that necessary?" he said.

"I'm afraid so." All Marshall's dislike of Kingham flared up. The bastard could wait. "I have," he said meaninglessly, "personal reasons."

"Very well," said Kingham reluctantly. "But we've got to get things rolling. I'd like your answer by first thing Monday morning." There was a slight pause. Having carried out his purpose, he was left with nothing more to say. "How about another drink?" he asked without enthusiasm.

"No, thanks," Marshall said, taking his cue. He was no more anxious to prolong the conversation himself. "I ought to be leaving. I have a date for dinner."

CHAPTER III

He joined the stream of traffic on the parkway, easing his car into the more sluggish outside lane. He was in no hurry. Past him, in an endless procession, nose to tail, drove the more ambitious commuters; each evening they poured out of Manhattan like a defeated army, bolting for refuge in the suburbs. In a score of neat, prosperous, ever-growing villages, a hundred thousand wives in a hundred thousand houses waited, and wondered whether it was time to start fixing a martini. Twice that number of children played on the lawns behind the houses or poised themselves in a cataleptic trance before the mystery of television. Soon Dad would be home. And Dad, all tensed up after a hard day at the office, took one hand off the wheel of his new two-hundred-horsepower sedan and fumbled for the last remaining cigarette in his coat pocket. The sun was setting on another American day.

As he drove along, Marshall thought again about Kingham's offer. Why had he been so hesitant about accepting it? Had he, after all, so much to lose? There was a danger that his personal dislike of Kingham might be turning into an obsession, so that everything that came from him, no matter how superficially desirable, was treated as a matter of course with suspicion. It was important to see Kingham's point of view, to visualize yourself as a man in authority, plagued by a useless, unco-operative subordinate whom circumstances made it impossible to remove. You did your best to keep him away from real responsibility, but so long as he was around he remained a stone in your shoe, a bad example to others. What more obvious approach to the problem than to send him abroad?

It seemed the most likely explanation and one that he would be unreasonable to resent. Yet still he found himself unwilling to make a decision. Why? Could it be that he was afraid of returning to Paris? But surely that was over and done with. He had admitted his failure as a man might eat some nauseating meal, managing somehow to keep it down, hoping that at least he might absorb from it some benefit for the future. His father had, characteristically, spared him nothing, offered him no consolation. And he had asked for none. He had accepted his present position with resignation, because it was the logical thing to do, once you had lost, to accept the terms of the victor. He had even once hoped that in due time he might come, not perhaps to enjoy it, but at least to regard it without active disgust. Now he knew that this was an illusion. After five years he still hated New York, he hated the business, he hated Kingham. It was hard to see how any change could possibly be for the worse.

It was almost half-past eight when he reached the house. It was a rambling Dutch-colonial mansion which had been far too big even when his father was alive. The old man had seen it going cheaply during the depression and had snapped it up on a quick deal. He had had very little feeling for it except in so far as it had been a bargain, and he always felt affectionately toward a bargain. He had taken a pride in keeping it in good shape, though he had spent little of his time there. Since his death, his widow had lived there constantly, loving the house, and done practically nothing to keep it in repair; she seemed to prefer an atmosphere of mild dilapidation. The garden was overgrown, and some of the window frames needed painting. As he got out of the car an old great Dane lumbered reluctantly from his place on the porch, walked over, and nuzzled his hand. He was growing fat and sleepy. Very soon he would be just watching from the porch, too lazy to get up.

Marshall walked through the hall to the living room. His mother was sitting at a card table, playing solitaire. It was as he had expected to find her.

"Hello, Mother."

"Hello, Chris." Though she had lived in the North for years, she still bore traces of the accent she had brought with her from Petersburg as a bride. Nowadays it seemed to him, if anything, more noticeable, possibly because she went around so little and spent so much time talking to the servants.

She put down her pack of cards and allowed him to kiss her on the cheek. "How's everything?"

"Oh, fine, fine." He looked out of the open french doors. The shadows on the lawns were warm and scented. "The country certainly is wonderful at this time of year."

"Yes." Her face was handsome even now, her voice pleasant, her smile charming, her movements graceful. Yet somehow she had always been slightly unsatisfactory as a mother. There was a certain vagueness about her affection for her two children which seemed at times, particularly in Jeff's case, almost to amount to indifference. Though interested in their affairs, she was primarily occupied by her own. As boys they had been grateful for her lack of possessiveness, and yet at the same time they had felt vaguely cheated, as if they had missed some warm maternal experience which they had a right to expect. "You should come out here more often," she said casually, as if talking to an old friend, some near but not very intimate relation. "We're not as cut off as we used to be. It's only an hour on the parkway."

"An hour and a half."

"Your father used to say he could make it in an hour."

"He was a liar."

"Chris——" she protested mildly.

"Well, he was, wasn't he?"

"He might perhaps have exaggerated a little . . ."

"That nonsense about doing New York in an hour was typical of him. He liked to show off, like a child. When you pointed out to him that he wasn't telling the truth, he got mad and tried to shout you down." And then of course he wasn't like a child any more. Marshall remembered those rages (who could have forgotten them?), the flushed face, the glaring pale blue eyes, the short stocky figure rigid with determination. That determination had been his most lavish asset; he had had it to burn, as another man might have intelligence or imagination. And he had burned it. He had used it to compensate for a dozen other disadvantages—impulsiveness, lack of education, deficiencies in charm. Like any man with an abundance of something, he had almost seemed to take pleasure in wasting it. The smallest disputes within the family were enough to call out the utmost violence of his nature. The recalcitrance of a golf ball could arouse within him agonies of frustration.

"I don't think," said Mrs. Marshall mildly, "that you should talk about your father like that."

"I don't know why not." He began to mix himself a drink. "He always said what he liked about me."

She turned on him reproachfully. "He thought the world of you, Chris."

It was true, of course. As a boy he had been the smart one and his father had worshiped smartness—up to a point. "Oh, sure. So long as he thought I'd do what he wanted, we were great pals. When he found I wouldn't, he hated the sight of me."

"No, he didn't. He——"

"I'm not complaining. It's just that he had to do everything a hundred per cent. Or rather more if possible."

"It made him what he was."

"Yes, by God." There didn't seem to be anything more to say about that. After a short silence his mother said, "Are you staying for the weekend?"

"Until Sunday night—if that's all right with you."

"Of course." A transient sense of social obligation came over her. "Perhaps you'd like to invite some friends over one afternoon. We could mark out the tennis court . . ."

The tennis court had not been weeded or marked out since his father died. He said: "Don't worry, Mother. There's no one around I want to ask."

"As you say, dear." She could not disguise her relief. At least she had made the gesture. "It probably would be better for you to take a rest. I'm sure you lead a very hectic and unhealthy life in New York."

"Not really."

"No? Somehow I always think of young men in service apartments living on cigarettes and highballs. And you look so thin——"

"I always was, you know."

"That's true. Well, perhaps I'm completely wrong. And when a man's getting near thirty he has to lead his own life—there's no object in trying to influence him any more," she said. She was obviously glad to be released of any obligation to do so. "Shall we go in for dinner?"

"I thought Jeff and Paula were coming."

"Not until afterward. Paula called up to say they'd had some trouble with baby-sitters. But they'll be over for coffee." With unconcealed satisfaction she added: "So we can have an hour on our own." Getting up from her chair, she suddenly raised her voice and called, "Virgie!"

"Yes'm," came a voice from the kitchen.

"Is dinner ready?"

"Been ready for some while now."

"We'll be coming right in then."

The big dining-room table was laid for two places only and lit by an enormous silver candelabrum, one of whose arms had fractured in the middle and had been temporarily splinted with wire. The meal was served by Virgie, the colored woman who had come North with his mother from Petersburg. Now aged and almost entirely toothless, she shuffled to and from the kitchen with the dishes, humming snatches of some old song and occasionally talking to herself in a low voice. Her husband, Joe, acted as chauffeur-gardener, driving Mrs. Marshall around the district in an old Cadillac almost as gaunt and dilapidated as himself. As they all grew older, the tempo of life at Falls Ridge was running down. Gradually in her old age Mrs. Marshall was returning to the old, sleepy, sunny, careless way of life of her childhood.

The food, however, was still good. There was fried chicken for Marshall; his mother, who had taken to vegetarianism and bridge as hobbies suitable to her widowhood, was served an avocado-pear salad.

During the meal he said, "There's some possibility that I may go to Europe fairly soon."

"On a trip?"

"No. I've been offered a job. As European representative."

"When was this?"

"About an hour or two ago. Kingham—do you know him?"

"No. Should I?"

"He's head of the International. He occasionally asks after you."

She thought and then shook her head. "I don't know him. Perhaps he came here to one of your father's parties in the old days. So many of them did. I could never remember . . ." She asked plaintively, "What exactly *is* a European representative?"

He waited for Virgie to take away his empty plate and then said, "Well, as you may know, we deal with Europe mainly through agencies and distributors. They sell our goods for us and take a percentage. Theoretically they're separate firms, but most of them are in some degree or other dependent on the corporation. The British one, and that's the largest, is a subsidiary in everything but name. The European representative of Marshall's is based in London and acts as a liaison between these firms and the main office in New York. It used to be a man called Wilcox, but he's due for transfer. Today Kingham asked me if I'd like to go in his place."

She paused for a moment, as if searching for a means of interpretation. "And what did you say?"

"I said I'd like to think about it."

She looked at him more sharply. In spite of her vagueness she was by no means an unperceptive woman. "You have some doubts about it?"

"Yes." He was hesitant. They were doubts he hardly felt able to express.

Fortunately she did not ask him for details. "I wish I could help you," she said after a pause, "but I know so little of what goes on in the company nowadays. This person Kingham, for instance——" In her world, thought Chris, everything was seen in terms of personalities. He had at one time laughed at this naïve type of approach. As he grew older he was not so sure. "What does Mr. Bernstein say?" she asked.

He smiled. She was certainly a little out of touch. "The company's much bigger nowadays, Mother. I hardly ever see Mr. Bernstein."

She shook her head in wonderment. "It seems funny, Alfred Bernstein being so important. I remember him from the old days when he and Sarah used to come round for a game of bridge in the evening. He could never make up his mind what to call and your father used to get so impatient that we had to stop inviting them. Poor man, he had no card sense. I think he only played to be agreeable." She was silent for a moment and then suddenly asked, "Is this European job an advancement?"

He was momentarily disconcerted. This was an aspect which he had hardly considered. "Oh yes. I'd say so——"

"What's the salary?"

"I'm afraid I forgot to ask."

She looked at him in surprise. "*Really*, Chris."

"But, hell," he protested, "the money doesn't matter. It only goes in taxes anyway."

"I know that." She went on patiently, as if to a child, "But it's still important. The more they pay you, the more you count for. If you're prepared to work for nothing, they'll think of you as a nobody—you've got to keep up your prestige."

"Oh, sure," he said ironically. "I'm loaded with prestige right now. Co-ordinator of publicity."

"What's wrong with that?"

"It doesn't mean anything, that's all." She opened her mouth to speak, but he went on quickly, "Now don't get the idea that I'm beefing about it. It's really very kind of them to have me around at all."

"You can do anything that Jeff can," she said with spirit. "And now he's on the Board."

"I know." His voice was tired. This was an old argument. "Jeff's no ball of fire, we'll agree on that. But he works hard and he believes like hell in his job. And that's what matters."

"Your father used to say——"

"Please, Mother—please!" He got up from the table in his agitation. "Don't quote Father to me. It just makes me mad."

"I don't know why——"

"Because I'm not prepared to accept anything he said—or anything he did, for that matter——"

"He did a lot for us."

"He made money—that's what you mean."

"Is that nothing?"

"It isn't enough."

She sighed. "Nothing's ever quite enough, you know. We have to do the best we can."

"Okay, I'll agree with that." He sat down again. "But he didn't. He was a liar and a cheat and a bully. And, what was worse, he was proud of it." He said with disgust, "Anything to win a trick."

"No." She shook her head. "You're not being fair to him. He could be like that, I know—he made me very unhappy, especially when I was younger. In those days I didn't understand the sort of problems he had to face." She explained slowly, "Your father had a great deal to do in the world. He was a man who couldn't stand still—he had always to be acting, moving, fighting. He couldn't help that—it was his nature. To keep up his self-confidence he had to win as often as possible. And to win——"

"He had to cheat."

"Sometimes," she admitted. "Sometimes he behaved very badly. And naturally it was a great shock to him when you wanted to go to Paris and paint pictures——"

"I wasn't talking about that. I was talking generally." Seeing the look of disbelief on her face, he added irritably, "You never seem to understand that people can be talking generally."

"Perhaps not." She was undisturbed by his annoyance. It was impossible to quarrel with her; in the world she inhabited now, nothing was sufficiently serious. She smiled. "Your father used to complain about that too."

The tension between them was relaxed. Soon she changed the subject and began to talk about her health. She was a mild hypochondriac and at the present moment under the sway of a certain Dr. Aronson, who claimed to be a specialist in allergies. She had a long list of various substances, any one of which might do her irreparable harm if inadvertently eaten or inhaled, and carried it with her everywhere. It made her whole life a sort of gigantic obstacle race. A copy of the list had also been posted in the kitchen, but Virgie, she complained, was proving unco-operative.

"I can't imagine why she's so awkward," said Mrs. Marshall, peering suspiciously into her fruit cup. "It's impossible to trust her any more. I must have told her a hundred times that I'm sensitive to pineapples."

Jeff and Paula arrived in time for coffee. Their entrance was always an impressive ceremony, as if Jeff, instead of living ten miles away, had been off on safari for at least a year. He was a large, heavily built man in his middle thirties. At college he had been a footballer of distinction, but since then he had put on some weight. The dark, smooth-shaven chin had lost a good deal of its sharpness. His wife was small, fair, and very pretty.

"Hi, Chris."

"Hi, Jeff." Marshall moved forward and allowed his hand to be gripped. Extricating his bruised fingers, he said, "Hello, Paula. I hardly saw you."

This got a laugh, as he knew it would. The contrast in their sizes was an endless source of delight to them both. "How are the kids?" he said.

"Terrible!" shrieked Paula proudly. "They're driving me crazy. First they want fur hats, then space helmets and death-ray guns. Now they're all steamed up about some sort of a mouse. I don't get it at all."

"She spoils them," said Jeff. "They get too many gadgets nowadays. Why, when I was a kid——"

"But, honey, what can you do? All the other kids have them."

"Yeah, I guess so," he agreed indulgently. As they went into the living room he said, "Congratulations on the new job, Chris."

"Oh—you heard?"

"Yes, Harry Kingham just called me up."

"I haven't officially accepted yet."

"Oh, but you will, won't you?"

Mrs. Marshall was pouring the coffee. "Do you think he should, Jeff?"

"Why, surely." He added earnestly, "This is tailored for you, Chris. Wilcox was all right, but he just didn't have the necessary class."

"You think I can make something of it?"

"Sure I do. And so does Kingham."

"I wouldn't have thought I was his type."

Jeff shook his head knowingly. "That's where you're wrong. Kingham's a smart guy—he's not so conventional as some. I'm telling you—you rate higher than you think."

"Well—that's encouraging."

"I know you won't take it wrong if I say this, Chris—but, the way I look at it, all you lack is self-confidence."

Chris looked at him, taking in the smooth, solemn face, the Rotary Club voice, the dull, tenacious, satisfied mouth. "You think so?"

"Sure. Just because Dad——"

"Never mind about Dad," he cut in sharply. "In fact, never mind about Kingham, or Bernstein, or Handley, or Lewis, or all the rest of the vice-presidents. They're all great guys and as smart as whips. There isn't a finer board of management in the whole of American industry. Am I right?"

Jeff eyed him doggedly. "I believe so."

Suddenly he was tired, not of Jeff, but of himself. Who was he to be getting so smart and cynical about everything? The clever younger brother who never grew up, who hadn't managed to make anything of his own life but consoled himself by sneering at the beliefs and enthusiasms of other people. It was easy enough to do—too easy—especially when the people you were sneering at were your own family and too kindhearted to hit back where they knew it would really hurt. . . . What he really needed, he thought, was to get away. Away from the people who knew his history, and remembered his father, and had formed preconceived ideas about everything concerning him. Somewhere else he could start afresh with a different set of people. They would look at him with new eyes and perhaps he would see himself differently too. Perhaps for once spring was right, there *was* something round the corner. . . .

He put his arm affectionately on Jeff's shoulder. "Don't worry," he said. "I was only kidding you. I'm going to accept."

CHAPTER IV

On the Monday morning he called Kingham as soon as he reached the office.

"Yes?"

"This is Chris Marshall. I called you to say I'd like to take the job."

"The job? Oh yes——" He was expected to draw the inference that Kingham had so many things on his mind that he had momentarily forgotten about the job altogether. "Good. That's fine. Now, wait a moment—I'd like to talk to you but I'm busy right now. What about lunch?"

"I'm free."

"Okay. Twelve forty-five?"

He rang off sharply. Marshall started to go through the morning's mail. It was a fairly average sample—the usual proofs of public relations handouts, foreign press cuttings, some advertising material, an invitation to a trade function. It was pleasant to think that he would not be doing this kind of work much longer. When Rose came in he handed the correspondence to her.

"You'd better handle this," he said. "I'm leaving."

She raised her eyebrows. "To do what?"

"Wilcox's job."

"Congratulations," she said. "You'll like it, won't you?"

"I hope so."

"It sounds like a lot more fun than this. Traveling around . . . Though I'm sorry you're going."

Looking at her, he realized with surprise and gratitude that she was genuinely sorry. "You won't notice much difference," he said. "You always did all the work anyway."

She didn't bother to deny it. "Just the same, we've had some good times."

"They may even promote you."

"I doubt it. More likely they'll push in some eager beaver who wants to make a reputation for himself by running us all ragged. Or even wash up the department altogether." She sighed. "No. I'm happy as I am. I just want to be left alone. But there's no sense in hoping for that in this outfit."

Over lunch Kingham said, "I felt sure you'd take it."

"You did?"

"Certainly. I couldn't see any ambitious man of your age passing up an opportunity like this. It's more than just an ordinary job," he said in an approach to lyricism. "It's a challenge." He popped an olive into his mouth. "And I know you're going to meet it."

"That's very kind of you——"

Kingham waved away gratitude. "The hell with that. I say what I think. And that's my guess about you. I may be wrong—but I don't think so." His mistake about Wilcox, thought Marshall, had evidently not affected his faith in his own judgment. "And now—perhaps I'd better give you some details about the setup over there."

The setup in Europe, he explained, was by no means as tidy as the company liked. Most of the trading arrangements had been made just after the war, when conditions were very confused and there was a shortage of reliable information. The essential thing had been to get into the new markets quickly. There were difficulties to overcome concerning the importation of materials and the remission of dollars.

"Those were difficult days," said Kingham reminiscently. "When your father went over there in 1946 everything was in chaos. The ordinary rules of business didn't apply. You couldn't look for a reputable, long-established firm to handle your goods. They didn't exist any more. Or if they did you probably found that the managing director had bolted for the Argentine or been put in prison as a collaborator or something. You couldn't have a standard form of agreement, because what might be accepted in one country wouldn't work in another. You had to improvise, to pick your men and take a chance on them, to make what arrangements seemed possible at the time. That was the sort of situation where your father scored. He was prepared to jump in and gamble on his own judgment. He met with a good deal of criticism in certain quarters. But in the end he proved himself right. He sure was a great judge of men." Kingham paused reverently and then went on, "You never met any of the distributors?"

"No. They're just names to me."

"The countries that matter most are England and France. Gilbertson in London will be your nearest contact—he may seem a little formal and British at first, but underneath it all he's a very fine guy and a pretty shrewd businessman. I'm confident that he'll help you right up to the limit. But the really brilliant person over there is Furac, the Paris distributor. He's done miracles in building up business under extremely difficult conditions. Believe me, he's a really smart man. And very cultured too."

He went on to speak of others of lesser importance. Most of them received a build-up of one kind or another. They were either very sound or very smart or had unusual experience or first-rate connections. Marshall began to feel restless. No individual characters could be discerned through this fog of superlatives, no clear picture of his own place in the scene.

Kingham paused for a moment. He had finally come to the end of his list of significant personalities. It was time for the summing up. "Now," he said carefully, "what I want to emphasize is this. These are men we have confidence in, because they've produced results. I believe, as your father believed, that results are what matter. You'll pick up knowledge gradually as you go along—that's the only way. Don't get the idea that you're expected to reorganize the whole continent in a month. Take it slowly and be tactful.

Over there, they're only too ready to believe that Americans want to push them around. If their methods are different from ours, don't immediately assume they're crazy. What goes in one place doesn't necessarily go in another. Do you get me?"

"Yes, of course." The advice was sensible, if somewhat obvious. The implication was, presumably, that Wilcox had been overenthusiastic, had interfered, had trodden on influential toes in some fatal but unexplained fashion.

"Then that's fine." Kingham gave a satisfied smile. "I hope I've made everything clear?"

Marshall hesitated. "There's just one thing——"

"What's that?"

He asked rather diffidently, "Well, what do I actually *do?*"

"Do?" Kingham frowned, as if he were beginning to have doubts of Marshall's intelligence. "Well, you're there to look after the interests of the company. You'll report periodically, as Wilcox did. You'll receive instructions from here and act as liaison with the European distributors, especially with the English subsidiary. . . ." He added reassuringly, "You'll soon get into it. As regards the ordinary day-to-day routine, Gilbertson will be able to give you all the information you want. You'll find him most helpful."

"Yes, I'm sure I will," said Marshall. He was still not entirely clear about the position. For instance, what was to be his precise relationship with Gilbertson? However, there seemed little chance of getting any clarification from Kingham. "I suppose," he said, "I shall have a chance to talk to Wilcox before I go?"

"Oh, sure, sure. There should be lots of time for that," Kingham said. "He's being transferred to Domestic, you know."

"I didn't know."

"We think he'll fit in better that way. He'll have a few months' training out in the field, then they'll probably give him an area." He added: "He's going off to Detroit for a couple of days, but he should be back before you go."

"When would you like me to leave?"

"The beginning of next week would be early enough, I guess." Kingham added generously, "I always like to give people time to make arrangements."

It was almost three o'clock when he returned to the office, heavy with rich food and brandy. He had only a week to clear up all outstanding work, arrange his affairs in New York, and see about letting his apartment. He felt excited but confused; events were beginning to march more quickly than he was used to. He telephoned the travel agency to book his passage. The girl was dubious. The notice was short, and first-class berths were not easy to come by. However, she would make inquiries and perhaps call back later in the afternoon.

At half-past five she had still not phoned. He picked up the telephone and then put it down again. Personal contact was always more effective. He decided to call in at the agency on his way out.

The girl behind the counter was apologetic.

"I'm very sorry, Mr. Marshall. I had a note to phone you, but the reservation only came through a matter of ten minutes ago. Yes, it's okay. You were so lucky, just one stateroom left, a cancellation——"

"Well, that's fine. Thank you very much."

"You're welcome." As she made out the ticket, she said: "I really feel badly about not calling you up, but we've been so busy . . ."

"That's quite all right."

"Mostly from your office too. It's really one person's work just looking after the Marshall reservations. And always at the last minute. They think we can work miracles. It's not so difficult on some of the routes. But it's a busy service to Los Angeles——"

To make conversation he asked, "Who's going to Los Angeles?"

"Mr. Wilcox."

"Wilcox? I thought he was going to Detroit."

"Well, yes he is. He had a Detroit return and then we were told this afternoon that it was to be changed to a through ticket to Los Angeles with a forty-eight-hour stopover at Detroit. I've managed it for him in the end, but I practically had to go on my *knees* to the airline——"

"So he won't be coming back to New York?"

"Well, no. At least that's how it stands at the moment. But don't quote me on that. For all I know, he may change his mind again. . . ."

She continued to chatter, but Marshall was no longer listening. The company was given to these sudden and unpredictable postings to distant areas; they gave an impression of urgency and drama, but this was carrying things to absurdity. Presumably the Domestic Division had changed Wilcox's itinerary without bothering to notify Kingham about it. It was a typical piece of administrative muddle. By the time Wilcox returned Marshall would have left for Europe.

He turned back to the girl. "When does Mr. Wilcox leave?" he asked.

"You mean his plane for Detroit?"

"Yes."

"The bus leaves the air terminal at six-thirty, but I gathered from Mr. Wilcox that he wasn't taking it. He said he'd take a cab from his home directly to La Guardia."

"When does the plane actually leave?"

"At eight o'clock. But of course you have to check in twenty minutes earlier."

"Thanks." There was time to drive out to La Guardia if he wanted to. There might be nothing to be gained, but it seemed crazy to go out on a new job without at least having a talk with the man who had been doing it for the past two years. There might be some useful advice he could pick up. He turned away from the desk.

"Mr. Marshall, your tickets." The travel clerk's voice was plaintive. She was having a difficult afternoon. "And here are the baggage tags——"

"Send them up to my office."

He took his car out of the garage and drove to the airport. At first he found himself hurrying and then slowed down, realizing that it was pointless. Even so, he arrived much too early. He lit a cigarette and sat down by the gate for the Detroit flight. It was nearly half an hour before he noticed Wilcox threading his way through the crowd.

"Why, hello!" Wilcox looked at him in surprise. "I didn't figure on a send-off," he added, not too pleasantly.

"I just wanted to have a talk with you before you left."

"Sure. Glad to. Though I haven't much time. . . . I'd better check in first."

When he had checked in they went upstairs to the bar.

"I only just heard," said Marshall, "that you were going through to Los Angeles. It occurred to me that we wouldn't have a chance to talk——"

Wilcox nodded. "It was a rush decision." His speech was a little faster, his face pinker, his whole manner a little less guarded than usual. "I wasn't any too pleased with it myself, but what the hell can you do? There's no sense in arguing."

"It was stupid of them not to tell Kingham."

Wilcox looked at him skeptically. "He didn't know?"

"No. He told me at lunch that you'd be back from Detroit in a day or two."

"Well, what do you know," he said. He gave an unsuccessful little smile and said: "What can I do for you?"

"I was hoping to hear something from you about the European job."

"Were you?" Wilcox picked up a cocktail stick and prodded moodily at the ice in his glass. "There's not much I can tell you in a quarter of an hour. Besides," he added obscurely, "you may know more about what goes on than I do."

"Meaning what?"

Wilcox looked at Marshall as if wondering whether to be wise or to forget about discretion for a change. There was more than one whisky on his breath. He said: "Maybe I was wrong. I had the idea that all this was being arranged for your benefit. Isn't that right?"

"You mean that you were moved out to make a place for me?" Wilcox nodded. "No," said Marshall, "I don't think so. If it was, I knew nothing about it, I can promise you that."

Wilcox regarded him for a moment with the unembarrassed stare of the slightly drunk. "All right," he said eventually. "I believe you. Though God knows why I should." Almost to himself he said: "I guess it must've been the other business. . . ."

"What other business?"

Wilcox paused and then rubbed a hand across his face. He

yawned. "Nothing," he said indifferently. "Nothing that you have to worry about anyway. God," he went on with apparent irrelevance, "I won't be sorry to get back to working on American soil. No, sir."

"You didn't like it over there?" asked Marshall, seeing a possible opportunity of getting back to the point.

"No." Wilcox was suddenly assailed with melancholy and self-doubt. "Maybe Kingham was right—I just don't connect with Europeans. I don't speak their language. All I want to do is to go ahead and get a job done. But it seems that's not enough," he said bitterly, "not for those boys. Have you met Gilbertson?"

"No."

Wilcox shrugged his shoulders. "You may get along all right with him. To me he's just a stuffed shirt."

"Kingham said he was a good businessman."

"He's not such a fool as he looks, I'll give him that."

"What about the other countries?"

"Well, as you probably know, the agencies in Scandinavia and Italy aren't worth much. Nor are the Germans—they can make instruments just as good as ours, and cheaper. Apart from England, France is the only place that counts." He was silent for a moment. "You've heard of Furac?"

"Yes."

"You'll like him," he said sarcastically. "He'll give you a wonderful time. But when you shake hands with him, just count your fingers afterward, that's all." He added with feeling, "Boy, I hope I never see France again."

He drained his glass and looked at Marshall.

"All right," he said sourly, "I know what you're thinking. Poor old Wilcox—he flopped out, and now he's blaming the rest of the team. Correct?"

"No, not at all. I——"

"I didn't look so good at the meeting—I know that. But, brother, you wait till they want to fix you the same way. You just have to sit there and take it—there isn't a goddamn thing you can do. They made it look as if I fell down all along the line. But there was only one thing I did wrong. Do you know what that was?"

He leaned toward Marshall, tapping him on the chest. "Do you know what it was?" he repeated.

"What?"

"I tried to play it the straight way, the American way——" he said in a maudlin voice. "Yes sir, that was my mistake."

This obscurity was maddening. "Tried to play what?" Marshall asked impatiently.

Wilcox withdrew, shaking his head. "Let's leave it there. I've got my future to think of." He was suddenly cautious. "My old man didn't leave me a million dollars, you know."

It was fifteen minutes to eight. Urgently the loud-speakers began to call passengers for the plane to Detroit. Wilcox picked up his brief case from the floor with an air of relief. Obviously he was determined to say no more. Nor did Marshall feel like pressing him. He was out of patience with Wilcox, with his mysterious allusions and his drunken self-pity. Obviously he had antagonized the distributors in Europe and they had used their influence with Kingham to have him replaced. Looking at him now, Marshall found it possible to sympathize with them. Coldly he shook hands and then watched Wilcox disappear through the door toward his plane. Then he went out of the building to look for his car. It had been hardly worth while making the journey.

PART II

CHAPTER I

HIS FIRST SIGHT of Europe was at Cherbourg. The town was a gray, jagged pattern in the misty evening light, with that air of shabby abandonment so characteristic of the ports of northern France since World War II. A few new blocks of concrete flats had appeared, standing on plots of waste ground like skittles in an alley, waiting despondently for the next invader to come and knock them down. The harbor seemed almost deserted as the great ship moved in. Ashore, a few pale lights twinkled sparsely in the main streets of the town. Marshall could visualize the narrow streets, the cafés, the indomitable old women in shiny black clothes poking about for bargains in the shops. He could see the walls covered with tattered posters and scrawled with slogans, the dockside bars in which men sat for hours in political argument or playing belote with greasy packs of cards. The ship drew into the quay, a puff of wind blew from the shore, and he smelled once again the odor of France—something vaguely compounded of coffee and old furniture and dubious sanitation, and the baking of bread in basement kitchens. . . . A few bronzed figures stood lounging on the quay, picturesque in their berets and fishermen's linen trousers, scowling into the clicking cameras of the tourists. A gangway went down and a handful of passengers hurried ashore to catch the train to Paris. The gong for second dinner boomed up from the saloon. Marshall stayed on deck for a little while, feasting on nostalgia. But the air was cold, the diet thin and lacking in sustenance. Presently he left the rail and went down to dinner with the rest.

A few hours later they were in Southampton. Here it was just as he remembered it, only rather smaller. After New York, the houses, the streets, the trains, the automobiles were like a collection of miniatures, delightful in their tidy completeness but hardly to be taken seriously. Even the polite formality of the people seemed to be somehow related to this smallness—the necessary courtesy of individuals compelled to live together in a confined space. He watched them in the train as it traveled toward London, seated within inches of each other in the narrow carriages but carefully avoiding each other's eyes, taking elaborate steps to avoid being drawn into conversation. Outside in the darkness was the tame, trim countryside of Hampshire, punctuated now and then by a flash of lights from an occasional market town. The food in the dining car was cheap but bad, and they were running late; no one knew why. He felt himself growing attuned once more to the rhythm of British life.

It was after midnight when the train drew into Waterloo. He was standing on the platform looking for a porter to collect his luggage when he noticed someone pushing his way through the crowds toward him. It was a young man of between twenty and thirty, wearing a loose tweed suit and a small mustache of a vaguely military appearance. He leaped over a pair of suitcases and presented himself with the satisfied air of a man breasting the tape at the end of an obstacle race.

"Mr. Marshall?"

"Yes?"

"How do you do, sir?"

Marshall was about to say, "Fine—fine" and then remembered in time. "How do you do?"

The young man shot out an arm and shook hands with him, squeezing quite unnecessarily hard, as if he had once been advised to cultivate a strong, positive handshake. "My name's Travers. I'm Mr. Gilbertson's personal assistant."

"I'm very glad to meet you."

"Mr. Gilbertson asked me to apologize for him. He had a dinner engagement outside London which he couldn't very well skip. . . ."

"Please don't apologize," said Marshall. "I never expected him to be here. Or anyone, for that matter. It was very good of you to come along."

"Delighted. Delighted." He spoke with apparent sincerity. Perhaps he was the sort of person who enjoyed meeting trains at midnight. "I'll just see about your luggage." Travers waved to a porter who had been waiting some ten yards away, deaf to all other requests. The disposal of the luggage was arranged with ostentatious briskness and efficiency. Plainly, Travers was out to make an impression. It occurred to Marshall for the first time that over here they might have the mistaken idea that he was a person of importance in the organization. He had the feeling of gaining attention under false pretenses.

Outside the station there was a hired car with a chauffeur. As they drove away Travers said: "We fixed a room for you at the Savoy, sir. I hope that's all right?"

"Oh, sure." He wished Travers would stop calling him "sir." It made him feel foolish—and rather old. On the other hand, this was the better of the two extremes. In New York, Travers would have been calling him "Chris."

"I took a look at the room myself. It's quite a good one, facing on to the river."

"It sounds fine."

"I wasn't sure whether you might not prefer a suite. But then I thought, well, you could always change——"

"Sure. That's right. Thanks a lot." He was beginning to feel suffocated with so much thoughtfulness. He looked out of the window. It was raining—as it should be, he thought, on one's first night in London. They were crossing Waterloo Bridge, with the lights of the Embankment stretched in a great arc before them, outlining the north bank of the river. Somerset House, the Shell-Mex Building, the Houses of Parliament, covered with scaffolding as usual, damp, shining streets, so silent after midnight. The river was high —a tug passing upstream with a string of coal barges seemed to be sitting on the same level as the road. . . . He turned back reluctantly to his companion.

"Have you been with the organization long?" he asked.

"Two years only." Travers gave a brisk and rather meaningless smile.

"And before that?"

"Before that I was"—he paused and then went on rather obscurely—"connected with the motor industry." Selling cars? wondered Marshall. It seemed rather likely. "It was quite fun, but rather a dead end, you know. Then this chance of a job at Marshall's came up and naturally I jumped at it. Enormous piece of luck, really."

"You like the work?"

"Oh, rather." He added earnestly, "I mean—I do feel there's an enormous excitement in working for a really alive, *growing* concern. Some of the English firms are pretty stick-in-the-mud, you know."

"Oh, I wouldn't exactly say that——"

"Yes, I'm afraid we have to admit it. We have certain virtues, it's true, over here, but we haven't the energy, the streamlined efficiency, the sense of dedication, if you know what I mean——"

"Yes, I know what you mean." The frightening thing was, there was some truth in it. Not about the efficiency so much—the New York office seemed to spend most of its time in a state of bureaucratic confusion—but about the dedication. His father had been a dedicated man. But dedicated to what?

"And the other thing is, I'm glad to be dealing in something important, something really new, not just soap powders or vacuum cleaners—those are all very well in their way, but these instruments of ours are things of the future. Nobody knows what their eventual implications may be——"

He went on to give his views on possible developments in the use of transistors. It sounded like a speech he had made often before.

Marshall yawned. Faith, he thought, faith and loyalty in another country and another language. He had traveled four thousand miles to be confronted once again with his own isolation. His first pleasure at being in England began to leave him.

Travers stopped quite abruptly, sensing a failure of response. Had he laid it on a bit too thick? Was he talking too much? After a short pause he looked out of the window and said: "This is the

Strand we're turning into now. But perhaps you know London?"

"Fairly well. I was over here in the Army Air Force for a little while. Then after I was released I spent a year or two at Cambridge."

"Oh, really?" Travers sighed fondly. "Wonderful place, Cambridge. I was there for some time myself."

"Is that so?" Marshall's interest was momentarily aroused. "Which college?"

"Well, I wasn't exactly at the *university* . . ."

The car drew up in front of the Savoy. As Travers made a move to get out behind him, Marshall said, "Don't bother to come in. I can manage."

"Oh, but——"

"No, I insist. It's late and you must be very tired. I know I am." He could feel Travers' disappointment. He had been looking forward to a late-night drink, a little chat. This was his chance to get on easy terms with a supposedly influential American, perhaps to strike up a personal friendship. You never knew, it might lead to anything—one of these days Marshall might be talking to some nameless demi-god in Rockefeller Plaza and say casually, "I know just the man you want. I met him in London—young, keen, smart as a whip." That was how big careers were made, by attracting attention, making the right sorts of contacts. . . .

Marshall was not attracted to Travers but he felt a moment of sympathy for him. He was probably as able as Wilcox or Richardson if the truth were known. But nobody had ever heard of him and nobody would, except through a lucky chance. One could hardly blame him for doing his best. Just the same, there was no obligation to sit up all night with him.

Marshall held out his hand. "Good night," he said, "and thanks a lot."

"It's been a pleasure," said Travers. He sank back, thwarted, into his hired limousine. "Will you be in at the office in the morning?"

"Sure."

"You have the address?"

"Yes."

"I'll tell Mr. Gilbertson. He's looking forward to seeing you."

CHAPTER II

Gilbertson and Cowles, the partly owned British subsidiary of the Marshall Corporation, occupied a pleasing Georgian house in a square about midway between Oxford Street and Piccadilly. These, at one time, had been the town residences of the great people of a vanished age. Now not a single one remained in private occupation. The cold winds of the twentieth century had blown with devastating effect through these magnificent double reception rooms, up the elegant staircases and tall, drafty corridors. Supertax and death duties, high wages, inflation, and rent-restriction acts had succeeded in beating the ancient aristocracy to its knees. Social change, more ruthless than any foreign invader, was gradually stripping the great families of their possessions. One by one they had fled, to country houses half closed down, to "amusing" converted stables in Kensington, to farms in Kenya or tax-free villas on the shores of the Caribbean.

Their homes had been taken by various forms of national or commercial enterprise. In parts, wholesale destruction, either speculative or bureaucratic, had led to replacement by concrete office blocks. In more fortunate areas, such as in this particular square, there had been determined efforts at preservation. With a delicacy that was almost oppressive, façades had been repainted, chandeliers cleaned and replaced, rooms repapered in the style of the appropriate period. Window boxes flourished. Furniture hardly distinguishable from real Sheraton added dignity to waiting rooms and executive offices. Many of the houses had not looked so well cared for in years.

The only thing that gave the game away from outside was the metal plates on the doors. Although unobtrusive and in the best of taste, they could not avoid generating a certain disillusion. Or so it seemed to Marshall, glancing idly at the names of the occupants as he passed by. Accrington Jute Spinners, Susie Gay Modes Ltd. (K. Schumberger), Ministry of Agriculture and Fisheries (Cattle Cake Section)—they were all doing first-rate work, no doubt, the sort of work that needed doing in this modern world. And yet, somehow . . .

Gilbertson and Cowles, he was pleased to find, had one of the best houses, with a front elevation rather strikingly picked out in gray paint. Inside the hall an attractive receptionist was standing behind a desk, putting the finishing touches to a bowl of daffodils. He introduced himself.

"Mr. Marshall?" She threw him a brilliant smile. "Please come this way. Mr. Gilbertson is expecting you."

She led him upstairs to a room on the first floor and knocked on the door. There was an indefinable sound from within. She opened the door.

"Mr. Marshall."

Gilbertson rose to his feet as Marshall entered the room. He was a man in his forties, very tall and thin, with a kind of languid, whiskery distinction. His trousers were narrow, his coat full-skirted, his shoes almost certainly handmade. His hair was thick and dark and brushed back over his ears in a faintly theatrical fashion.

"Marshall?" He loped forward, extending a thin hairy hand. It was curiously dry to the touch, like that of one of the higher primates.

"Delighted to see you. You found the office without any trouble?"

"Yes, thanks."

"Excellent. Now do sit down." He gripped Marshall's shoulder and impelled him into a chair. "Cigarette?" He snapped open a case. "I hope young Travers looked after you properly last night?"

"Oh, certainly. It was most kind of him. But there was really no need——"

"My dear fellow, he was delighted to do it. I was sorry I couldn't be there myself, but I live rather far out and my wife had a dinner party arranged sometime before, you understand." He sat down behind the desk and folded one spidery leg over the other. "Otherwise, of course——"

"I quite understand," said Marshall. As Gilbertson lit a cigarette for himself, Marshall glanced around the room. It was large and high-ceilinged, with an Adam fireplace along one wall and two sets of french windows leading out on to a wrought-iron balcony.

"Quite a place you have here," he remarked.

"You like it?" Gilbertson grinned delightedly. "I'm so glad. We got it for a song—by your standards, that is. They wanted a good tenant on a long lease and I happened to be a friend of Charlie Porteous, the owner. Naturally he didn't want to let it go to a somebody who'd turn it into a corset factory or something." He sighed. "Impossible to run as a house any longer, I'm afraid. Charlie was heartbroken. His family had lived here for two hundred years."

"That's pretty tough."

"Yes. But he doesn't feel too badly about it now. He looked in the other day, as a matter of fact. He told me it was the first time it had been properly decorated since the First World War. They couldn't afford it, you see."

"I suppose not."

"And it suits us perfectly. A little chilly in winter on the upper floors, perhaps, but the girls don't seem to mind. And they love the address. It gives them cachet in some extraordinary way, to work in Mayfair. It means that we can get a good class of girl." He paused, as if seeking an illustration. "You met Miss Carvill-Sykes, our receptionist?"

"Momentarily."

"Charming, don't you think?" With a significance which Marshall failed to grasp he added: "She's a vicar's daughter." He suddenly swung around in his swivel chair and recrossed his legs. Then he grinned again at Marshall. His whole behavior somehow gave the impression of being a performance, as if he was always rather amused at the idea of himself sitting behind a desk, playing the part of a businessman and had to be careful not to let the performance degenerate into burlesque.

"Did you have a good crossing?" he asked.

"Very good, thanks."

"I'm so glad. You know," he said reflectively, "I think you were most sensible to come by boat. Between ourselves, there's far too much chasing about in airplanes nowadays. There's a tendency to work oneself into a premature grave. . . ." It was a tendency, Marshall imagined, which Gilbertson himself had so far managed to resist. "I hope you're going to enjoy yourself over here."

"I hope so too." Not to be outdone in courtesy, he added: "I fully expect to."

"Good. Naturally we'll do everything we can . . ." Gilbertson suddenly rose from his chair. "I expect the first thing you'd like to do is to have a look at your office. I'll take you along and introduce you to some of the boys and girls. You'll find them all very anxious to help you. We're a pretty happy family here, on the whole."

His own office was on the floor above Gilbertson's, not quite so grand, but with a view of the square—presumably it had been one of the better bedrooms of the house. When the tour of the building was over, Gilbertson deposited him there, having first invited him to lunch.

"I'll give you a chance to settle down," he said. "If there's anything you particularly want, just shout for it." He indicated a buzzer on the telephone table. "This calls your secretary, Miss Lancing. She works in a room just across the hall. A very experienced girl. I'm sure she'll be a great help to you."

When Gilbertson had left, Marshall sat down behind the mahogany desk and tried to fit himself, as it were, into his new part. There was a palatial emptiness about the office which he found intimidating. The desk was completely bare, the drawers empty; there were no filing cabinets in the room, though one corner held a bookcase filled with trade journals and almanacs and a copy of last year's *Who's Who*. There was not a trace of anything personal. Nothing to remind him of Wilcox. Of course it was a little while now since Wilcox had left London, but he had somehow expected *some* degree of continuity, a feeling of taking over rather than starting afresh. . . .

He was just engaged in wondering who had been doing Wilcox's work during the last two months, when there was a knock on the door.

"Yes?"

"Mr. Marshall? I'm Miss Lancing."

The girl who came in was small and slight, her thin oval face moderately and somehow discreetly good-looking. Her hair was cleverly arranged to make the most of her face, her blouse and skirt suitable and becoming to her trim, tight-waisted figure. Her eyes were smiling, but sharply interested, making only a formal effort to disguise their curiosity.

"Glad to meet you, Miss Lancing." They shook hands. "Do sit down."

"I don't want to interrupt——"

"That's all right." He waved a hand over the naked desk. "As you see, I'm not very busy right now. Perhaps this is a good time for us to get to know each other. You used to work for Mr. Wilcox, I take it?"

"Yes."

"I saw him just before I left. He's got a new assignment in the Domestic Division, you know."

She nodded, showing respectful interest. Then she asked innocently, "A promotion?"

"Why, yes——" He was slightly off guard. His voice, he realized, sounded confused; almost, for no logical reason, guilty. "Yes—I imagine so. Though of course I don't know too much about that end of the business——"

"I suppose not." Her interest in Wilcox's future seemed to have been no more than perfunctory. She glanced around the room. "I hope everything's all right for you," she said. "Mr. Gilbertson told me to be sure to see you had everything you wanted."

"That was kind of him."

"He's a very kind man," she said demurely. She looked down at her notebook, the merest trace of a smile on her lips. He had the feeling that beneath the façade of respect she was secretly laughing at something or somebody. Himself? Gilbertson? The whole organization?

"Is there nothing," she asked, "that I can get for you? Please don't hesitate to ask for it if there is. Most of the executives," she explained almost reproachfully, "have certain little peculiarities of their own."

Already, thought Marshall, before he had been much more than an hour in the building, he was beginning to disappoint people. It was true enough that he found his working quarters lacking in something, but he could not immediately put his finger on what it was. The successful man of affairs did not accept everything, as he was tempted to do—he made demands, demonstrated his own methods, set up a form of organization, stamped any new environment immediately with the mark of a distinctive personality. Even the secretaries knew it and expected it.

On the defensive, he searched his mind furiously for something to ask for, some memorable but not too outrageous demand.

"Since you ask," he said, "there are one or two matters——"

"Yes?" Miss Lancing's pencil hovered expectantly over her notebook.

"I like a box of cigarettes on my desk. One of those leather ones—you know the kind? And fill it with Chesterfields. You'll need about a hundred a week. Can you arrange that?"

She made a few squiggles in her notebook.

"And some English cigarettes for visitors."

"The charwomen will pinch them."

"Never mind." This was something, but hardly enough. Another idea came to him. "And it seems to me that the offices in this building are hard to find. Why don't we have name plates?"

She looked serious. "Mr. Gilbertson doesn't like them. He says they disfigure the doors."

"Well, I like them." He was determined to be decisive. "Fix one for me, will you?"

"I don't think I could, not unless you would clear it with Mr. Gilbertson first. I believe he promised Sir Charles Porteous——"

"The hell with Sir Charles Porteous."

"Yes, sir." She made another squiggle in the notebook. Once

again a secret trace of a smile, little more than a movement of the lips, crossed her face. He wondered if she had seen through his bluff. Suddenly he was tired of this childish game.

"No, I don't mean that. Forget it." He looked around him. "I guess he has a point of view, at that."

"You like the house?" she asked.

"Yes indeed." He contemplated the fireplace, the high, carved ceiling. "It's certainly a change from New York."

She put down her pencil and relaxed in her chair. She became suddenly less prim and more human. "You wait until the cold weather sets in. Though it's nice at Christmas, I have to admit that. Mr. Gilbertson gives a party to the staff in that great office of his—it used to be the drawing room, of course, in the old days——"

She was interrupted by a knock on the door. The receptionist came in, carrying a tray of coffee. She gave a cup to Marshall and then turned to Miss Lancing questioningly.

"Shall I take yours through to the back room, Jane?"

Miss Lancing did not immediately reply. It was as if she had misheard or misunderstood. It was a few seconds before Marshall realized that the question had been silently transferred to him. Presumably this was a matter for his own discretion.

He had no wish to seem undemocratic. "Why not drink it here?" he said.

When the receptionist had left, Miss Lancing looked at him over the top of her cup.

"That," she said, "was Miss Carvill-Sykes."

"So I understand."

"Our receptionist." With a touch of malice she added, "She's a vicar's daughter."

"Mr. Gilbertson told me."

She raised her eyebrows, and once again he saw the faint, secret, mocking smile. But this time it was not quite so secret and it occurred to him that he was invited to share in the joke if he chose. Unfortunately he was not quite clear what the joke was, except that it was at Gilbertson's expense. Whatever it was, it seemed a good thing to ignore it. He decided to move the conversation back to business.

"Have you done this job for long?" he asked.

"About eighteen months."

"Then you probably know the routine better than I do at the moment." This, he thought, was putting it mildly. So far he had only the haziest idea of what he was supposed to be doing. He sought for a way of obtaining information from her without exposing his ignorance too nakedly. "Is there anything I ought to be attending to right now? Anything urgent?"

"Not really. There's a certain amount of mail. Would you like to see it?"

"Yes, please."

She went out, taking the empty coffee cups with her. A few minutes later she came back with a pile of letters and trade journals. He looked casually through the letters. There was about a dozen of them, mostly routine inquiries.

"Not much here," he said.

"No."

"Surely this isn't all since Mr. Wilcox left?"

"Oh no. The rest are dealt with. Mr. Gilbertson told me to answer as many as I could myself and pass the rest over to him."

"Oh—I see."

"Mr. Wilcox was often away on business trips," she explained. "He left a good deal to my discretion in the matter of correspondence. Of course it's up to you now. If you just tell me how you want things done——"

She spoke without a trace of officiousness, as if prepared to take responsibility if he wished it but not in the least concerned if he didn't. Nevertheless, he was cautious. It would probably be a tactical mistake to hand over too much at this early stage.

"Well," he said amiably, "perhaps we'd better see how it shakes down, shall we? In the meantime"—he picked up the letters—"I think I'll take care of these myself."

CHAPTER III

"I ALWAYS SAY," said Gilbertson, looking at his plate with appreciation, "that here they have the best cold beef in London."

"Is that so?" Marshall tried to make the phrase express not skepticism but rather gratitude for a useful piece of local knowledge. He himself, in a rash attempt to be thoroughly English, had ordered steak-and-kidney pie and was now regretting it.

"Yes. Of course the secret is to cook it and let it go cold. Once you cut into it——" He smiled in acknowledgment to an acquaintance who passed their table. "That's Tom Phillipson, the Q.C., most interesting fellow, perhaps you'd like to meet him later on." He took an exploratory sip from his glass of burgundy. "I hope you'll like this. I've always considered it a really first-rate Chambertin."

Fortunately it was. It was also a wine of high alcoholic content, and a couple of glasses of it had the effect of generating a certain warmth of spirit to counteract the forbidding effect of the club itself. Marshall found himself able to look around the cavernous dining room with something approaching equanimity. It was, even now, not exactly friendly—but it was rather less sepulchral than the nave of Westminster Abbey.

Having declared his support for the food and wine, Gilbertson began to explore a series of conversational gambits. He spoke in a high-pitched, slightly exhausted voice, with prolonged, strangled vowels, and he had a tendency to drop his voice into a weary mumble at the end of each sentence. This, together with his clothes, his club, even his walk, had the effect of placing him, to anyone familiar with English social distinctions, as a member of a certain economic and cultural caste. It was a caste with which Marshall had never felt entirely at home, since he had always sensed within it an atmosphere of patronage. He was repelled by the complacent lack of curiosity about strangers, the evasion of any attempt to build up a relationship on a personal basis. At this moment, for instance, he had the impression that Gilbertson was carrying out a mere performance; he had a certain routine for visiting Americans, appropriate topics of conversation, a little flattery because they were simple people and known to like it, a joke or two . . . The needle was put into the groove and the record was played—it bore no relation to himself at all.

Nor did it give any clue about Gilbertson's own attitudes. His formality of manner was effective in concealing not only his personal reaction to Marshall but his views on the system of European representatives as a whole. It seemed important to get a clear picture of this as soon as possible. Marshall was wondering how to move the conversation politely back to business when Gilbertson made the change himself.

Raising his wineglass, he said, "To success in your new job."

"Thank you very much."

"I'm sure we shall be able to work together very smoothly," he said. "Naturally it will take you a little while to settle down. I don't want to interfere in your affairs, but it may be that I can help you over some matters——"

"I was hoping you might. When I spoke with Mr. Kingham in New York before I left, he told me that you would be able to explain a good many things to me."

"Glad to." Gilbertson added appreciatively, "A very capable fellow, Kingham, don't you think?"

"Oh yes."

"I was most impressed by him the last time I was over there. A very acute mind."

They remained silent for a moment, meditating on the acuity of

Kingham's mind. Suddenly Gilbertson became more confidential in manner. The record had been switched off; even his voice had lost some of its affectations. For the first time he appeared to address Marshall as an individual. "He wrote me a personal letter about you, as a matter of fact. Gave you an enormous build-up."

"That was good of him."

"I must say that when I read it I was relieved. It encouraged me to hope that we might be getting just the sort of person we needed."

"I hope I shan't disappoint you."

"I'm sure you won't."

"You hardly know me yet," Marshall pointed out. He felt a little uneasy at so much approbation.

"Perhaps not." Gilbertson smiled at him benignly. "But one feels these things. And you've lived in Europe before. That's an enormous help—far more than you probably think."

"Are we Americans quite so foreign as all that?"

"I used not to think so. But recently . . ." He sighed, as if remembering a regrettable episode. "You take young Wilcox, for instance. A charming fellow—keen as mustard—excellent businessman. He'll be a big success in the States. But, let's be honest, he didn't really fit in over here."

"No?" Marshall waited expectantly.

"No. Of course he was—young."

Gilbertson almost whispered the last word, as if youth were a disease one didn't mention in public. "I was sorry for him, really. He often seemed rather bewildered."

"By what?"

"Oh—conditions generally. I'm not saying it's anything against him—much more probably something wrong with us." He grinned to make it clear that this was a joke. "But there you are. In an organization of this kind, one of the most important things is to be able to adapt oneself to varying conditions. Flexibility," he said with the air of a man summing up a complex situation in a single word. "Flexibility, above all things, is what is required here."

Marshall nodded in a dazed way. Gilbertson's words, though delivered with the utmost solemnity, seemed to him to mean practically nothing at all. Perhaps, he thought, the wine was responsible for some degree of failure in communication.

"You see," Gilbertson went on after a pause, "business here isn't quite the same as it is in the States. Over there it's a fairly straightforward problem. You make a good article, fix your price in relation to the competition, and then use your sales organization to get as much of the market as you can. Correct?"

"Yes." It was not only correct, it was elementary.

"And if you know your job and put your back to it, you make money, and society applauds you for it?"

"More or less."

"Well, here," said Gilbertson, "it's not quite so simple. In England, business, and particularly American business, is regarded with suspicion by a large part of the community. If you manage to make money, the assumption is that you've stolen it from somebody. Most of your profits go in taxation, and as for the rest, it's extremely difficult to get it out of the country owing to the Exchange Control. Politics come into everything, even when they don't immediately appear to." He paused to allow the waiter to clear away the cheese and serve them with coffee and brandy. Then he went on, "So you see, the main problems here are ones that don't exist for you at home. You may think they shouldn't exist here either, but there's nothing we can do about it. Personally, I've long since lost interest in discussing the rights and wrongs of a situation which I can't change. But"—he leaned forward earnestly; his eyes were hard and the languid note had left his voice—"the main point I want to emphasize is that you have to accept it. It's no use getting exasperated and saying it couldn't happen at home."

Marshall nodded. So this, presumably, was where Wilcox had gone wrong. He had refused to accept local customs and had been punished for it. The situation was becoming to some extent clarified. The rather curious aspect of the affair was that officially the European representative was supposed to be supervising the subsidiaries on behalf of New York, but evidently it was dangerous to supervise them too closely. It seemed likely that Wilcox and Gilbertson had disagreed on some matter of policy, that the matter had been taken to New York for arbitration, and that Gilbertson had won. That would explain everything, including Wilcox's attitude when they had talked together at La Guardia. Only the details of the struggle were still obscure.

"You'll find," said Gilbertson, reverting to a more relaxed manner, "that it isn't easy to do anything here in a hurry. Before you make any sort of move you have to consider the possible reactions of various influential bodies—government departments, business associations, trades unions—we can't afford to get across any of them."

"You make it sound tough going."

"One gets used to it. It's largely a question of getting accustomed to a more"—he searched for a word—"a more *deliberate* approach. There isn't, in any case, the same incentive toward developing absolutely maximum efficiency under present circumstances."

"Not worth the effort, you mean?"

"Well—not worth killing yourself, shall we say? After all, life is there to be lived, to be enjoyed . . ." He looked fondly at his brandy glass, at the spring sunshine pouring in through the tall windows. "When you get to my age you begin to have some idea of what's worth while, of what's possible and what isn't. It's hard sometimes to be patient with people who want to go through the whole process again, just to find out for themselves. It's very satisfying to come across somebody who can grasp not only the possibilities of an enterprise but the necessary limitations." He added reminiscently: "Your father was a man like that."

"Was he?" Marshall looked at him skeptically. This conception of his father was new to him. "That wasn't how I saw him."

"Oh yes," said Gilbertson with assurance, "of course he was very forceful and energetic, and he liked to play that side of himself up—he was a bit of an actor, I think you'll admit. But when it came to the point, you could always make him see reason. He had no taste for beating his head against a brick wall."

There was a silence. As so often when he listened to the opinions of other people about his father, he found himself withdrawing, like some threatened crustacean, into the confines of a shell which was not quite large enough to give him complete protection. Gilbertson was wrong, of course, just as his mother and Kingham and

Jeff were wrong—the vivid, colorful personality of the old man had been too strong for them. Like a conjurer, he had so succeeded in dominating their attention that he could attract it at will in any direction which suited him, while at the same time diverting it from other activities which he wished to conceal. He had been able, at various times, to pass himself off as the bluff, honest, jovial self-made man; the rough go-getter with a heart of gold beneath all his toughness; the shrewd operator; the capable administrator conscious of his lack of education but with a talent for picking up technical knowledge as he went along; the sympathetic listener; the loyal friend; the lost child sitting lonely and forlorn in the midst of all his possessions. . . . And the curious thing was that those closest to him were deceived along with the rest, perhaps even more than the rest. They found him out and still continued to believe, as if the belief had become as necessary for themselves as for him. Only a few, thought Marshall with a certain pride, were incapable of such easy forgiveness.

But there was no question of explaining this to Gilbertson. Marshall was more interested in trying to get a clear picture of the present situation. These obscure hints were beginning to get on his nerves.

"I follow your point in general," he said. "But I'd appreciate it if you could give me a little more detail. I presume you must have some particular problems in mind—some specific examples——"

Gilbertson flapped his hand in a gesture almost of panic. "No, no, I can assure you I had nothing specific in mind—nothing." He appeared quite horrified at the suggestion. "I was speaking purely generally. My advice is simply this—settle down here. Get to know us. Make the necessary contacts, see how the land lies, and don't be in too much of a hurry to change everything. Rome wasn't built in a day, you know." He looked up at Marshall through his bushy eyebrows and said with significance, "I'm sure Mr. Kingham agrees with me."

"I guess so." So, he thought, Gilbertson knew what the line was, knew what Kingham had said to him in New York. The line was: Plenty of tact, no interference, and remember what happened to Wilcox. He was to be what he had been in the past—nothing. And

Gilbertson knew it. It was only on the Travers level that there remained any illusions about his significance in the company.

He told himself, not for the first time, that he must expect nothing else. He was the unbeliever at the séance whose very presence was a threat to those assumptions on which the whole performance was based. They could not be blamed for distrusting him, for trying to hide him away in some unimportant corner of the organization where he would have no reponsibilities and be the least possible nuisance. Nevertheless, he felt a fierce, illogical blaze of anger at being held so cheaply.

Gilbertson had moved on to firm ground. "How do you like the idea of living in England?"

"Very much."

"Of course you were here before, weren't you? But that was not long after the war. You'll find everything greatly changed. Do you know many people in London?"

"A few."

"Excellent. I feel sure you'll enjoy yourself enormously. This is quite the best time of year, you know. There's everything—cricket, tennis, golf, the theater——" He waved his hand expansively. "I really envy you. And if I can be of any help with introductions——"

"That's very kind of you."

"Not a bit, my dear fellow, just say the word. I suppose you'll be living in town?"

"I imagine so."

"Quite the best thing for a bachelor. Though for a family man like myself there's a lot to be said for the country. I have a house in Sussex—not a large place, you know, that's quite impossible nowadays—but it's very pleasant out there. You might like to come and spend a weekend with us sometime."

"Very much."

"Excellent. I'll have a talk with my wife and then we can fix a date."

Gilbertson looked up at the clock. "Good God—it's three o'clock. If you'll excuse me I think I ought to get back to the office." He added with solemnity, "I don't like to set a bad example."

CHAPTER IV

AFTER THE RAIN which had greeted his arrival the skies had suddenly cleared, and London was enjoying a period of spring weather of unexpected magnificence. The air was crisp and fresh, the trees in the squares were coming into leaf, and the parks at midday were crowded with office girls in summer frocks, eating picnic lunches on the grass. It was not difficult, in these first few weeks, to take Gilbertson's advice, to let things go and enjoy himself. He was happy to explore the labyrinth of narrow streets, to visit the curbside market of Soho, to eat alone in the taverns of Fleet Street or the chophouses of the City. It was at first pleasant to be unknown after the compulsive sociability of New York.

He rented a furnished apartment in a small old-fashioned block in St. James's. The narrow, twisting stairs, the manservant he shared with another bachelor, even the eccentric arrangements for heating the water generated an atmosphere pleasantly reminiscent of Cambridge. He bought a few pictures and a great many books. Now at last, he persuaded himself, he would have time, in these placid solitary evenings, to catch up on his reading. *Madame Bovary, David Copperfield, The Brothers Karamazov* . . .

But shortly he grew restless with his own company. He began to look up old friends. He was surprised to find how many of the people he knew were no longer traceable. Those who were still in London were delighted to hear from him. They were mostly married by now, with small children, and lived out in the suburbs. Evenings in town were not easy to arrange, but he must certainly come out one evening for dinner. Potluck, of course . . .

The dinners always turned out to be unnecessarily elaborate, the wives harassed, servantless, and mildly resentful of university reminiscence. The men seemed to Marshall to have aged to a quite unreasonable extent under the pressure of family responsibilities. Conversation would flourish gallantly for the first hour or so as they talked of old times, then quite suddenly it would wither and die, to be replaced by an atmosphere of mutual dissatisfaction. He found them stodgy and began to suspect that they in turn looked upon him as frivolous and immature. There was no longer any point of contact.

He had known loneliness in New York, but it had been a loneliness of the spirit; there had been almost an excess of physical companionship. Now for the first time he began to find it difficult to fill in his days. There was little to do at the office, and it seemed to be a matter of indifference to everybody whether he went there or not, but it was at least an anchor, a place where he felt, however insignificantly, a part of something. And there was always Miss Lancing to talk to. She was, he found, one of the few people in London with as much time to spare as himself.

"Don't you find this work boring?" he asked her once. She raised her eyebrows. "After all, there isn't very much to interest you."

"That's true," she admitted. "But then all work's pretty boring, isn't it? And at least it's better than living at home."

She was, she told him, a fugitive from the provinces, the daughter of a solicitor in Stoke-on-Trent. She lived alone in a bed-sitting-room in South Kensington.

"I used to share rooms with a girl friend, but she left to get married," she explained.

"And you're not lonely?"

"I'm used to it now. At first I didn't like it much. I have quite a few friends. Among the other girls here, for instance . . ."

She made no mention of men friends. It was likely that she had them—she was undeniably attractive in a curiously detached, independent way. Perhaps that might explain her cheerful acceptance of what seemed a fairly depressing and uneventful existence. She was also, he found out, extremely curious. Almost imperceptibly she managed to lead him into disclosing a good deal of information about himself. In exchange she handed out titbits of gossip about the various inhabitants of the London office. At times he felt guilty about these conversations. It was, when all was said and done, none of his business if Travers was in the habit of padding his expense sheet or if Gilbertson had been seen dining tête-à-tête at a restaurant in Charlotte Street with Miss Carvill-Sykes. He should be above taking an interest in such matters.

But (one had to face facts) he *was* interested. And Miss Lancing knew he was interested. She also knew that in this field he was like some timid virgin, ashamed of the force of his own curiosity. She never told him very much at a time. When he showed signs of being shocked she would withdraw, like an expert seducer, biding her time, waiting confidently for him to invite further advances.

But gradually his idleness began to get on his nerves. He could not contemplate an existence so utterly futile as this. Whether Gilbertson liked it or not, he would find some kind of work to do. How, for instance, had Wilcox managed to spend his time? He decided to ask Miss Lancing.

"Oh, he was always on the go," she said in a voice which combined admiration and amusement. "Conferences with Mr. Gilbertson, sales estimates, memoranda on this and that, visiting the distributors on the Continent—we had a high old time, I can tell you." She shook her head reminiscently. "You couldn't keep Mr. Wilcox out of anything."

That, Marshall thought uneasily, was how it ought to be. He, Marshall, was obviously considered to be a man who could be left out of anything and everything. It was true that Wilcox's energy appeared to have done him more harm than good. On the other hand, he had at least achieved a kind of respect.

A few days later he approached Gilbertson.

"I've been here a month now," he said, briskly businesslike, "and I'm quite settled in. I feel completely at home. Now I think it's time I did something."

Gilbertson stroked the hair back over his right ear in an exasperated way. "I'm not quite sure that I follow you. What exactly——"

Marshall was prepared for this. "I'm anxious to get a complete picture of the business over here. I'd like to go through the books, see the sales records for the last few years and the estimates for the coming year. Also the production reports, the proportion of turnover due to re-exportation, and so on. After that I can go up to Lancashire and visit the plant. And then . . ."

It sounded good, he thought. Gilbertson was visibly disconcerted.

"Yes, yes, of course. Naturally we'll be delighted for you to see anything you wish, my dear fellow." He spoke as if Marshall were some distinguished but rather tiresome visitor. "Though I don't know that you'll get very much out of it. Still, if that's what you'd like . . . I'll get Travers to make you out a summary." He sighed. "He's fairly busy at the moment, but I imagine he'll be able to fix it within the next week or two."

"You don't have to bother Mr. Travers," Marshall said firmly. "Just send down the original figures. I'll make my own summary."

"You'll find it heavy going, I'm afraid."

"Never mind. I'll have a try. If I get stuck I can always call on you or Mr. Travers."

"Oh, definitely—definitely."

Even after this there was an inexplicable delay. When the figures failed to appear, Marshall telephoned Gilbertson's office, only to be told that the managing director had gone away on some unspecified business trip and omitted to leave any instructions with the Accounts Department. When Gilbertson returned he seemed slightly exasperated to find the matter still under discussion.

"Of course—I'm so sorry. Most annoying for you. I'm sure I left instructions with somebody, but there it is. One can't be everywhere oneself, more's the pity. One has to delegate responsibility."

When the books were finally brought to his office Marshall regarded them with the satisfaction due the trophies of a minor victory. He did not suppose there would be anything very exciting or unusual in the figures themselves, copies of which would have been long since sent to New York for analysis. He imagined that Gilbertson's passive resistance to showing them to him had been largely a matter of principle.

Nevertheless, on going through them he discovered one thing which surprised him. He made some notes in longhand and went back to see Gilbertson.

"I don't know whether you'll agree with my interpretation, but as I see it, the figures show that on the sales in this country and the Commonwealth we hardly pay our way. The profits only just cover the fixed overheads."

"Oh, come." Gilbertson smiled uneasily. "I think you'll agree that our final returns are excellent."

"Certainly. But that's almost entirely due to the sale of instruments assembled here and re-exported to France. Without that, we should be nowhere."

Gilbertson thought for a moment and then nodded. Marshall, he conveyed, had been a clever boy and should not be denied his appreciation. "Yes," he said, "you're quite right—though, as you can imagine, we don't go around advertising the fact. The truth is, our things are too expensive. They can't really compete in the sterling area." He added cheerfully, "I've pointed that out to New York on innumerable occasions."

"You don't seem very concerned."

"Well, there's no point in making ourselves miserable about it, is there? And the business is doing all right on the over-all figures. The great thing is to judge by results—don't worry too much about the details. As your father used to say, let's take the broad approach."

"But," said Marshall, "supposing you lost the French business?"

"Time enough to worry about that if and when it happens." He gave an unexpected guffaw. "Perhaps you chaps in New York would have to cut down your prices a bit, eh? But don't worry," he said reassuringly, "old Furac's a first-rate man. He's got the Paris connection very nicely sewn up."

"You don't think there's any risk of our being priced out of the market in France?"

Gilbertson gave a confident shake of the head. Then he said with aristocratic tolerance, "The French are a queer lot. I don't profess to understand them myself. Personal connections seem to count for a lot over there."

It seemed to Marshall as he pondered this conversation afterward that here at last was an opportunity for him to take some part in affairs. However casually Gilbertson might regard it, the position was plainly unsatisfactory and should be called to New York's attention. It would have to be done tactfully, not in the form of a criticism of any particular person, but as a review of the trading difficulties peculiar to the area. After that it would be up to Kingham to decide whether anything should be done.

He rang for Miss Lancing.

"I want you to take a memorandum," he said. "It's to Mr. Kingham. Head it: 'Trading Position in Western Europe.'" He hesitated. Did that sound pretentious? Never mind. "'An analysis of the records for the past two years, together with a breakdown of present sales estimates, appears to indicate the following . . .'"

He began to dictate slowly, referring now and then to his notes for the relevant figures. He was just warming to his thesis when he looked up and noticed that Miss Lancing had stopped writing. She was regarding him in a faintly apologetic way.

"What's the matter?" he asked. "Is there something you can't follow?"

"Oh no. It's just that—I don't really know whether I ought to say this—but I think you should know——" She stopped, waiting for encouragement.

"What is it?"

"Well, Mr. Wilcox already did a memorandum saying all this, soon after he came here. He made more or less the same points as you have."

"I see." He slumped back in his chair, unable to conceal his frustration. It was hard to resist the conviction that there was something like a conspiracy in the company to make his every action appear futile and ridiculous. His anger, foiled of any other object, directed itself toward Miss Lancing.

"It might have been a good idea," he said acidly, "to have shown it to me before this. Don't you think so?"

"Yes, I'm sorry, but——"

"I distinctly remember asking to see any important letters or memoranda from Mr. Wilcox's back correspondence. Naturally I assumed that any documents of this kind would be included. Otherwise I'm simply wasting my time going over old ground." She tried to speak again, but he was too angry to listen. "Now, before we go any further, would you mind getting for me the *complete* files, with all the copies of the Wilcox correspondence, memoranda, and so on—just so I can get some idea of what happened here before I came?"

"I'm awfully sorry, Mr. Marshall, but I'm afraid I can't——"

"Why not?"

"Because it isn't there. The memoranda to New York were in a different file. I went through all the records when you arrived, but I couldn't find that one anywhere."

"You mean you lost it?"

"No. I'm sure I put it in the right place in the cabinet. It just wasn't there when I went back for it."

"You'd better have another look." He got up impatiently from his chair. "I'll come along and help you."

As they passed the general office the clerks were covering their typewriters and putting on their coats preparatory to leaving. It was half-past five. They went on to the filing room on an upper floor, a dark room with flowered wallpaper and two small windows which looked out on to a bombed site.

Silently they began to go through the filing cabinets in an atmosphere rendered oppressive with dust and resentment. He read through old letters, desperate, staccato cables about long-forgotten crises, tedious, inflated reports about unimportant problems—but nothing from Wilcox. After half an hour he slammed the last drawer of the last cabinet and said irritably:

"All right, then, I agree—it isn't there. But where is it?"

"Mr. Wilcox may have taken it away with him."

"Is that likely?"

"It's possible. Or Mr. Gilbertson may have taken it." She shrugged her shoulders. "I don't know," she said coldly. "It's really nothing to do with me."

She sat down and looked at him, waiting for orders. Her expression said plainly that since he had decided to act like a boss he had better tell her what to do next. Suddenly he felt ashamed of himself. He had done what he had so often criticized others for doing—vented his personal chagrin and annoyance on a subordinate. It was particularly despicable after he had encouraged her to treat him as a friend.

"I'm sorry," he said. "I shouldn't have bawled you out like that. It wasn't your fault."

Immediately her expression changed. She was evidently not a girl who liked to bear a grudge. "I should have told you before that the file was gone."

"I don't think so." One could hardly expect her to have done that, he realized, particularly if she thought Gilbertson had taken it—not unless she was looking for trouble. He heard the clock strike in the square. "I'm afraid I've kept you late."

"It doesn't matter."

"I hope you didn't have a date or anything——"

"Oh no."

He was persuading himself that he owed her something for putting up with his ill temper, for keeping her almost an hour after the others had gone. It was hardly fair to send her home now. Also, she was a woman and attractive, and he was lonely.

"It's almost half-past six," he said. "Would you care to join me for dinner?"

Anticipation flashed for a moment in her eyes. Then she looked down at her blouse and skirt. "I'm not dressed."

"Don't worry about that. We'll go to some small place."

Suddenly he realized how close they were together in the narrow space between the filing cabinets. High up in this silent, deserted house, every word, every movement seemed to carry a heightened significance. She raised her right arm to push back a lock of hair which had fallen across her face while she was working. Her faint, feminine scent hung in the still, dusty air of the room. She smiled at him in a way slightly but indescribably different from before, as if she were adjusting her conception of him, trying to evaluate him for the first time, not as a man across a desk, but as a possible friend, even a possible lover. . . .

"I'd love to come," she said.

CHAPTER V

It was a curious and slightly awkward sensation at first. His relations with women usually started off according to a fairly conventional routine. There was the process of exchanging confidences, discussing attitudes and tastes, becoming gradually more intimate if things went favorably, and signing off at a fairly early stage if they did not. But on this occasion a great deal of the preliminary spadework had already been done. They had learned a good deal about each other, but without considering that this knowledge might ever be a preliminary to anything. It was like watching rehearsals of a play and then suddenly being expected to take a leading part in the first act.

She was, or at least appeared to be, a good deal less ill at ease than he was. She was also noticeably less discreet than she had been during their conversation at the office.

"You know," she said, "between ourselves, I think it was pretty certainly Gilbertson who pinched that memorandum."

"Why? After all, it was only a copy. New York must have received the original."

"Perhaps he didn't want you to see it."

"I don't know why. I'm not so important. Anyhow," he said impatiently, "it doesn't matter. If New York has the information, that's all that concerns me. If Gilbertson wants to act like a screwball . . ." He added uncomfortably, "It made me a little sore at the time. I feel very badly about speaking to you the way I did."

She smiled. "That was nothing. I'm really far tougher than you think." After a pause she said, "Do you mind if I say something rather personal?"

"Go ahead."

"I think you worry too much."

"About what?"

"All sorts of things. That was just an example. You were momentarily rude to me—well, what of it? Nobody behaves well all the time. I never thought you were St. Francis of Assisi."

"Now you make me feel silly."

"I didn't mean to. I just didn't want you to set yourself too high a standard, that was all. People are more at ease with you if you behave badly now and then. Don't you think so?"

"It depends who you are. Some people can get away with it. My father, for instance, behaved abominably most of the time. He insulted his friends or his business associates or members of his family whenever he felt inclined. Then an hour or two afterward he would see them again, tell them a joke, offer them a drink, just as if nothing had happened. And he got away with it. They made excuses for him. They used to say he didn't mean it. But he did mean it. I know he did. How do you explain that?"

"He was a powerful man, wasn't he? Everybody wants to think powerful men are good—it's less frightening that way."

"Nobody makes excuses for me," he said. "If I insult them they take it for granted that I mean it. You think I'd be more popular if I were more powerful?"

"Yes, of course. Do you want that?"

He shook his head. "No, thanks. That's not for me."

When they left the restaurant she said, "Thank you very much for the dinner. I enjoyed it enormously."

He was reluctant to end the evening but did not know quite how to prolong it. In New York it would have been easy, but here —what did one do after dinner?

"Shall we go someplace for a drink? Or dance, perhaps? I don't know exactly where——"

"No, really, I'd sooner go home if you don't mind. I can catch the tube just around this corner——"

"The hell with that. I'm certainly going to insist on taking you home. Let's see if we can find a cab."

The taxi stopped outside a big terrace house in South Kensington.

"This is where I live," she said. "Would you like to come in?"

He was not sure what he ought to reply. Was her invitation merely a polite formality which he was expected to refuse? The house looked shabby and depressing—a sort of rooming house. He noticed the movement of a curtain, the suspicion of a face peering out of a ground-floor window. He was curious to know what sort of life went on within.

Noticing his hesitation, she said, "It's not very luxurious, I'm afraid." Her tone was amused rather than defensive. She had contrived to solve his problem for him. A refusal now would seem snobbish.

"Well, thanks very much. If that's okay. . . ."

She opened the door with a latchkey. As soon as they were inside the hall, a small white-haired woman poked her head out of a door on one side of it.

"Oh, hello, Jane dear. I'm sorry—I thought it might be Mrs. Venables." Her eyes were on Marshall, devouring him with ferocious curiosity. "You haven't seen her, have you?"

"I'm afraid not."

"She went to a séance at that place in Lancaster Gate. I hope nothing's happened to her." She said to Marshall, "Excuse my impertinence, young man, but are you any relation to Miss Bellamy's fiancé?"

"Not so far as I know."

"No? You have quite a look of him, you know. Where are you from?"

"New York."

"Oh, that's quite impossible then. He was from Cardiff." With a sharp, disappointed nod she popped back into her room.

"Who was she?" asked Marshall as they climbed the stairs.

"Just a woman who lives here. She's lonely, and I feel sorry for her. Mind you, it's a mistake to give her too much encouragement." She added reflectively, "London's full of old girls like that. They live in bed-sitters on a little capital and every year sell out a few more shares to cover the increase in the cost of living. They haven't anything to do but peep out of windows and quarrel with each other and complain to the landlady about the hot water. With any luck they die before they go broke." She stopped outside a door on the top floor where a card read: "Miss Jane Lancing." "Could you hold this for a moment?"

She handed him a leather bucket-bag containing a novel, a rolled-up plastic raincoat, a small soft parcel from Swan and Edgar's, and two more solid ones from Selfridge's. She took another key out of her handbag and unlocked the door. The bed-sitting-room was a fairly large one, with a curtain drawn across the bed and a screen to hide the washbasin—two pairs of stockings were hanging over the top of it. There was a cheap sofa and an armchair, a threadbare carpet which covered little more than half the floor, and a gas fire serviced by a shilling in the slot meter. A dormer window looked out on to the glistening wet roof of an adjoining house.

She waved at the armchair. "Make yourself at home." She took off her coat, whisked the drying stockings into a drawer, dropped a coin in the meter, and turned on the gas fire. The boards creaked as she walked about the room.

"I've got some gin and orange squash, but there's no ice and I really wouldn't recommend it. The usual thing round these parts is coffee and biscuits."

"That's fine with me."

She made two cups of instant coffee and opened a tin of biscuits.

"How long have you lived here?" he said.

"Two years. Ever since my girl friend got married." There was mockery in the smile she gave him. "I expect it looks a bit gruesome after the Savoy."

"I don't know," said Marshall awkwardly. "You seem to have——"

"You think I've made it nice and homey?" She shook her head. "I did have a try once, but the wallpaper beat me. There seemed so much of it somehow." There was a short silence. Then she said, "But I don't really mind. If you have to be badly off, London's the place to live in."

"Why?"

"Because nobody cares. The city's so crammed with decayed gentility that you don't have to keep up with the Joneses—the

Joneses are in the same mess as you are. It's a nice, restful feeling."

"Does everyone feel like that?"

"No." Her voice hardened. "It would be better if they did. This country's poisoned with self-pity. Old people who do nothing but look back to the days before the war, young men who've had things too easy since the war and sit around bellyaching because life isn't exciting enough. I'm sick to death of people complaining about things they can't alter."

"That makes you sound pretty tough."

"I'm not really. It's just that—it's in the air. I suppose I'm afraid it might get me too. Have another biscuit?"

"No, thanks."

"They're not very nice, are they? I think the damp must have got at them." She put the tin away. "Do you like this job you're doing?"

"Not much."

"I didn't think you did. You find it a bit pointless perhaps?"

"Yes."

"You mustn't let it get you down. So far as I can see, the way to be popular is to do as little as possible. You'll soon get the hang of it."

"You seem to know a lot about what goes on."

"I keep my eyes open. And I see most of the correspondence, you know. And I talk to the other girls. You'd be surprised how much the secretaries know."

"I suppose so." He was silent for a moment. Then he said: "It's not just this particular job as far as I'm concerned. I've always felt completely out of place in the organization."

"Then why don't you leave?" she asked bluntly.

"I don't know quite what I'd do. I never wanted to go into the business. I tried to paint once, but I was a failure. Somehow I can't bring myself just to do nothing."

"What you're doing now makes a pretty close approach."

"I know. Naturally they realize I haven't got my heart in the game, so they won't give me anything worth while to do. You can hardly blame them."

"Why are you so against it—the business, I mean?"

"I just don't feel identified with it. Do you?"

"On my salary you don't feel identified with anything. But it should be different for you. You can get somewhere."

"Pushing people around," he said bitterly. "That's all it amounts to. That's what they get their fun out of. They call it administration."

"I suppose it has to be somebody's job."

"Not mine. I've seen enough of it."

"So what are you going to do? Stay as you are?"

"I don't know," he said wearily. "Sometimes I try to think it out, but I get nowhere. I suppose you think I'm hopelessly confused——"

"Just a crazy mixed-up millionaire?"

"I guess I asked for that."

"No, please." She sat down beside him on the sofa. "Really, I'm terribly sorry. Please don't be angry."

"That's okay. You were right."

"No, it was unforgivable. I invited your confidence and then sneered at you. I didn't even mean it. I just put on an act—pretending to be hard-boiled. I'm not really that sort of person at all."

"No?"

"No. Really, I suppose I'm frightened—scared stiff, just like so many of us, but I daren't admit it to myself. Once you do"—she looked at the dingy yellow walls, the spluttering gas fire, and shivered slightly—"in a place like this——"

"So in fact," he said, "you're just as weak as I am?"

She looked up at him, her eyes suddenly dark and sad, her defenses abandoned. She said: "If you only knew . . ."

It was then that he kissed her. She made no attempt to resist. Compliantly she turned her face upward and pressed her lips against his. Her eyes were shut, her body immobile—she seemed hardly to be breathing. There was something curiously exciting to him in the strangeness of the situation—the bare room, silent above the roof tops, the bed behind the curtain, the washbasin behind the screen. Here in this room her whole life was laid out in front of him. Here she dressed and undressed, brewed her solitary cup of coffee, read her novel, and entertained her friends. All her intimate possessions were around him, open to his gaze. There was something almost indecent, to his eyes, in such a lack of privacy. But to her there was nothing extraordinary about it. In her world it was not considered in any way unusual to entertain a man in your bedroom. As a rule, it was the only room you had.

Presently she got up and began to tidy away the cups and saucers.

She said, "Shall we pretend that didn't happen?"

"Why?"

She was determinedly matter-of-fact. "Because if I'm any judge you're going to feel like hell going home. Once you get into your taxi, you'll break out into a cold sweat and wonder how things are going to be in the morning. Am I going to be saucy and knowing and difficult to handle? Am I going to blow the works to the other girls?" She went on reassuringly, "Don't think I blame you. I hate women myself. But, honestly, you don't have to worry."

"I wasn't worrying," he said angrily. "You can tell anyone you damn well please."

He walked over to her and kissed her again, furiously this time, as if to avenge the insult she had thrown at him. But as he held her, his resentment faded and was lost in tenderness. He was suddenly conscious of the supreme importance of this moment, struggling against the force of his own emotions to record it and preserve it in his memory. The scent of her hair, the touch of her silk blouse against his fingers, her back slightly arched under the pressure of his hand. Never again would her flesh seem quite so warm or her lips so moist. In that first surrender she was mystery, she was desire, she was consolation, she was danger and opportunity, she was life. At one time he would have pressed impatiently on, eager to possess her that very night. He would have destroyed the moment—or tried to. But in this one respect at least he was wiser than he had been at twenty. When she made a gentle effort to move away from him, he let her go. As he did so, he heard the sound of footsteps on the stairs. A door opened and closed on the landing, and the footsteps continued in the next room, clearly audible through the wall, succeeded by the noise of water running. A high cracked voice began to sing "Abide with Me." Mrs. Venables had returned home safely.

CHAPTER VI

OUTSIDE, in St. James's Square, the gas lamps began to go on one by one, casting shadows on the ceiling of his living room.

"Darling Jane . . ."

"Darling Chris . . ." Suddenly she said, "Damn, I shall have to move, my arm's gone to sleep." She got up and began to massage the fingers of her left hand. "Shall I draw the curtains?"

"What about going out for dinner?" he said.

"I'm not hungry just yet. Are you?"

"No."

"I'll make you an omelet later on."

She drew the curtains and switched on the lights. Looking around the room, she said, "You're so lucky."

"Why?"

"To have this little flat. I suppose it costs the earth."

"Well . . ." He was uncomfortably aware that the rent he paid was considerably more than her weekly salary. "It's only really fun when you're here."

"You don't have to say that, you know."

"It's true. Nothing's quite the same when I'm on my own. I used to sit here in the evenings and wonder what to do. Or I'd go out to restaurants and read a book with my dinner. Often I used to wish I were back in New York."

"You told me you liked Europe."

"When I was here before I did. I had lots of fun—until the last part. . . ."

"In Paris?"

"Yes. I think the very fact that I loved Paris so much made it worse when I found that I hadn't any place there."

"But are you sure——"

"Sure enough. You see, my father made a bargain with me. At first, when I wanted to paint, he shouted and swore and tried to ridicule me. Then, when he saw it wasn't working, he suddenly became reasonable. He said, 'Okay, if you're set on it, I won't stop you. But knowing you, I'd say you want to be good. You don't want to just sit around in a beard and velvet pants playing at it. Am I right?' I told him he was right. So he made me a typical businessman's proposition." He made a helpless gesture. "And it sounded reasonable enough. By his standards—and by mine, too, at that time, I guess. He would finance me for two years at the best art school in Paris, then at the end I was to show my work to the best art teacher in Paris—everything had to be the best, you notice, he could afford it—and then accept his opinion. We chose a man called Mayer."

"And what did he say?"

"Mayer?" He laughed, as he had trained himself to laugh when telling this story. "I can see him now—a little bald-headed man in a linen jacket covered with grease spots. He had false teeth and he kept pushing his upper plate back with his thumb the way people do when they don't fit very well. But he knew about pictures all right. I explained what I wanted and he told me to bring along what I thought were my ten best pictures to his studio. He asked an extortionate fee, of course."

"And he didn't like them?"

"He let me put them up, one after another. He didn't say a word—just nodded when he'd finished looking and wanted me to put up the next one. When he'd seen them all he said, 'Tell me, Monsieur Marshall—have you ever contemplated any alternative career?' "

"And then?"

"That was all. He didn't need to say any more."

"But he might have been wrong. They don't always know——"

"Let's not talk about it, shall we?"

"Sorry."

"That's all right. It's just that—well, I've thought about all those things myself, and it gets me nowhere. I was beaten. I gave up. Let's leave it at that."

"Even so, you needn't have come back into the business."

"I thought I might as well keep my side of the bargain. Not that it mattered, as it happened. My father died soon afterward."

"But you still carried on?"

"Why not?" he asked indifferently.

"Why not?" She was incredulous. "Because you hate it—because it doesn't mean anything to you. Surely there's every reason in the world for packing it up and doing something else. What you have now isn't a life at all——"

"There was only one sort of life that mattered to me and I failed at it." When she said nothing, he went on: "What do you suggest I should do?"

"Anything!" She looked at him desperately, in furious impatience at his inactivity. "Surely you must see that anything's better than what you're doing now. You can't just throw your hand in at your age and admit you're beaten. What you're saying is that if you can't have the thing you wanted most you're going to stop trying. Isn't that it?"

"In a sense, yes."

"Well, I think you're crazy." She got up and walked away from him. "You never stop criticizing your father, but at least he had some fight in him——"

Was even *she* on the side of the old man? "You think that's all that matters?" he said. "To fight—no matter what you're fighting for? At least I'm doing no harm——"

"It might almost be better if you did. Better for yourself, anyway." She turned on him. "Anything rather than sit here inert, doing nothing—suffering——"

The impatience in her voice was surprisingly painful to him. So this, he thought, is how I appear. Without ever admitting it, he had held in the back of his mind a picture of himself as a Byronic figure, withdrawn in a tragic and dignified isolation. With this image he had comforted himself for years. Now, in a few words, she had destroyed it.

"I shouldn't have said that," she said. Her voice was so unhappy that it was hardly audible. "I don't know what it is. There's something about you which seems to force me into hurting you."

"Perhaps," he said bitterly, "you see in me a natural victim."

"No, I don't." She shook her head. "Not in the least. I just think you're behaving not as yourself at all, but as a sort of idea of yourself built up on the basis of a lot of things that happened years ago. Don't you see what I mean?"

"Everybody does that to some extent."

"Yes, I know. But with you it's such a—well, such a *negative* idea, isn't it?"

He laughed. When everything else failed it was always possible to take refuge in a joke. "It's a little hard to come four thousand miles to be told about the Power of Positive Thinking."

Later she said, "You don't hate me, darling, do you? Tell me you don't hate me."

"For what?"

"For saying what I did."

"Of course I don't hate you. You may even be right."

"You're happy now?"

"Yes. As happy as I've ever been."

"You'll get tired of me. We see too much of each other." He smiled at the stereotyped, woman's-magazine wisdom. "Yes, we do. Every day. Almost every evening." She shook her head. "It can't last."

"Don't you enjoy it?"

"Yes, of course——"

"Then why go looking for trouble? Are you so afraid of being happy?"

"In a way." Now it was her own experience speaking. "Nothing's all that good in this world."

He pulled her gently onto the sofa. He kissed her and said, "I love you, Jane."

"Don't say that."

"Why not?"

"We've known each other such a short time."

"A moment ago you were saying——"

"You know what I mean. Give yourself time. It's best to be cautious."

"I don't feel cautious. I feel proud. I want to tell people. Though I don't know why one should feel so proud of being in love. It's the one thing any fool can do."

He meant it as a joke, but she answered him quite seriously. "Yes," she said. "That's true, isn't it?" She moved suddenly away from him, frowning a little. It came to him that she would want more from a man than mere devotion, just as she in her turn would wish to give more. There were other things as important as love—respect, admiration, the promise of adventure. She seemed about to explain some of this and then changed her mind. "I'm hungry now," she said. "Why don't we have something to eat?"

She made omelets and laid the table in front of the fire. As they were eating she said, "By the way, I forgot to tell you. Gilbertson was looking for you this afternoon."

"Yes, I saw him just before I left the office. He was unusually friendly. The ice seems to have thawed a bit." Ever since the incident of the accounts there had been a noticeable coldness between himself and Gilbertson. "He asked me out to his place in the country next weekend."

"Did you accept?"

"Why not? We have to work together, don't we?"

"Have you ever spoken to him about that memorandum of Wilcox's? The one that was missing from the files?"

"No. I decided there wasn't anything to be gained——"

"You're going to let him get away with it?"

He frowned. "I haven't much alternative. If that's the way New York wants it——"

"You have to be a good boy and do as they tell you?"

"Up to a point." He rebelled against the implication. "No, that isn't entirely true. I have a certain amount of discretion. But obviously only within limits. And it's not easy to see what's to be done right now. I get the feeling that things are being kept from me and that Wilcox was moved out because he got too nosy—all right. But it's all very insubstantial. . . ." He could hear his own voice as he felt she must hear it—excuses, excuses for doing nothing. She thought he was afraid of action. Could it be true? he wondered with his always fatal readiness to see the other person's point of view. This Olympian detachment of his, which affected to despise the squalid personal feuds, the petty jealousies, the constant struggle for advancement, for money, for power—was it, when it came to the point, no more than an excuse for laziness and cowardice? "It might be different," he added defensively, "if I had some facts."

She looked at him questioningly. Her eyes seemed to be asking him, "Do you really mean it or is it just part of the act?" In business, she knew, it wasn't always advisable to take statements at their face value. Promises were made, plans were outlined, more as a pious hope for the future than as a definite undertaking; they were easily forgotten and it was considered tactless to remind anybody of them at a later date. But he looked back at her defiantly, daring her to disbelieve him. It was as if, without saying anything, an agreement had been made between them, a contract signed.

She lit a cigarette. "If you're interested, I could tell you some other things," she said slowly, "about Wilcox. . . ."

"Such as?"

"He used to send confidential reports to New York. Did you know that?"

"No."

"He didn't even let me type them. He would stay behind in the evening and use my typewriter. Then in the morning he'd hand me a sealed envelope marked 'Private and Confidential.' "

"Who were they addressed to?"

"Kingham, usually. He kept the copies himself, of course."

Marshall felt a spasm of envy for Wilcox. Nobody had ever asked him to send confidential letters. Ever since his childhood he had experienced this feeling of being excluded from certain inner circles of trust. He had always comforted himself with the conviction that the secrets involved were for the most part unimportant as well as frequently ridiculous. It had, after all, done little good to Wilcox, being so confidential. Nevertheless, he was piqued.

"So you don't know what he said?"

"No."

"Then where does that lead us?"

She hesitated for a moment. Then she picked up her bag and took out a notecase. Behind the few pound notes she carried was a piece of paper folded into four. She handed it to Marshall.

It was a typed list consisting mainly of dates, with various odd words and code letters opposite each one. Most of the words were quite simple—"Budget," "Estimates," "Pricing," "Production," and so on. Many of the dates had the letter K next to them. A few were marked K(C).

Marshall looked at it in perplexity. "I don't understand. What *is* this?"

"It's a record Wilcox made of his letters to New York."

"He gave this to you?"

"No. After he left I was cleaning out and I——" Seeing the look on his face, she said, "All right, I know I should have torn it up. You can, now, if you want."

He should, of course. It was undoubtedly the correct thing to do, as well as the easiest. For a moment, unknown to him, the lives of not only himself and Jane but of Gilbertson, Furac, Kingham, Jeff, Bernstein, and some thousands of men he had never even seen or heard of stood suspended, waiting for his decision on this minor ethical point. It was mainly curiosity which decided him.

"What do these letters mean?" he asked.

"I can only guess. But some of them are obvious. Those without the C are the ones he dictated to me. K refers to Kingham. The ones marked K(C) are almost certainly the confidential memoranda. As you see, they got more frequent toward the end."

"Yes." His attention was attracted by the last three entries. They referred to letters written only a few weeks before Wilcox was recalled to New York. The first two were marked "A.V." The last, two weeks later, "A.V.—immediate action."

He looked up at Jane. "Have you any idea what A.V. refers to?"

"No. That's one of the things I wondered about. All I know is that he'd just returned from Paris about that time. It might refer to something there—or some person. I don't know."

There was a silence. He turned the piece of paper over. There was nothing on the other side.

"This is all there is to it?"

She nodded.

"Well, I don't see where it gets us, frankly," he said. "He wrote some confidential letters—so what?"

"Toward the end he and Gilbertson were always quarreling. We could hear them through the door sometimes. It was worse after he came back from Paris the last time. Then he wrote that last letter, calling for immediate action. A few days later he was recalled." She added with significance, "Don't you think there's anything in that?"

"Maybe," he admitted. "Maybe. But I still can't see anything I can do about it. There's nothing to go on." After a pause he added, "If we had any idea what A.V. referred to, it might be different."

CHAPTER VII

"My idea," said Gilbertson, "was to have a quiet, restful weekend. Completely informal. I hope that's all right with you."

"Surely."

"We can get up when we want to. Lounge about in old clothes. I'll introduce you to some of the local people. . . . My wife's looking forward enormously to meeting you."

Marshall made a suitably appreciative noise. It was Friday evening and they were driving down to Sussex in Gilbertson's 1936 Rolls-Royce, color maroon, coachwork by Hooper. Gilbertson himself made a fine sight at the wheel, with his long bloodhound face, his Homburg and lemon-yellow wash-leather gloves. They traveled slowly but in style.

"It's a grand old bus," said Gilbertson with obvious affection. "Never lets you down. A bit heavy on petrol, but I don't do a big mileage. Most days I take the train into town—it works out rather quicker."

"I see you have commuting problems here too."

"Yes indeed, my dear fellow." He went on to describe in somewhat tedious detail the traffic congestion on the Southern Region. It seemed to Marshall that the weekend was likely to turn out a little dull. On the other hand, it was pleasant to be on good terms with Gilbertson again. He seemed to be taking the view that Marshall, after a short phase when he had shown signs of being "difficult," was now settling down to behave in a suitable fashion. Did he know about Jane? Marshall wondered. Probably—people always knew more than you thought. No doubt he regarded the affair indulgently, in view of his own efforts with Miss Carvill-Sykes, or even with active support, as a healthy method of keeping Marshall's mind off more serious matters. . . .

"It takes me well over an hour to get to the office every morning," Gilbertson was saying, "but it's worth it—for me, at any rate. I have to work in London, but I'd always want to make my home in the country." He meditated for a moment. "Of course that's where you Americans have it over us. You actually *enjoy* business."

Marshall looked at him with interest. "Don't you?"

"Between ourselves," said Gilbertson, "it bores me to death. One has to make a living, of course, so there's nothing else for it. But if I were in your position, for instance——"

"You'd give it up?"

"My dear boy, you wouldn't see me for dust."

"Do you think you'd be able to enjoy life without an occupation?" Marshall asked doubtfully. "Just doing nothing?"

"I don't see why not," said Gilbertson almost peevishly, "my father did." He went on, "The trouble with you people is that you've accumulated enormous wealth without creating a proper leisured class to spend it. The upshot is that you become richer and richer all the time, and nobody knows what the hell to do with you. Most inconsiderate."

They were well out of London now, driving across the Downs. As they drove over a hill Gilbertson pointed to a large house partly hidden by a clump of trees. "You see that house?"

"Yes."

"I was born there. It's a beautiful place—sixteenth century. We had to sell it when my father died, to pay the death duties." He said regretfully, "The house we have now is pleasant enough, but when you were brought up in the old place . . . Do you know what I'd really like to do?"

"What?"

"I'd like to make enough money to buy it back and retire there—end up my days as I started. God knows if I shall ever be able to pull it off, what with the inflation and one damn thing and another, but still, there's no harm in hoping." With some defiance he added: "I suppose you think that's absurd?"

"No." Marshall was taken by surprise. He had never thought of Gilbertson as a passionate man. Plainly, beneath his desiccated exterior there lay unsuspected depths of romanticism. On the face of it, in this highly taxed, servantless post-war world, it was a mad ambition. Yet there was a certain gallantry about it which prevented it from being entirely ridiculous.

The house in which the Gilbertsons now lived was only a few miles away and was fairly imposing in its own right. It was an ivy-covered Georgian mansion with an acre of garden and a small paddock. Mrs. Gilbertson was almost as tall as her husband, angular, harsh of voice, and with an abruptness of manner which attempted unsuccessfully to conceal her natural shyness. As she showed Marshall to his room she told him once again that it was to be an informal weekend. There were to be no other guests. The two children, a girl of seventeen and a boy of fourteen, were away at school.

Dinner was a protracted and unappetizing meal, served by a gloomy, semi-moronic village girl who had been dressed up unconvincingly for the occasion in a cap and apron. There was a multitude of tiny courses—soup, fish, meat, dessert, savory, cheese—the changing of plates was punctuated by unexplained delays and the sound of voices raised in argument from the kitchen. The lamb was overcooked, there was a skin on the egg sauce, and some unspeakable disaster had occurred to the summer pudding. Mrs. Gilbertson sat on the edge of her chair, following the maid constantly with her eyes and occasionally hissing furious instructions through her teeth; her response to any form of conversation was no more than fragmentary. Every now and then an expression of despair would flit transiently across her face. Marshall felt sorry for her. He wanted to tell her that he understood all about the servant problem and the impossibility of maintaining pre-war standards—he would have been quite happy to serve himself and dry the dishes afterward. Was she, he wondered, going through this rigmarole to please her husband? Or were they partners in self-delusion? Did she, too, feel the necessity of preserving this ritual of the Good Old Days?

When the cheese was cleared, she got up from the table and left the two men alone. They sat dutifully for some time over port and cigars, trying to find something to say to each other. Marshall grew bored and sleepy. It seemed to him that he was taking part in some tedious game which Gilbertson was staging to appease his own nostalgia. Perhaps he could find other Englishmen who were happy to play with him, to pretend that the income tax was only five shillings in the pound and the landed gentry still relatively secure in their possessions, and that in the servants' quarters were a cook and two housemaids instead of a half-witted girl and a daily woman who stayed late once in a while as a special favor. Marshall felt himself miscast. He did not know the rules and he found the game without interest. He was beginning to lose sympathy with this obvious yearning for the past, and he suspected that Gilbertson was finding him equally unsatisfactory. He refused a second glass of port and they went to join Mrs. Gilbertson, but when they looked in the drawing room she was not there. Marshall had a shrewd suspicion that she was in the kitchen, helping with the washing up. As soon as was decently possible, he excused himself and went to bed.

The next morning they breakfasted late and went for a walk through the village. Marshall was relieved to find that his sports coat and trousers were sufficiently shabby to be acceptable—his stock went up slightly when he appeared in them. They lunched at the local pub, spent the afternoon at a cricket match, and dined with a retired stockbroker who was endeavoring to adjust his tax position by breeding pedigree cattle at a loss. As they left the stockbroker's house Gilbertson said to him, "We'll see you tomorrow evening then, Charles? Any time after you've finished dinner." To Marshall he said, "We're having a few friends in—I'd like you to meet some of the people around here. Nothing elaborate, of course."

Elaborate or not, it appeared to entail a good deal of preparation. Mrs. Gilbertson was hardly to be seen on the Sunday. In the afternoon Travers drove up. His position at the party seemed to be something between guest and part-time butler. He prepared drinks, moved furniture, flattered Mrs. Gilbertson, and made brightly predictable remarks on general subjects.

They dined lightly off cold ham and salad. Soon afterward the guests began to arrive. Apart from the vicar and the doctor and the land agent of a local nobleman, they were mostly men like Gilbertson. They spent five days of the week in town, banking or underwriting or sitting on boards of directors, in order to earn the money to play at being country gentlemen on Saturday and Sunday. The talk was mainly of gardens and horses and church bazaars—any mention of business was an obvious social blunder.

By eleven o'clock it seemed to Marshall that the party had been going on for several days. He found himself in the grip of a determined matron who had once spent a week in New York and was counted in consequence as an authority on American social customs.

"In our view," she said, baring her dentures and adroitly intercepting an attempt at escape, "the women over there get far too much of their own way. It isn't good for them. Basically, as a sex, we need to be dominated. Don't you agree?"

"Perhaps. I——"

Ignoring what she appeared to regard as an interruption, she went on to illustrate her point with an anecdote about a prize-winning Labrador bitch, now unhappily deceased. Above the hubbub of conversation, the telephone rang.

Gilbertson motioned to Travers. "Take it in the dining room, would you, Travers?" Travers disappeared. Gilbertson, suddenly conscious of Marshall's predicament, walked over to rescue him.

"Marcia, I believe Henry wants to ask you about the next meeting of the R.S.P.C.A." As she moved hurriedly away he said apologetically, "Rather a bore, I'm afraid—but a wonderful hand with Labradors. I remember—— Yes?"

Travers was standing at his elbow. "It's from Paris, sir. Monsieur Furac."

"Oh—excuse me, would you?" He left the room.

Marshall carried on a desultory conversation with Travers. After a while Gilbertson returned, his manner noticeably abstracted.

"Anything serious?" Marshall asked.

"Oh no, not really." He looked down at Marshall's glass. "But you're not drinking, my dear fellow. Travers . . ."

"I don't want any more, thanks." He put the glass on the mantelpiece behind him. "Was it about business?"

"Yes——" Gilbertson hesitated. "In a way . . ."

"Does he often ring up on Sunday nights?"

"Oh no—quite unusual really." Gilbertson half turned away, with the obvious intention of terminating the conversation. He had administered a snub, and if Marshall was to behave like a well-conducted Englishman he would blush and regret his own inquisitiveness. But Marshall had suddenly grown tired of Gilbertson's conception of good behavior. He was bored and irritable. His resentment at the atmosphere of concealment and delay at the office flooded back. He would not be treated like an inquisitive child.

"I'm sorry if I sound intrusive," he said sharply, "but if it was a matter of business I am naturally interested. You must appreciate that I have a direct responsibility to New York for the Paris agency."

The determination in his tone surprised even himself. Gilbertson turned back toward him, startled at this unexpected attack. Travers had disappeared.

"Have you?" Gilbertson was undecided. His instinct was to question Marshall's authority to demand information. On the other hand, one could not be sure. Kingham was not the only powerful man in New York. And there was the magic of the name. Cipher though he was reputed to be, this was still Marcus Marshall's son. It might not be safe to go too far.

"Yes." Marshall spoke firmly, conscious of the other man's indecision. "So, naturally, I want to be kept abreast of what happens there."

"I see." Gilbertson acknowledged defeat. He went on coldly, "Well, I don't know whether you'll find this particular piece of news of great significance. It's mainly personal." He went on in a voice of exaggerated casualness, as if describing the sort of trivial incident which was always happening. "It seems that one of Furac's employees has gone off his head and taken a shot at him with a revolver."

Marshall looked at him in astonishment. "That doesn't sound exactly insignificant to me. Is he seriously hurt?"

"No, no, just a flesh wound." Gilbertson assumed an expression of distaste. These excitable Americans . . . "The chap was evidently quite mad. Afterward he turned the gun on himself and tried to blow his brains out. With only partial success, apparently."

"He's still alive?"

"Yes. He's unconscious in hospital. They say he probably won't survive."

"Does anybody know why he did it?"

Gilbertson shrugged his shoulders. "He just went crazy. Furac says he always was what he calls an introspective type."

There was a silence. Gilbertson was regarding him with hostility, as if to say: "Well then, what now?" Marshall suddenly began to feel ashamed of his curiosity. It was true—the information meant nothing to him. A tragic, sensational accident involving two people he had never met; no more than that. He found himself trying to justify himself in his own mind. It was a consequence of this absurd secrecy. If so much had not been kept from him previously he would never have been so insistent. And why had Gilbertson been so unwilling to tell him?

"Are you satisfied?" said Gilbertson ironically. "Or is there anything else you'd like to know?"

Marshall flushed. He was being put hopelessly in the wrong. In a final burst of obstinacy he said, "What's the man's name?"

"Nobody you've ever heard of. He was a salesman called André Verrier."

PART III

CHAPTER I

The plane climbed through the uppermost layer of fleecy cloud into a world of limitless blue sky and glittering sunlight. It was like suddenly going into heaven through a trap door. The note of the engines changed slightly as they leveled off. The stewardess began to pass up the aisle with coffee and biscuits. In less than an hour they would be in Paris.

Gilbertson said, "I still think it's a little unnecessary for us both to go chasing over like this."

"I told you," said Marshall, "that I didn't mind going by myself."

"Oh no." Gilbertson sounded shocked. "I couldn't let you do that—not the first time. It wouldn't be the thing at all. Much better for me to take you over, introduce you—and so forth. I'd intended to do that later on in the year," he added reproachfully.

"I'm sorry if I upset your program."

"That's all right. One must be flexible, I suppose." He sighed. If one was condemned to deal with lunatics, he managed to suggest, flexibility was the only answer. But there was no object in pretending to enjoy it. "It's just—at such short notice—rather inconvenient. . . ."

These, Marshall realized, were hard words. In Gilbertson's world it was a very serious matter to be accused of causing inconvenience. Marshall was given to understand that he had failed dismally to live up to the advance publicity he had received from Kingham.

Instead of accepting things as he found them, in an appropriately man-of-the-world fashion, he had been tactless and interfering.

Marshall was a man who, on the whole, liked to be popular. He had never achieved any satisfaction from arousing dislike, nor had he been able, in the way of most successful men, to accept it with either indifference or resignation as the necessary price of action. But over the past few months he had been tried too hard. Too often he had been reminded of his own insignificance, told (by inference, if not in so many words) to mind his own business. Now he was weary of being tactful and no longer cared whether Gilbertson liked him or not. Kingham's instructions were forgotten. His own pride demanded satisfaction. And his curiosity also. For he felt certain that André Verrier must be the A.V. referred to in the list of Wilcox's confidential correspondence. Wilcox had written three letters to New York about him, letters which he preferred to type himself and of which no copies had ever been filed. Shortly before his return to New York he had made a visit to Paris, quarreled with Gilbertson on his return, written a last letter about A.V. demanding action—and then been immediately recalled. Now Wilcox was in California and Verrier had tried to kill himself. Marshall could not imagine what the explanation might be. But he was certain of one thing, that it was his duty to talk to Verrier if it was humanly possible.

"If we'd waited till it was convenient," he pointed out, "it might have been too late."

"Too late for what?"

"You tell me Verrier's critically ill. I am particularly anxious to speak to him."

"I can't imagine why," said Gilbertson testily. "You don't know him, do you?"

"Not personally—no."

Gilbertson glanced sharply at him. Deliberately he had tried to put as much significance as he could into his last remark. With luck, Gilbertson might suspect that Wilcox had confided in him or that he had, while in New York, read the confidential memoranda. Without doubt, his bluff had had some effect. Gilbertson dropped the subject immediately.

"Furac will be meeting us at the airport," he said. "I told him it wasn't necessary, but he insisted. He's a very hospitable person. Almost overwhelming at times."

Once again Marshall felt the desire to shock, to push a vulgar finger through this veil of discretion.

"Do you like him?" he asked bluntly.

"Like him?" Gilbertson floundered for a moment. "I don't really know him very well—I mean, ours is just a business relationship, you understand. He's a shrewd man, there's no doubt of that. And very cultured, too, I believe—speaks several languages." He added obscurely: "Not perhaps everybody's cup of tea . . ."

"In what way?"

Gilbertson fluttered his fingers. "It's not easy to explain." He paused and then said carefully, "He's a bit of a law unto himself, if you see what I mean."

"I don't, quite."

"You will when you've met him, I think."

Furac was waiting for them at the customs barrier. He was a tall man with a bald head and a long reptilian neck. At a distance he could be easily mistaken for a relatively young man, but on closer inspection his real age became apparent. Above the neat, dapper body the face was old, with anxious, vertical wrinkles; it seemed to look down on his elegant gray suit, the handmade shoes, the pale manicured hands, and derive from them nothing more than a grim satisfaction. He smiled perfunctorily and apologized for not shaking hands. His right arm was in a sling.

"It's very kind of you to meet us," said Gilbertson. "There was really no need——"

"Not at all." He spoke English with only a very slight accent. "I have been looking forward very much to meeting Mr. Marshall."

"But your arm——"

"Oh, that is nothing," said Furac positively. "A mere scratch. It causes only slight inconvenience, nothing more." He added, "Fortunately Verrier was unused to firearms. He was a poor shot."

"How is he?" asked Marshall.

"Still alive—but unconscious, I believe." He added with indifference, "The doctors say his condition is extremely serious."

Gilbertson shook his head solemnly. "A shocking business."

"Yes. Most unfortunate."

"Have you any idea why he did it?" said Marshall.

"How does one account for the actions of a madman?" Furac accompanied his words with short, sharp gesticulations. It was plain that, for all his protestations, he had been badly shaken up by his experience. "You must understand that Verrier was always a man of unstable personality. We've had trouble with him frequently before."

"What sort of trouble?"

"Oh—hysterical outbursts, paranoid delusions. He brooded a great deal and fancied that people were against him. I myself am an amateur student of psychology and I did my best to help him, but without success unfortunately. In fact, it seems that I turned his delusions to some extent against myself. That sometimes happens, you know."

"He thought he had a grievance against you?"

"Presumably. I cannot imagine what it was, since he made no attempt to explain himself. He simply took out this revolver and shot at me." Furac shook his head and frowned; a diagnostician confronted with a difficult problem. "The whole case is extremely complex. He had, I know, certain other troubles—private difficulties, you understand. . . . No doubt under the circumstances it was foolish of me to continue to employ him, but I was sorry for him. He would have had difficulty in finding another job. So"—he gave a curious nervous wriggle, as if dislodging a fly from one of his shoulder blades—"I have been punished for my foolishness. It is perhaps a lesson to me."

Outside the airport was a large chauffeur-driven Mercedes. As they drove away, Marshall said, "I'd like to see Verrier if I could."

Furac's eyes regarded him questioningly. Beneath his grim, humorless self-possession there were signs of strain.

"Certainly," he said. "Though, as I said, he is unconscious at the present time. You would not be able to speak to him."

"Just the same——"

"I will try to arrange it for you. Meanwhile, my wife is expecting us all to lunch at our apartment. I hope this will be convenient?"

"Of course," said Gilbertson. "We shall be delighted. I hope we haven't put Madame Furac to too much trouble?"

"On the contrary, it will be a great pleasure," he said with formal, toneless courtesy. "My wife is most anxious to meet Mr. Marshall."

If that was so, Marshall reflected later, it was certainly not immediately apparent. Madame Furac was a woman many years younger than her husband, with white-blond hair, a Riviera tan, and an appearance of exhausted boredom with her surroundings which was curiously infectious. Having dressed and groomed herself with considerable care for her luncheon party, she obviously considered that she had done all that could possibly be expected of her. She made little attempt to conceal the fact that she found them all, Furac included, extremely dull company.

The apartment was large and luxuriously furnished, the meal served in a magnificent dining room overlooking the Bois. There was a great deal of food and wine. By the time they had finished drinking their coffee it was after three o'clock. Gilbertson just managed to suppress a yawn.

"Perhaps we should be checking in at our hotel," he suggested to Marshall.

Furac stood up. "Of course. There are rooms for you at the Plaza-Athenée—I will drive you there." He paused. "This evening I would very much like you to meet a friend of mine, Monsieur Patou. He is a deputy." He turned back to Gilbertson. "Patou is an extremely influential man."

"Naturally," said Gilbertson formally, "we shall be delighted. . . ."

"Excellent. I have a reservation at eight o'clock at the Tour d'Argent. I could perhaps pick you up at the hotel a quarter of an hour before that." He looked at Gilbertson's flushed, sleepy face, at the sun pouring down on the street outside. "In the meantime you will probably wish to rest a little."

The thought of a few hours on a bed in a luxury hotel was undeniably seductive. Marshall had to force himself to intervene.

"What about visiting the hospital?" he said.

There was a silence. Furac regarded him sourly, Gilbertson half closed his eyes as if in pain. It was as if some appalling social indiscretion had been committed which they hoped he would at least have the decency to retract. But he said nothing. Finally Furac said reluctantly, "I will try to find out what can be arranged."

"Is it necessary to arrange anything? Couldn't we just go along there?"

"I am afraid not. You would almost certainly be refused admission. Not being a relative or, for that matter, even an acquaintance of the patient, you would have no standing. On the other hand, I, as his employer, might be able to persuade the hospital to admit you. If you would care to wait another few minutes I will make a telephone call now."

He went out, leaving the two men alone. Gilbertson said: "Of course, I'm sorry for the poor fellow and all that, but if he's unconscious——"

"He may not be unconscious when we get there."

"Perhaps not. But even so—I mean, we don't even know the fellow."

Gilbertson's embarrassment was genuine, if slightly absurd. Even in these circumstances it seemed he recoiled from the idea of an interview with a person to whom he had not been introduced.

"You haven't met Verrier before?"

"Never in my life. I've heard Furac mention his name occasionally."

"If that's how you feel," said Marshall, "why don't you stay and rest in the hotel? I'll go alone."

"No, no," said Gilbertson hurriedly. "I wouldn't hear of it. If you're set on going, of course I'll go with you." He added in a discouraging voice, "Let's hope it isn't a complete waste of time."

In a few minutes Furac returned.

"Nothing is possible until six o'clock," he said. "Then we may see him for a short while."

"How is he?" asked Marshall.

"His condition is very serious."

"But hell——" He grew angry. He was being stalled again. This supercilious old camel was stringing him along. And not knowing the language well enough, there was nothing much he could do about it. "That's nonsense! He may be dead by six."

Furac waved his hands, palms upward, fingers outspread, to indicate his own impotence in the matter. "The rules of the hospital are very strict." Seeing that Marshall was once again preparing to protest, he added with absolute finality, "My chauffeur is waiting to take you to the hotel. I will call for you there at five-thirty."

CHAPTER II

THE HOSPITAL was a massive structure built entirely of dark gray stone. It consisted of a series of parallel rectangular blocks six stories high leading off a central administration building; running around the buildings and between the blocks were graveled paths and a few ill-kept flower beds. The whole was enclosed within a protective circle of high spiked railings.

They drove along beside it for almost half a mile before arriving at the entrance. The huge double gates were surmounted with barbed wire and securely locked. "This is a very poor district," explained Furac. "There are many criminals . . ." He and the chauffeur became involved in an argument with an aged concierge—apparently the instructions for their reception had not been passed sufficiently far down the scale of authority. After a good deal of talk and gesticulation, terminating in the furtive passage of money, they were finally allowed in.

"This is not the normal visiting hour, you understand," said Furac. "One has to make special arrangements."

Inside the hospital there was a dank, tomblike atmosphere. Their footsteps echoed on the stone flags of the main corridor. There was none of the bustle which Marshall had always associated with hospitals at home. The sunlight struggled hopelessly through high dusty windows, illuminating strips of wall from which the paint was peeling and Gothic archways like those of an old seminary. Nobody interfered with them or asked who they were. It seemed that, once past the barrier of the main gate, their presence was accepted without question.

They found the ward with some difficulty. It was on the third floor of one of the side blocks, up a narrow stone staircase with different smells, ranging from carbolic acid to stew, on each landing. By this time they had all begun to feel much less important than they had felt a quarter of an hour ago. Effortlessly this gaunt, archaic building had cut them down to size. Here nobody cared for them. Their bank accounts and expensive cars and homes and clothes meant nothing. The hospital was not impressed; it saw them merely as men, like all the others. It seemed to be awaiting with grim expectancy the day when it might see them again under less favorable circumstances.

They were in a small corridor with doors opening off it on either side. At the far end were large swing doors leading into the ward proper. The corridor was deserted. More than ever, they felt like intruders.

"What do we do now?" asked Gilbertson.

Furac looked about, exasperated. The lack of interest in their arrival was like a personal insult to him. It reflected on the efficiency of his organization and the importance of his contacts. Marshall was slightly amused. In international business it was a point of prestige to demonstrate to foreign visitors the extent of one's influence. Furac had lost face.

"I cannot understand it," he said. "The superintendent assured me that we would be expected. He promised to notify the sister of the ward. No doubt she is in her office." He approached one of the doors and stood before it indecisively. Suddenly it opened and a tiny, aged man in a flannel nightgown shuffled out and walked past them toward the ward. There was the sound of rushing water, stifled as the door sprang shut again.

"I can't help feeling," said Gilbertson, "that it was perhaps a mistake to come at this time. It may be rather inconvenient. . . ."

He looked longingly at his lines of retreat, which were, his voice reminded them, still open. A quick change of plan and they could be drinking champagne cocktails in the Tour d'Argent, with this ridiculous escapade completely forgotten. . . . Marshall's own confidence was beginning to ebb. After all, what was he really trying to do? What conceivable object was there in this visit to the sick-bed of an unconscious man whom he had never met and whose existence had been unknown to him until a week or two ago? Supposing Verrier did regain consciousness, what then? What questions could he ask? Would the two of them be left alone? Most unlikely, he decided, especially if Furac had anything to hide. And, in any case, would Verrier be able to understand English?

The ward door opened and a tall woman of about thirty-five in a blue uniform came out. She looked at them questioningly.

"Excuse me," said Furac. "That is the sister."

He hurried up to her and engaged her in conversation. Marshall and Gilbertson followed. After they had listened uncomprehendingly for a while to the rapid conversation, Furac turned to them.

"He is still unconscious," he explained. "It is impossible to speak to him."

The sister nodded sharply two or three times and led them to the ward door. She pushed it open to show a long row of beds, one of which was encircled by screens.

"She says he has been screened off because he is seriously ill. Also, his wife is with him. He cannot receive any visitors at the moment."

Marshall nodded despondently. That certainly seemed to settle the matter. It was hard to see what more he could do. Would Jane understand? he wondered. He remembered her excitement when he had spoken to her on the telephone just before leaving for Paris, her unconcealed delight at the knowledge that he had roused himself from his inertia and decided to take the initiative. The thought of her confidence in him had given him strength to withstand the hostility of Gilbertson and Furac. It would be hard to tell her that it had all come to nothing. It was no fault of his, of course, he had every excuse. But there came a time when no excuse was good enough.

He summoned together the last remnants of his determination.

"Perhaps," he said, "we could wait a little while——"

Furac frowned. "But there is no object——"

"We don't want to make ourselves a nuisance," put in Gilbertson.

"That's for Sister to decide." Marshall was conscious of the weakness of his position. He could not himself give any reason for staying, except that to go now would be to admit that he was beaten. "Will she allow us to wait?" he asked Furac.

Furac, with a sigh of exasperation, spoke again to the sister. She gave a shrug. "*Si vous voulez . . .*"

"Okay," said Marshall. "Let's do that."

She opened a door on the left-hand side of the corridor and showed them into a small bare office. Marshall was conscious of being the focal point in an atmosphere of disapproval to which the other three contributed in some degree. It varied from the impersonal irritation of the sister to downright disgust on the part of Furac. When the sister had left, Gilbertson arranged himself in a chair and offered cigarettes.

"We might as well be as comfortable as possible," he said. "Goodness knows how long we shall have to wait."

"Our dinner engagement," said Furac pointedly, "is in one hour's time."

Marshall said nothing. It seemed to him that anything he might say would only make matters worse. His chair was beside a desk on which the sister presumably did her clerical work. There was a litter of memoranda and half-completed temperature charts, a pile of case sheets. He glanced over them idly. They were meaningless to him, but at least it was better to look at them than to meet the eyes of his two companions. Suddenly he noticed the name on the top case sheet.

André Verrier, age 32. Occupation: Salesman. Address: 49C rue Zurbaran; married; no children; next of kin—wife, Louise Verrier, same address. Date of admission to hospital: . . . . Date of discharge: . . . . Mode of discharge: . . . .

That was all, on the front sheet. Presumably the details of his medical condition were on the other side. Marshall was tempted to turn over the page in search of further information but could not bring himself to do so. As he looked away, he saw Furac's eyes upon him. He also had seen the case sheet.

They had been sitting there for almost half an hour in complete silence when they heard the sound of voices in the corridor outside. Then, without warning, the door was thrown open and a young man in a white coat, with a stethoscope round his neck, came into the room. He looked at them in surprise, muttered excuses, and walked over to the desk. Picking up Verrier's case sheet from the desk, he took a fountain pen out of the pocket of his coat and in the column labeled "Mode of discharge" he scribbled: "Mort." Then he tossed the case notes into a wire tray for disposal.

Furac said: "You are the doctor in charge of André Verrier?"

"Yes." The doctor raised his eyebrows questioningly. He could not have been more than twenty-five or so; his clothes were cheap, his collar soiled and crumpled. Even in death Verrier was in no position to demand the best.

"Are you friends of his?"

"Yes. I am his employer."

With a spark of interest the doctor looked at the sling on Furac's right arm. "The one he . . . ?"

"That is so."

"You were lucky. It was a dangerous weapon——"

"He was mad. I knew it as soon as he came into the room."

"Really?" The doctor was only mildly impressed. "That may be so. For myself, I had no chance to speak to him. You understand, I suppose, that he is dead?"

Furac nodded, his long bony face composed in an expression of solemnity. "It is very tragic."

"Yes." The doctor made no attempt to be anything other than perfunctory. He looked at Gilbertson and Marshall as if wondering whether to ask who they were and what they were doing here. Then he seemed to decide against it—he was too busy and too indifferent to care. He gave them all a thin, tired smile and left the room.

"I guess we might as well leave now," said Marshall. Despite himself, he was conscious of an apologetic note in his voice. The affair was finished; Verrier was dead, wiped off the face of the earth with a stroke of red ink. . . . With the air of a man in retreat, he walked out into the corridor.

As they stood there, waiting to take their leave of the sister, a woman came out of the ward. The light was poor, and Marshall formed no more impression of her than that she was fair and slight in build, with a pale, oval face. As she passed by them Furac nodded at her, smiling uncertainly, like a man who remembers a snub on some previous occasion. The woman showed no sign of recognition.

Marshall looked at him sharply. "Is that his wife?"

"Yes. I have met her once before." His tone was disparaging. "She is not a bad girl—though somewhat provincial——"

"Excuse me."

She had almost reached the outer pair of swing doors when Marshall overtook her. Hearing his footsteps, she half turned to meet him.

"Madame Verrier?"

"Yes."

She regarded him coldly, without welcome or encouragement. He found himself at a loss for words. It was necessary to make some contact, some show of human sympathy. Whatever the truth about Verrier or the meaning of his dealings with Wilcox, he had nevertheless died in horrible circumstances, perhaps in madness, perhaps in despair. It was not possible to go out to dinner and forget about it, to allow his widow to walk past in a corridor without a word. But he was discouraged by her lack of response. Everywhere he found himself surrounded by suspicion and hostility—even in the eyes of the person he was trying to befriend.

"I would like to say——" he began in his halting French. As he searched for words, he cursed himself for his own idleness, his failure to learn the language. How was it possible to gain understanding or express sympathy under such conditions? He started again. "*Je veux offrir*——" What was the French for condolences? But even that was too cold, a card on a wreath, black-edged. "*Je suis triste*——" he began again.

She had no mercy for his embarrassment. "Perhaps," she said coldly in English, "you should speak your own language."

"Oh, I'm sorry. I didn't realize——" He added with relief, "That will be much easier——"

"You are a friend of Monsieur Furac?"

"Yes. Of course, how stupid of me, you don't know who I am. I should introduce myself. My name is Marshall—Christopher Marshall. I'm from the New York office of the corporation. I was in London and as soon as I heard——"

"You are Marshall?"

She spoke softly, but it seemed to him that at that moment her attitude of indifference had changed to something much more positive. She looked at him almost with loathing.

"Yes. This has been a terrible tragedy. I wonder if there is anything I can do to help."

"To help? In what way?"

He floundered. He had not intended to discuss details. Nor, he began to realize, had he any clear idea of what his intentions were. "Well, I don't know exactly just now. Perhaps we could have a talk——"

She shook her head. "No." The eyes that regarded him were red-rimmed, shadowed, implacable. In her voice there was hate, not only for him, but for his organization, his country, everything he might be taken to represent. "There is nothing I want from you—nothing whatever."

She turned and walked hurriedly away, her footsteps echoing along the stone walls of the corridor. He thought of following her and then stopped himself. He would only expose himself to further humiliation, and at this time, at least, she had the right to be alone if she wished.

In the silence that followed, Furac was the first to speak. "Perhaps we should go now," he said. "It would be impolite to keep Monsieur Patou waiting."

CHAPTER III

WHEN HE AWOKE next morning his head was throbbing and his mouth was dry and sore from innumerable cigarettes. Memories of the night before came back to him, combining with his physical condition to induce a mood of extreme pessimism. He had gone to bed late, and after the first hour or two of heavy sleep owing to the wine, he had passed a restless night. He looked at his watch on the bedside table. It was after nine o'clock.

It had been a dreadful, nightmarish evening. Monsieur Patou had turned out to be a florid, middle-aged man with a thick, coarse voice and an uncertain temper. He spoke no English. When they first met him he was in a bad mood for some reason which was never clearly explained, but began to thaw a little under the influence of alcohol. Gilbertson and Marshall, after the first introductions, he practically ignored. He ate and drank on a Rabelaisian scale, stopping only to shout at the waiters or wipe the sweat from his forehead with the napkin he wore tucked in his collar. Every now and then he would laugh harshly, explosively, for no obvious reason. Marshall watched with mounting indignation as he ordered bottle after bottle of champagne without consultation with the other members of the party. As the wine took hold of him, his voice rose and he banged on the table with his fist to emphasize his points. Furac smiled and nodded agreement; occasionally he would translate snatches of Patou's conversation into English in the patient but patronizing manner of a professor of psychiatry showing off a mental case. As Patou sank farther into drunkenness, Furac amused himself by making contemptuous remarks about him in English to Marshall and Gilbertson. It was as if in this way he was somehow able to disclaim responsibility for his own part in the spectacle.

The entertainment had ended at a night club in Montmartre, where Patou had capsized among the bottles and glasses which littered the table, to be eventually borne home unconscious.

Marshall heaved himself wearily out of bed, drank a glass of Perrier to clear his mouth, and opened the shutters. The sunlight hurt his eyes. The bedroom was magnificent, with a balcony facing on to a courtyard and a fountain—it was part of a two-bedroom suite which he was sharing with Gilbertson. He put on his dressing gown and walked into the sitting room.

Gilbertson was already up, eating croissants and reading the *Continental Daily Mail.* He looked as neat as ever and none the worse for the previous night. His coldness of manner had now entirely disappeared. He seemed to be taking the attitude that Marshall had behaved badly yesterday but had, after all, been punished for it by being made to look foolish. It was not for him to kick a man when he was down. He waved a hand in greeting.

"Good morning," he said. "Help yourself to breakfast. Wonderful day, isn't it?"

"Yes." Marshall poured coffee for himself. He looked at the food and decided against it. Instead, he lit a cigarette. "How do you feel after last night?"

"Fair," Gilbertson said judicially. "But I couldn't stand it very often. I'm not much of a man for the night life, myself. I suppose," he added with large tolerance, "the French have more stamina for that sort of thing."

"What I can't understand is what we were doing there at all."

"Prestige, my dear boy, prestige. These distributors like to show you around. It convinces chaps like Patou that there *is* such a thing as the Marshall Corporation and that Furac isn't just knocking those machines of yours up himself in a converted garage at Passy. I suppose it's of some value," he added dubiously.

"Where does this Patou come in, anyway? Government contracts?"

"I shouldn't be surprised. Though I don't know much detail of what goes on over here. He was certainly a dreadful bore."

"You said it." But he didn't want to sound too holier-than-thou. It was the kind of attitude that got Americans disliked abroad. "Mind you, we have them like that at home. I guess it's pretty much the same everywhere."

Gilbertson nodded noncommittally. Evidently he was not prepared to speak for England in the matter. Marshall went over to the window and looked out into the courtyard. He found he could manage to stand the light a little better now. "What goes on today?" he asked.

"I had a ring from Furac a little while ago. He's tied up this morning, it seems. That's understandable, since we came at such short notice. But he's going to send his assistant, Colbert, round in the car. He thought you'd like a little drive around the city. You know the sort of thing—the Champs Elysées, the Bois——"

Marshall shook his head. "I'm sorry." An idea that had been lying around in the back of his mind since they had left the hospital the previous afternoon was beginning to take shape. "I'm afraid you'll have to give him my apologies. I can't come for a drive this morning."

"Oh dear." Gilbertson was perturbed. "Are you sure? I mean —it's really very kind of Furac to offer—— He may be rather offended——"

"He should have asked me personally."

"You were asleep."

"Well, that's too bad. Tell him I'm sorry," he repeated. "I've got something else to do."

He waited for Gilbertson to ask him what it was. But of course an Englishman couldn't ask that sort of question, no matter how curious he might be, no matter how much he might raise one bushy eyebrow, waiting for you to volunteer the information. . . .

"Perhaps," said Gilbertson finally, "you could manage to meet us later?" He picked up a napkin and carefully dried the coffee out of his mustache. "We shall be at the office at one o'clock."

Marshall glanced at his watch. There should be enough time, provided it was not too far away. "I guess so."

"We'll expect to see you then."

Marshall went back to his room and bathed and dressed hurriedly. He took an aspirin for his headache and a benzedrine for the depression which usually accompanied it on these occasions—he was a poor drinker. Shortly afterward he imagined he felt better. As he passed through the lobby on his way out of the hotel he saw an anxious-looking olive-skinned young man at the reception desk, asking for Mr. Gilbertson. Colbert? The Mercedes was waiting outside, but the chauffeur seemed not to recognize him. He called a taxi.

"Forty-nine rue Zurbaran."

The driver took out a tattered street guide and leafed through it. After a while he gave an ill-tempered grunt and started off.

They crossed the river and headed south. At first they were in the Montparnasse area, where Marshall had lived and worked—many years ago, it seemed to him.

He remembered the excitement with which he had first explored the quarter. There, on the right of the Boulevard St. Germain, was the café where he had spent so many of his evenings. He had sat drinking cognac with Ken Pearson and Rafael da Silva, wearing berets and linen trousers and hoping people would take them for Frenchmen. Nobody ever did. Now Rafael was an insurance assessor in São Paulo and Ken was an executive in an advertising agency, drawing women with forty-inch busts for the glossy magazines. Neither of them had minded very much. It had been fun while it lasted, but when the fun was over you went back home and married and got down to a real job of work. When they had got themselves enough money they would come back for a vacation with their wives, hinting (as would be expected of them) of wild, unspecified adventures, of mistresses casually shared by impecunious students. Except that they hadn't been impecunious, and, no matter how you tried to kid yourself, Paris in the 1950s wasn't really very much like *la vie de Bohème*. Perhaps it never had been.

But soon they were beyond the area he knew. The streets were narrower, the stucco was cracking on the walls of the tall gray buildings, pieces of washing hung out from the windows of the apartment houses. Even the sun seemed to lose its brilliance, filtered through a cloud of poverty.

He felt obscurely intimidated. It was like making his way into a jungle peopled with savages he could never understand. He began to regret the impulse which had led him into making this expedition, the quirk of memory which had held in his mind the address he had seen on Verrier's case sheet. Why, after all, was he doing this? By any ordinary standards he had no longer any obligation to Madame Verrier. He had offered to help her and his offer had been rudely rejected. And yet, somehow, remembering her eyes in that last moment before she had turned away from him down the hospital corridor, he could not find within himself any genuine resentment against her.

Forty-nine rue Zurbaran was a house like all the others in the quarter. Inside the doorway there were slots containing four cards, one of which said "Verrier." Marshall paid off his taxi and then regretted that he had not asked the man to wait. There was, after all, no more than an even chance that she would be there.

The concierge's lodge was empty. He walked up the stairs. The building seemed quite uninhabited—probably all the tenants were out at work. His footsteps echoed on the carpetless stairs.

On the third floor there was a door marked "49C." The silence was such that he felt sure she was not at home. When he rang the bell he thought at first that he heard the sound of movement, but when it was not repeated he decided he had been mistaken. He rang again to make sure and was just about to turn and go down the stairs when she opened the door. She was wearing an apron over the same black dress she had worn at the hospital.

"Good morning," he said.

She seemed surprised to see him and at a loss to know what to say or do. At the hospital she had shown herself completely in command of the situation; now her assurance had deserted her. In the middle of her housework, her hair uncombed, her face not completely made up, she was unprepared for battle.

"What are you doing here?" she asked finally.

"I came to have a talk with you."

"About what?"

They were still standing in the doorway. He said, "Do you mind if I come in?"

She said nothing, but moved aside and allowed him to enter the apartment. It seemed to consist of no more than three rooms. The living room was small and cheaply furnished. She motioned toward a chair.

"You will excuse me for one moment?"

While she was away he looked around the room. The furniture was of light pine, highly polished, thinly upholstered with imitation leather. You could almost see the store where it had been sold on such accommodatingly easy terms. Part of the suite was a glass-fronted bookcase, fitted mainly with back numbers of *Paris-Match*. On top of the bookcase was a photograph. Madame Verrier was on the deck of a *bateau mouche,* arm in arm with a man, presumably Verrier himself. He was a delicate-looking man, dandified in the ready-made way of the traveling salesman. Behind the smile which the photograph had demanded there was a lingering trace of anxiety which he had found it impossible to conceal. He was rather smaller than his wife.

He had picked up the photograph and was looking at it when she came into the room.

"Your husband?" he asked.

"Yes." She had discarded her apron and made up her face. Her moment of confusion was over. She sat down in one of the shoddy chairs and regarded him uncompromisingly. When he hesitated, wondering how to begin, she grew impatient.

"Well?" she asked sharply. "What is it you wish to say?"

"Yesterday," he said slowly, "I offered to help you and you refused. I'd like to know why."

She sighed irritably. "I was very upset, you must understand."

"I understand and sympathize. Just the same——"

"I am sorry if I have offended you." She was offhand and perfunctory. If his vanity was hurt, she was prepared to make amends as the price of getting rid of him. "I apologize. Now please go."

"I didn't come here for an apology."

"What for, then?"

"An explanation. You appear to have something against me—or my company——"

The word "company" seemed to spark her into aggression. "Mr. Marshall, my husband is dead. I have no connection with your company any more."

"You prefer it that way?"

"Yes."

"Why? I may be able to help you——"

She shook her head, as if he were trying to sell her something. "This is a waste of time. I am busy."

"Listen." He was suddenly exasperated with her. Pride was all very well, but she was carrying it to the point of affectation. He would make one more attempt, and if she wasn't interested he would wrap up the whole Verrier affair and forget it. "I don't know what the situation was with your husband. But I got an idea from Wilcox——"

At that moment the doorbell rang. He stopped, waiting for her to answer it. But she did not move. The bell rang again, insistently.

"Aren't you going to answer?"

"No. It will not be important." She nibbled nervously at her upper lip. The person outside grew tired of ringing and began to bang on the door. The noise reverberated throughout the house.

Suddenly her endurance gave way. She got up and went to open the door. From the living room Marshall could hear her engaged in bitter argument with a man outside. The conversation was in French far too rapid for him to follow. It continued for a surprisingly long time, with the constant repetition of certain phrases. It sounded like a dispute in which neither side was prepared to give way.

Finally he got up and walked out into the hall.

"Anything I can do?"

She turned round. "No—it is nothing."

"It doesn't sound like nothing."

The man at the door slapped an account book he held in his hand, and pointed to one of the columns. "*Dix mille,*" he said violently. "*Dix mille six cents quarante.*"

"You owe him money?"

"Please—you must not interfere——"

Conscious of the cheapness of his gesture, he took some notes out of his wallet and handed them to the collector. Her efforts seemed to have exhausted her; she made no attempt to stop him. When the collector had gone he said: "I hope you didn't mind. It seemed the only way of carrying on our conversation."

She shook her head and sat down. It occurred to him that she was close to tears.

"Was it the rent?" he asked.

"No—the furniture. I had to pay the rent yesterday." She shrugged her shoulders. "Naturally they are all afraid I shall leave without paying them."

"You're going to leave here?"

"I think so."

"Where will you go?"

"I don't know yet. Somewhere smaller."

It was difficult to imagine anything much smaller. He said wonderingly, "Have you no money at all?"

In her unhappiness she had forgotten her bitterness against him. Now it was suddenly revived.

"I have enough, thank you."

"Enough for what?"

"To pay for the funeral. After that I shall get a job. Then I will pay you back your eleven thousand francs."

If his action in paying the money had been theatrical, her intention to repay it was even more so. He said, "Don't be silly."

"I am not silly!" She flushed indignantly. Her aloofness was gone; she was an unhappy little girl insisting on her right to be treated as an adult. "You do not want me to pay you back, I know. The money is nothing to you and you would like me to be grateful. In America you can buy anything—even people. But not here."

"You can't buy a hell of a lot of gratitude for thirty dollars, even in the States. And some people are for sale everywhere. Isn't that so?"

"Yes, that is so." Her voice was suddenly tired. "After all, you bought my husband, didn't you—so very cheaply."

"I don't quite know what you mean by that."

"No?"

"No. Your husband was employed by Furac."

"On your business."

"That's true. And of course indirectly I suppose we paid his salary." He looked round the room uneasily. "Incidentally, what was his salary?"

"Fifty thousand francs a month."

"Fifty thousand?" About four hundred to the dollar. "That——"

"A hundred and twenty-five dollars," she said bitterly. "Thirty dollars a week. Not very much, is it? Even for a poor country."

He strove to remember—there was some arrangement about salaries in the International. Money was paid from New York to the distributors to cover payment of staff, but he could not recollect the details.

"That can't be right. Why, my secretary——" Miss Tracy had earned a hundred a week and was not oversatisfied at that. "Do they know about this in New York?"

"I don't know. I think so. André didn't tell me much. But I know he spoke to Mr. Wilcox."

"And what did Wilcox say?"

"He said it was quite wrong. He told André that Furac received money from New York to cover his expenses and that it was sufficient to pay his staff very well. He promised to raise the matter with your head office. André was very hopeful. Then Wilcox left Paris and we never saw him again." She added with boundless cynicism, "I think perhaps he forgot."

"He didn't forget. He tried."

"You have spoken to him?"

"Not about that. But I happen to know he wrote to New York several times about your husband——" He had to admit to a feeling of disappointment. He had hoped for something more dramatic. Was this all there was to it—a sordid, petty swindle involving a few thousand francs a week?

She seemed to read his mind. Perhaps she had seen the same expression on the face of others. "Yes," she said, "that's all it is. Hardly worth your trouble, is it?"

"I didn't say that."

"You were thinking it. I could see you. That's why I didn't want to talk to you in the first place. I knew it would be like this." She sighed hopelessly. "But to us it was important."

"Of course it's important." He spoke violently, angry with himself. He had almost fallen into the same trap as the others. Human injustice was never trivial. The smallness of the sum involved made the affair more rather than less serious, since it could have been so easily put right. Why, he wondered incredulously, had it not been? Why, if she was telling the truth, had nothing been done?

"So you think Furac was cheating you?" he asked.

"Of course."

Her acceptance of it as a matter of course was more painful to him than any reproach. "And us too?"

"How should I know? André didn't tell me everything about his job." She hesitated, as if struggling with the impulse to confide in him. "He was not always an easy man to understand. He had a tendency to brood, to make secrets. He would say sometimes that he would not accept such treatment forever, that Furac should be careful, he would drive him too far, he could make trouble if he wished, and so on and so forth. I must confess I didn't take him too seriously. Furac had become something of an obsession with him. He talked of him all the time."

"Did he ever go direct to Furac about the money?"

"Oh yes. They had many arguments. But André always lost. He hated Furac but he was afraid of him too. Eventually he decided the only thing to do was to go over Furac's head. After he had spoken to Mr. Wilcox he had great faith that everything would be all right. He was very simple in some ways." She glanced at the photograph. The delicate face, fixed forever in a nervous half-smile, gazed uncertainly back to her, eager for reassurance. "I told him not to trust the Americans."

Half an hour ago she could have made him angry. Now he felt only pity for her. He said, "You don't like us much."

She shook her head. "I don't understand you."

"We're not so difficult."

"Oh yes. With people like Furac it is easy. They take everything and give nothing. One knows what to expect. But the Americans are so anxious to be fair and generous and for everyone to love them. But, in the end, somehow we are still poor and they are even richer than before."

"Look," he said desperately, "you've got to understand about Wilcox. He was on the level. It wasn't his fault. I know he felt very badly——"

"Very well," she said impatiently. "It was not his fault. But my husband is dead. And Mr. Wilcox is—where?"

"In California. They put him on a job——"

"California—that must be a very nice place."

"He was sent there. He didn't want to go."

She said nothing for a moment. Then almost to herself she said, "He never even wrote a letter."

"He didn't? I can't understand that."

"The first we knew was when André heard from Furac that Wilcox had been replaced. After that he knew there was nothing to hope for any more."

"Surely that wasn't the reason——" But, after all, why not? He looked around at the pitiful little room, the mortgaged furniture. In this world he was a stranger. Here a man's home, his self-respect, the fidelity of his wife could hang on the same amount of money as you tipped the headwaiter at your hotel. You paid him five dollars a week less than he could live on, and he killed himself. He asked her, turning to her experience, "Is it possible?"

"How can I say? He didn't tell me he was going to do it." She stood up, dismissing the subject and Marshall with it. There was no hatred in her voice now, only a dignified finality less possible to ignore than hatred. "But, after all, it is done and there is no use to go on talking about it. You have heard everything I have to tell you. I do not dislike you any more. This was not your fault, I see now. You have been kind." She prolonged the word, with no more than a trace of irony. "Now you should go back to the Georges Cinq and drink your cocktails."

"No." He shook his head. "I didn't come here just to give myself a good conscience." Though perhaps he had—he could not be sure.

Certainly, now, there was no possibility of such an easy solution. "I'm going to do something. . . ."

"I do not know what there is to do."

He was not very sure himself, he realized. If Varrier had still been alive it would have been different. He could make trouble, insist on an inquiry into the whole of Furac's dealings with his staff—that would help certain other people, but what about her? Some form of compensation, perhaps? On the other hand, he had heard only her side of the story. It was necessary to be cautious.

"It's early to talk about that. But I won't let it go. You can rely on that."

"Thank you."

The clock above the mantelpiece showed half-past twelve. There was nothing else to say, no reason to stay any longer. He got up to go.

"You can find your way back?" She gave him a thin smile. It was suddenly clear to him that she had believed nothing. He would find his way back, as Wilcox had done; into his own world, the world of big deals and important men and large sums of money. In the comfort of his hotel her problem would seem less important. A good meal, a bottle of wine, a word of reassurance from Furac or Gilbertson, and he would begin to wonder whether it had ever existed. Helpless though she was, she could at least take pride in being undeceived; she had learned the value of promises. With a dignity born of total disillusion she was waiting calmly for him to betray her.

CHAPTER IV

Out in the street there was no sign of a taxi. An old woman at a tobacco stand on the corner directed him to the nearest Métro station, but the walk was longer than he expected. He saw, to his relief, that there was no chance of his being able to reach Furac's office by one o'clock. Instead, he took the Métro to the Champs Elysées and had lunch by himself in a small café. Over his coffee he asked the waiter for some paper and envelopes and wrote a letter to Jane.

Toward the end he said:

> . . . So, as you see, this isn't going to be exactly a simple affair. Verrier may have been out of his mind, as they say—even his wife seemed to admit it as a possibility, though she suggests that anxiety may have made it worse. In any case, it seems that he had a genuine grievance, and I think the company should do something about it, even if it does mean antagonizing important people. I am going to collect any information I can in Paris and also possibly raise the matter point-blank with Furac—there has been too much politeness and covering up so far. It will be interesting to see what he has to say.
>
> Good-by, darling, and look after yourself. I think of you all the time. You were right in what you said about me—it isn't really enough to spend my life as a spectator. I am much happier now that I feel I have something worth while to do. It may not seem very important, but I think this is the sort of thing I am particularly fitted for. Fortunately it doesn't matter very much to me if I make myself unpopular. . . .

When the letter was finished, he posted it and took a taxi back to the hotel. He found Gilbertson and Furac in the suite, drinking whisky.

"Hello, Marshall." The friendliness in Gilbertson's voice was noticeably strained. "Where on earth did you get to? We waited for you at the office——"

"I'm sorry. I got tied up."

"Why didn't you telephone?"

"I'm afraid there wasn't one at hand."

His answers were perfunctory. His eyes were on Furac, who had so far said nothing. The Frenchman showed no sign of resentment or even of curiosity. His left hand mechanically stroked at the bald area on the top of his head, as if searching for something long since lost.

"I hope I didn't spoil your lunch," said Marshall.

"Not at all." Speech seemed to relax Furac. His hand dropped to his side. Three parallel red lines on the top of his head showed where he had been scratching with his fingernail. "Though naturally we missed you." He paused for a moment and then said, "How was Madame Verrier?"

For a moment Marshall was disconcerted. Surely he had not told anyone where he was going. . . . Then he remembered Furac's chauffeur—the man had been only a few feet away from him when he had given her address to the cab driver. He sat down and lit a cigarette. On reflection, he was encouraged by the fact that Furac had chosen to raise the question. It showed a certain anxiety.

"Not so bad," he said, "taking everything into consideration."

Furac nodded. "She has, of course, experienced a great tragedy. One has to remember that." His sympathy was perfunctory. "I trust you found her more co-operative this morning?"

"Definitely."

"She confided in you?"

"To a certain extent."

Furac looked at his fingernails. "Perhaps I should warn you," he said, "in your own interests not to set too much value on everything she tells you. She has the reputation of being"—he hesitated—"a little unreliable."

"That wasn't my impression."

"No?" The pale, watery eyes opened wide, politely astonished at Marshall's simplicity. "I suppose it might not be so obvious to somebody who did not know her very well."

"Perhaps you'd explain what you mean."

Furac gave a small exasperated sigh. "You place me in an embarrassing position, Mr. Marshall. Naturally one doesn't wish to say unpleasant things about a person who is in such unfortunate circumstances. However, since you seem so interested in her . . ." He shrugged his shoulders, disclaiming responsibility. "She caused poor Verrier a great deal of trouble at one time or another."

"What sort of trouble?"

"She worried him. She was persistent and ambitious—also somewhat extravagant. Always she tried to drive him into doing things which were beyond his abilities. She made him feel a failure—you know what I mean? Well, maybe he was a failure, but no man likes his wife to think so. I think it was partly because of this that he ended up the way he did." He shook his head regretfully. "He was not a man of strong character."

"You think it was because of her that he tried to shoot you?"

"I would not be so specific." He became slightly patronizing, the lecturer too experienced to be caught out by a bright student. "But it is by no means impossible. The human mind is very complex. Have you ever studied psychology, Mr. Marshall?"

"Not seriously."

"You would find it well worth while. To a businessman I would say it is indispensable. I have no claims to be anything more than an amateur," he said modestly, "yet I have gained from it more than I can say. So many of the obscurities of human behavior are clarified by psychology." He returned suddenly to more specific matters. "You appreciate, of course, that Madame Verrier did not care for her husband?"

"No."

"It is so, I can assure you."

"Then why did she——?"

"Why did she behave so strangely yesterday? Why is she unhappy? Why does she feel resentment against me—against you even, whom she has never met before? I will tell you why." He paused oratorically, his index finger raised in the air. "Guilt."

"Nonsense."

Furac was not put out. "That is what people always say when first confronted with the truths of psychology," he said complacently. "Nevertheless——"

"What reason would she have to feel guilty?"

"She did not love him. She cannot help this, but she is ashamed just the same. She reproaches herself. If she had loved him more he might not have killed himself. She cannot face this—she must reassure herself—she makes a parade of sorrow—she blames others——"

Marshall got up and walked toward the windows. There were shadows in the courtyard now, but a few people were still sitting about in cane chairs, drinking afternoon tea to the music of the fountain. There was a waiter with a trolley of cream cakes. One woman was trying to feed pieces of chocolate éclair to a satiated and indifferent poodle. He turned away from the window and looked at Furac.

"How much did you pay Verrier?" he asked.

The harshness of his voice cut violently across the silence of the room. It was as if anger had taken hold of him against his will, giving him, temporarily at least, a new personality of which he had little experience. It had happened to him on occasions before, and always afterward he had felt ashamed. It was so easy to lose control—and to enjoy it. Also to profit from it, on occasion. He remembered the purposeful, calculated rages of his father, so often invoked with no other purpose than to gain time, to prevent logical discussion of a matter about which he was in the wrong. . . .

The two men were looking at him in surprise. Furac blinked and began to stroke his head again. He was like a nervous lion tamer confronted by a disagreeable interruption in the rhythm of his act. He regarded Marshall indecisively, wondering what was required. A touch of the whip? Or a lump of sugar?

Eventually it was Gilbertson who spoke.

"I'm not quite sure what your object is in asking that question, Marshall," he said.

"Furac knows."

Furac shook his head. "I assure you I don't. Nor—and you must forgive me for saying this—do I consider it any of your business——"

"I seem to recollect an arrangement by which you have financial support from New York for payment of staff. Isn't that so?"

Furac rose from his chair. "Mr. Marshall, I don't wish to quarrel with you, but if I am to speak frankly——"

"Speak as frankly as you like."

"I consider your whole attitude offensive in the extreme——"

"I can understand that." He added grimly, "I know what you paid Verrier. I heard about it today."

"From his wife?"

"Yes." When Furac made a gesture of impatience he said, "All right, don't tell me—she's unreliable. Then prove it to me. Show me your books. Show me what you got from New York and how much you passed on to your men. And how much you took for yourself, and that apartment of yours, and your car and chauffeur——"

"Marshall, for God's sake!" Gilbertson's voice was sharp and determined, like a slap in the face to a hysteric. "Take a hold on yourself, man. You can't make accusations of that sort without proof."

This attack from the flank was slightly sobering. But he said stubbornly, "If it's untrue, let him prove it. I'd like to see his books."

"Now look here——"

"Please." At some point while the other two had been arguing, Furac had recovered his confidence. He spoke quietly and with dignity. "If I may be allowed an occasional word, I would like to clarify certain points. I think Mr. Marshall has become a little emotional under the influence of Madame Verrier and has lost touch with the realities of the situation." He turned to Marshall. "I should perhaps remind you that I am an independent man of business. I have close agreements with your corporation, but I am not employed by them. I cannot be easily bullied, or shouted at, or accused of theft or embezzlement merely on the unsupported word of a hysterical woman—no matter how attractive she may be——" As Marshall opened his mouth to speak Furac went on quickly: "That is my position, Mr. Marshall. Now—tell me—what is yours?"

"You know what my position is."

"You are the European representative—that I know. Are you anything more?" When Marshall did not speak, he went on with satisfaction: "Evidently not. Now, I have had dealings with quite a few European representatives in my time, as has Mr. Gilbertson. We have a fairly clear idea of the duties and responsibilities involved. It may be that you consider yourself in a special position because of your name and family connections, but I must tell you that these mean nothing to me. In my opinion you have grossly exceeded your authority." He picked up his hat. "I am prepared to overlook your behavior this afternoon on the supposition that you are in an unbalanced state of mind and have been influenced by an extremely plausible and deceitful woman. On the other hand, I certainly do not intend to discuss this question with you any further."

He bowed formally to both of them and left the room. When he had gone, Gilbertson said:

"You put your foot in it there, I'm afraid."

"He's a crook."

"Very probably," said Gilbertson without emotion. "But just the same——"

"He underpaid that poor bastard until he drove him off his head."

"Well—rather a strong reaction to a grievance about salary, don't you think?"

"You didn't see the way they were living. Why——" He began to describe the apartment, the sleazy, poverty-stricken district, the debt collector. Gilbertson was still dubious.

"It was ghastly by your standards, I can see. No fridge or dishwasher, sharing a bathroom, gold watch up the spout, and so on. But a lot of people live like that, you know. And if they all went round taking potshots at their employers——"

"Hell, this isn't a joke. I wish it were." He glared resentfully at Gilbertson. "You think the way he does, don't you? That she made a goat out of me?"

"I don't know. It's really not my affair. . . ."

"You have a sense of justice, don't you?"

"Of course. But I have to limit it to my own field of responsibility." The indifference dropped out of his voice. He leaned forward and spoke with unaccustomed intensity. "Let me tell you something, Marshall. I'm an older man than you, and I've seen a great deal of suffering and injustice in my time. I was a prisoner of war in Java for three years. When you were amusing yourself in college I was watching my friends being tortured and beaten and dying of starvation and dysentery. There was nothing I could do about it. I learned then that you can't go around feeling for everybody. A man has only so much sympathy to give. He has to ration it. Spread it too thin and it isn't worth a damn to anybody."

Marshall was taken aback. He realized that he hardly knew Gilbertson at all. He had tended to think of him almost as a caricature, a symbol of reaction, rather than as a separate individual subject to all the ordinary human emotions. He said defensively, "So you say—just let things go on as they are?"

Gilbertson relaxed into his old manner. "I wouldn't presume to advise you—especially since I'm quite sure you wouldn't take any notice. But, as a matter of interest, what's your alternative?"

"Take the matter to New York. Ask for an investigation. They won't like it when they find that they've been taken for a ride, I can promise you that."

"You'll need some facts."

"I can get them. There's Verrier's bank account for a start. And I'm going to get hold of some of Furac's other employees. I shall be surprised if he isn't playing the same game with them. What was the name of that man who took you around this morning?"

"Colbert."

Marshall wrote the name down in his diary. "I'll start with him."

"Are you sure," said Gilbertson dubiously, "that you have authority——"

"Perhaps not officially. But facts are facts. Once I give this story to New York, it'll be too late to ask about authority."

He put his diary away and smiled at Gilbertson. He felt suddenly very happy and very confident. The sense of malaise and boredom that had troubled him for so long had left him. He was invigorated by a sense of purpose. "I'm sorry," he said cheerfully, "that you're finding me such a nuisance."

"A nuisance?" Gilbertson raised his bushy eyebrows. "Not to me, my dear fellow—not to me."

CHAPTER V

THE NEXT MORNING he was awakened at eight o'clock by the bellboy with a cable. It read:

PLEASE RETURN NEW YORK WITHOUT DELAY REGARDS KINGHAM

As soon as he read it he was angry with himself for not having anticipated something of the kind. Furac was not the man to wait passively to be attacked without taking some form of counteraction. He would use the same method which had proved so successful with Wilcox, except that now there was more urgency. No doubt he had cabled, or more likely telephoned, New York as soon as he had left the hotel on the previous afternoon. He would have told Kingham that Marshall was making a fool of himself in Paris and ought to be recalled immediately, before he did serious harm. It was a warning which Kingham could hardly afford to ignore.

Marshall was conscious that he had been outmaneuvered. In matters of this kind it was important to get one's word in before the other man. *He* should have made the first telephone call. It was not too late, however, to hit back. If he moved fast he might still be able to redress the balance in his favor. He picked up his bedside telephone. "I want to make a personal call to New York." He gave Kingham's number. There would be half an hour's delay, they said. "And send me up some breakfast, would you?"

He had just finished dressing when the telephone rang again. "I am sorry, sir, we are unable to put through your call."

"Can't you find him?"

"We got through to Mr. Kingham, sir, but he refused to accept the call."

"Did he say why?"

"I gather it was because of the time."

"The time?"

"Yes." The voice was still bland and respectful, but with an undertone of amusement. "There is five hours' difference, you understand."

"Yes—yes, of course." He tried to sound unconcerned. "Thank you very much."

He put down the receiver. He had blundered again. In New York, he remembered too late, it was still only four o'clock in the morning. And Kingham had a particular objection to being called in the middle of the night, as he never ceased to remind people. He had a favorite story about a distributor who had conceived the idea of wishing him a merry Christmas, just after lunch in Manila. . . .

What was he to do now? he wondered. Certainly he had made the worst possible start. He could wait for five hours and call again—but somehow the idea of a telephone conversation with Kingham had lost its attraction. It might be better to cable. Using one of the cable forms on the desk, he wrote:

> URGENT BUSINESS HERE REQUIRING SEVERAL MORE DAYS TO COMPLETE STOP WILL EXPLAIN ON RETURN REGARDS MARSHALL

That seemed fairly satisfactory. It was in any case impossible to give details of what was happening. A point-blank refusal would cripple his case from the outset. The best he could hope for was to gain time. The showdown could wait till he got back to New York.

He handed the cable to the waiter who brought in his breakfast. A little later, when he was reading the papers over his coffee, Gilbertson came in. "I don't know about you," he said, "but I really ought to get back to London today. There are probably all kinds of problems waiting for me——"

"Sure, I understand. Why don't you do that?"

"What about you?"

"Don't worry about me. I'm staying here just for the moment. Then I'll probably fly straight to New York."

"You won't be coming back to London?"

"Not immediately."

"I see." Gilbertson's eyes flickered momentarily over the cable on the dressing table. "I hope everything's all right. No bad news or anything like that?"

"Nothing I didn't expect."

"Good. That's fine." He seemed a little ill at ease. He lit a cigarette and puffed at it with exaggerated concentration. "You still intend to go on with this—business?"

"Yes."

"I can't help feeling you're making too much of it."

"I don't know why you should care. After all, it doesn't really concern you," Marshall said with slight malice.

"Of course not," said Gilbertson sharply. "Nevertheless, I know from experience how easy it is to get involved in a great deal of unpleasantness without really knowing what you're doing. If you go around looking for trouble there may be—unforeseen consequences." He added heavily, "Since you came over from New York I felt we were getting to know each other pretty well—it seemed to me that you were going to fit in. In fact, I said to my wife only the other day . . ." He paused for a moment. "I wouldn't like to see you run into difficulties."

"You think that's likely?"

The creases in his bloodhound face seemed to deepen. He said in a melancholy voice, "Furac can be an awkward man to cross, I should imagine." When Marshall gave no signs of replying, Gilbertson got up from his chair and held out a hairy hand. "But of course it's entirely your affair. I shall be leaving on the midday plane, so I'll say good-by now." He added, not very hopefully, "I look forward to seeing you in London."

When he had left, Marshall rang up Furac's office.

"I wish to speak to Monsieur Colbert."

"Who is that, please?" said a female voice.

"My name is Marshall."

"Ah, Mr. Marshall. Good morning, sir."

"Good morning. Could you put me through to——"

"You wish to speak to Monsieur Furac? Yes. I will arrange——"

"Not Monsieur Furac—Monsieur Colbert. You understand? Colbert—C-o-l——"

"Yes. Yes. Very well. One moment." The line went dead. Then a new voice came on.

"Good morning, Mr. Marshall."

"Good morning. Is that Monsieur Colbert?"

"No, this is Furac speaking. How are you this morning?"

"Very well, thank you. But the operator must have made a mistake. I wanted to speak to——"

"Colbert. Yes, so I gathered. But unfortunately, you see, he is not in the office today. He has gone out——"

"Can you tell me where he is?"

"I am afraid not. He may be one of several places. He will not be back for two or three days at least, I am afraid. Can I give him any message?"

"No, thanks. Could you give me his home telephone number?"

"He is not on the telephone at home. Nor do I know his address. He has just moved. Most unfortunate——"

"Yes."

"So it seems you may miss him," said Furac. After a slight pause he added: "Did I hear that you might be going to New York very soon?"

"Who told you that?"

"I don't know. Perhaps I was mistaken. Shall I be seeing you again before you leave Paris?"

"I doubt it."

"Then I wish you a pleasant journey. And—one more thing——"

"Yes?"

His voice became suddenly openly unpleasant. "If you wish to interrogate any other members of my staff, you will please have the courtesy to notify me first. Thank you so much."

He rang off. So that hole had been stopped up, thought Marshall. At this rate his investigations were not going to get very far. He was not sure what to do now. He did not want to leave the hotel until he had heard from Kingham.

He read a novel until lunch time and then went down to the restaurant. At around two o'clock the cables started again.

REGRET CANNOT GRANT YOUR REQUEST TO STAY LONGER IN PARIS STOP YOUR PRESENCE REQUIRED HERE RIGHT NOW STOP DONT CALL UP IN THE MIDDLE OF THE NIGHT DAMN YOU REGARDS KINGHAM

The pressure was getting strong. It was true, of course, that he wasn't going to do much good here, now that he had failed to see Colbert. Just the same, it was important to talk to Madame Verrier again, if only to convince her that he intended to keep his promise. And Verrier's funeral was tomorrow. He would stay for that, at the very least. He wrote:

RATHER EXCEPTIONAL CIRCUMSTANCES HERE IMPOSSIBLE TO EXPLAIN ADEQUATELY BY CABLE STOP WILL LEAVE PARIS SOONEST CONSISTENT WITH CERTAIN OBLIGATIONS STOP SORRY ABOUT TELEPHONE CALL REGARDS MARSHALL

The reply came rapidly.

RETURN IMMEDIATELY REPEAT IMMEDIATELY WITHOUT FURTHER ARGUMENT CONFIRM FLIGHT KINGHAM

This time there were not even any regards—a serious sign. Kingham must be very angry indeed. Well, there was nothing to be done about it. Marshall went to the travel agency in the lobby and booked a seat on a plane for the following afternoon. Then he went to the hall porter and wrote out another cable. It simply gave the flight number and his time of arrival.

"Don't send it now," he said. "Hold it."

"Till when, sir?"

"Let me see." He wanted it to arrive just after Kingham had left the office. Then he would not pick it up till he came in the following morning—which would be early afternoon in Paris. That would stall things along for eighteen hours or so. He said: "Send it off about eleven o'clock tonight."

Marshall dropped a five-hundred franc note on the counter. The hall porter raised his eyebrows, but only momentarily. Americans were notoriously mad—but it was a profitable lunacy. He picked up the note in an absent-minded way, like a good housewife removing a speck of dust. "*Merci, monsieur.*"

Marshall went back to his room. There was something else he had to do. He picked up the telephone and said: "I want to make a call to London. Berkeley 4848."

He waited a few minutes. There was some crackling and snatches of muttered conversation in two languages. Then an English voice which Marshall recognized said:

"Gilbertson and Cowles speaking. Who is that, please?"

"Mr. Marshall."

"Oh yes, Mr. Marshall. You want to speak to Mr. Gilbertson?"

"No, thanks. He's back already?"

"He got in about an hour ago. Whom would you like to speak to?"

"Get me Miss Lancing, please."

"Very well, Mr. Marshall. Just one moment——"

A few seconds later he heard Jane's voice.

"Is that you, Jane?"

"Yes. Where are you?"

"I'm still in Paris. I didn't come back with Gilbertson. Did you get my letter?"

"No."

Of course, he thought, it was too soon, he had only posted it yesterday. It made explanation considerably more difficult. He heard a click on the line and the background noise sounded slightly different. Could somebody, say the switchboard girl, be listening to their conversation? Perhaps he was growing morbidly suspicious. But even the outside chance of being overheard made confidences impossible.

"You should get it within the next day or two. It explains most of what's been happening over here up to yesterday afternoon——"

"Did you see—the man you wanted to see?"

"No. I was too late. But I had a talk with his wife. She told me most of what I wanted to know." He went on hurriedly, before she could ask any more questions: "But you'll find all that in my letter, together with quite a few other things I can't tell you over the phone."

"Yes, I understand."

"But since I wrote to you, things have advanced a little——"

"Favorably?"

"Not entirely. There are certain interested parties I have to deal with—some degree of competition, if you understand me. It means I shall have to go to New York to straighten it out."

"I see." She was silent for a moment. "When are you leaving?"

"Tomorrow afternoon. In the morning I—I promised to attend the funeral. As soon as it's over I shall catch the plane from Paris. I'll write to you in detail. I just thought I'd let you know what was happening."

"Thank you. When you didn't come back with Mr. Gilbertson, I wondered——" Her voice was admirably casual. Anyone listening would learn nothing about them from her.

"Is everything all right in the office?"

"Yes." She paused momentarily. "When will you be back?"

"I can't say definitely. Soon, I hope. I'll keep in touch with you."

"I'll be looking forward to seeing you." Just for a second a trace of anxiety seemed to come through into her voice. "Come back as soon as you can."

"I will, don't worry." There was a short silence. There was so much to say but no possible channel of communication except on this prosaic, meaningless level.

"Good-by," he said.

"Good-by."

CHAPTER VI

There was nobody very much at the funeral—just himself and Madame Verrier and a few nondescript people from the neighborhood. The priest gabbled his lines and hurried off, like a man working on a tight schedule. Marshall could see another coffin, another seedy little group of mourners, waiting around a corner. Nobody, he thought, had ever had very much time to spare for Verrier.

Afterward they went to a little café by the cemetery. The waiter brought them two filters and they sat for a while watching the tepid liquid dribbling through the strainer. The air was stale and dusty. Someone in a back room was frying onions to the sound of a radio. There was a smell of onions and dust and sweet liqueurs. Everywhere in France, he thought, there was a smell of something.

"It was kind of you to come," she said.

"I wanted to."

Across the perfunctory phrases, the stilted, tea-table conversation, he regarded her anxiously, wondering what she really thought and felt. Unconsciously he found himself searching for a sign, something he could put a label on. In each country there were certain conventional ways of demonstrating emotion, a code of communication to which only those who had been brought up within that same community could hold the key. The language of words was one thing—but the language of sincerity, of courage and faith and sense of humor—what could the stranger know of that? If she had been an American woman, her reaction to her husband's funeral would have told him something about her feeling for him. Not much, perhaps, but enough for a starting point. Here, he knew nothing. He realized that she could tell him anything and he had no means of checking it. How could one recognize a lie in a foreign language?

"You must be glad it's over," he said. He searched for some way to console her and found only the old, tired phrases of a ready letter writer. Death was like love—everything had been said before, long ago. "It won't be quite so bad from now on."

"Because he's gone—put away? I can begin to forget him, you mean?" As he tried to protest, she went on: "But you're quite right. That's what will happen. Even now . . ." Always her eyes were away from his, regarding the table top, her cup of coffee. "He was a man, you know, who never made a strong impression. As you saw today, he had few friends."

"He was—shy?"

"Perhaps. He was afraid."

"Of what?"

"Of everything. Of being laughed at, of poverty, of losing his job. And of people too. Furac, of course. Even me." She suddenly looked up. "That sounds bad, doesn't it? As if I were cruel to him—but I wasn't. I was simply stronger, and he was afraid of strength. You can't do anything about that."

"Of course not." He was reminded of Furac's words—"She is ashamed." Anybody could be right sometimes about people. No matter how calculating or dishonest, no matter how addicted to cheap, secondhand psychology—they could still be right. He asked, "Did you love him?"

She was silent for a long time. "Why do you ask me that?"

"I'm sorry." They were always apologizing to each other, he thought. "I had no right to ask. It was a most personal question. . . ."

"I don't mind." She looked at him with a thin half-smile. "I am not so fragile, you know. I have not traveled through the world as you have, but I have experienced a great deal in some ways. When I first married André I was a silly young girl. I loved him then, I think. Of course I always understood that he was a little weak, but I was convinced that when we were married . . . Well, I was prepared to have strength enough for two, you understand?"

Marshall nodded. He remembered the photograph, the strong sunburned hand of the girl clutching the arm of the cheap gabardine jacket. She said, excusing herself, "I was only eighteen at that time. I did not understand very much."

"It didn't work out?"

"My parents were very angry with me. André earned very little money, and because my father disliked him he refused to help us. We were always poor. But that was not so important—when you are young and you are living in Paris, it is not so bad as all that to be poor. No—there is only one thing that is really bad in this world." She leaned her head forward and rested her chin on the palm of her hand. She was looking, not at him, not at the café or the anonymous, deserted street, but at some secret source of unhappiness within herself. "To be a failure."

"Maybe"—he spoke hesitantly—"some people just don't get the breaks——"

"*Comment?*"

"I mean—they just don't have any luck."

"You think that?"

"It happens, I guess."

She shook her head. "When you live with somebody, you know. André was a failure. He knew it. I knew it. Furac, even the people who lived in the other apartments of the house . . . And there was nothing I could do about it. I could not even go on loving him in the same way. Because, you see, when a man is a failure, failure is the most important thing about him. To love him, you have to love that."

When you had a wound, he thought, you might forget it for years, but there was no knowing when a chance knock might reopen it.

She was talking of Verrier, but she might just as easily have been referring to himself. He, too, when all was said and done, was a failure. He had thought of it as a private thing which he alone had to come to terms with. Now he realized for the first time that it was a problem which involved everyone he cared for or who cared for him. Failure was a disease with which he infected the ones he loved.

He thought of Jane, her fear of being committed, the urgency with which she had tried to persuade him to action, any action. Was she, too, conscious of the same danger? Was he the only one who was unaware of it?

Anxious to learn, he asked: "And you found you couldn't love —failure?"

"No." Beneath her shame he could feel the full impact of her determination. It was possible to sympathize with Verrier, conscious of his own weakness, ground between his wife on one hand and a hostile, merciless world on the other. "Not in the way I wanted—or he wanted. I was too sorry for him." She was silent for a moment. "I suppose it was Furac who told you?"

"About what?"

"About André and me. That is one of the reasons why he does so well—he takes great trouble to find out things about people. He has probably already found out a great deal about you."

"I wouldn't be surprised. Obviously he's prepared to fight me with everything he has. I might as well tell you," he said with an attempt at lightness, "that I've been recalled."

"Recalled? To New York?"

"Yes. Of course there may be no connection, but I think we can take it as Furac's doing." He described their conversation in the hotel. "Then, within a matter of hours, I got the cable."

"And this means you have to go?"

"I'm afraid so. I made one or two attempts to stall them, but——" He took the cables out of his pocket and showed them to her. "As you see, I didn't have much success."

When she had read them she said, "Who is this man Kingham?"

"He's my boss—the head of the International."

"What sort of a man is he?"

"Well—he's okay, I guess." Some half-forgotten loyalty to the organization prevented him from speaking freely about Kingham to an outsider. "Everyone thinks he's a pretty smart man."

"You don't like him?"

He shifted uncomfortably in his seat. "I wouldn't exactly say that——"

"Is he honest?"

"If you mean," said Marshall, "would he be a party to a piece of cheap chiseling on your husband's salary?" He shook his head. "I can't really see it. Even if he was prepared to do it, it would hardly seem worth his while."

"Then," she said with a persistence he was beginning to recognize as a characteristic of hers, "what about Mr. Wilcox?"

"You mean why was he taken away?" He shrugged his shoulders. "I don't know. I shall have to see what I can find out when I get to New York."

She pondered for a moment. "There is one thing," she said, "which I do not quite understand. Kingham is your boss, you say. Yet you are Marshall . . ."

He smiled. "A lot of people get mixed up that way. The company was my father's. He built it up. But when he died, the management passed away from the family. My brother's on the Board and we hold a certain amount of stock, naturally. But that's as far as it goes. Don't run away with the idea that I'm somebody very important."

"Oh."

He could sense her disappointment. "But don't worry," he said. "I'm not entirely without influence. They'll listen to what I have to say, all right."

"They will also listen to Furac," she said dubiously.

"Sure they will. But he's got a bad case and he knows it. He can't beat the facts. And incidentally—if you don't mind, I'd like to take some documentary proof with me, to show what your husband was paid. Have you anything—a bank statement, for instance?"

She hesitated. "I am not sure. I think that this will be required by the notary—for the will, you understand——"

"A copy would do."

She was still doubtful. "Perhaps we should look in the apartment. There may be something similar."

He paid for the coffee and they went back to the apartment. Eventually she found a few slips of paper on which Verrier had made records of his salary checks. Marshall put them in his wallet, then said, "I have to go now."

"You are flying this afternoon?"

"Yes." He looked around the tiny living room of the apartment. Each tasteless chair, each patch of damp on the corner of the ceiling was something he must remember. With some embarrassment he added, "I've put a sum of money to your credit in the Banque du Nord. That's on account of what you're owed by the organization."

She frowned, suspecting charity. "I do not know——"

"It's a purely business arrangement. You're obviously entitled to some form of compensation. But knowing our accountants, it may take some time to arrive. When it does you can refund my advance if it makes you happier."

"Very well. On those terms——" She suddenly laughed. "The bank will be pleased. They will think I am being kept by a rich American."

He was concerned. The idea had not occurred to him. "Would that be embarrassing? We can think of some other way——"

"No, of course not." It was the first time he had seen her at ease. At last she seemed to be able to talk to him in a casual, comradely way, even to laugh at him a little. "It is most considerate of you."

He got up to go. "I have to get back to the hotel and see about my luggage. My plane leaves in a couple of hours."

"I hope you have a pleasant journey."

"Thank you." As they shook hands he said, "Don't worry. I promise I'll do everything I can for you."

"I am not worrying."

She smiled confidently. That was why her manner had changed, he realized. She believed in him. Her cynicism had been no more than skin-deep after all. He was proud and yet a little frightened to feel the weight of her faith settling like a load on his back. These were the kinds of commitments he had avoided for so long. Gradually he was beginning to accumulate responsibilities.

PART IV

CHAPTER I

New York was a city in its shirt sleeves. Down the long avenues the July sunlight glittered in the still, heavy air, reflected from the sidewalks, the multitude of windows, the paint of a hundred thousand crawling automobiles. As always here, the heat seemed to arouse resentment rather than lassitude. The crowds jostled angrily, the taxi drivers blasted their horns and poked beefy faces out of their cabs, yelling abuse. The cops sweltered on traffic duty, their shirts sticking to their backs. The small, crowded island of Manhattan heaved, grumbled, sweated, like a man with a temperature.

Marshall, sitting in the back of a cab, wiped the palms of his hands on his handkerchief. He was nervous as well as hot. Ever since the plane left Paris he had been trying to prepare himself for the situation which lay before him. He had already rehearsed a dozen conversations with Kingham, but all of them had shared a certain lack of plausibility. He had no very clear idea what his reception would be, except that it was likely to be a cold one, judging by the cables he had received in Paris. It was just possible that Kingham might change his tune on hearing the facts of the case. He hoped so. He had no desire for trouble if it could be avoided. It occurred to him that, however bravely he might pretend, he was to some extent afraid of Kingham.

He paid the cabdriver and walked into the office building. Inside, the heat was less oppressive. He went through the glass doors marked "Marshall Corporation" and nodded to the girl at the reception desk.

"Why, it's Mr. Marshall." She smiled at him. "How was Europe?"

"Oh, fine—fine." She must make quite a game of it, he thought—remembering where everybody had gone. It was always the same—"How was Detroit?" "How was Johannesburg?" "How was Tokyo?" And the reply was always "Fine—fine." He said, "Is Mr. Kingham in?"

"I haven't seen him come in yet this morning."

He was ashamed of his own feeling of relief. But it was a breathing space.

"I expect he'll be in later. Would you like to check with Miss Curran?"

He nodded and walked along to Kingham's office. In the outer office Miss Curran sat at her typewriter. She didn't look surprised to see him and she didn't ask him how Europe was. But the look she gave him was rather alarming. It was almost compassionate.

"They tell me the boss hasn't arrived?"

"No."

"I suppose he got my cable from Paris, did he? I sent it off as soon as I knew the flight number. As a matter of fact, I was damned lucky to get on, it's pretty crowded this time of year——" He was talking too much. He pulled himself up. "When will he be in?"

She turned away and twisted a piece of paper out of the typewriter with a brisk, meaningless little gesture. "He won't be in, I'm afraid. He's gone away."

"Gone away? Where to?"

"Mexico."

"Mexico!" He looked at her in mounting exasperation. It seemed to him that whenever he wanted to talk to somebody that person took a plane to the other side of the world. "How was that? Was he called away unexpectedly?"

"I don't know. I don't think so."

"Well, that's most extraordinary. We must have got our wires crossed somewhere. He certainly gave me the impression that he was in a great hurry to see me. When will he be back?"

"He didn't say."

"Did he mention me at all?"

"Yes. He wanted you to see Mr. Richardson. I guess he must have left some instructions with him." As he turned to go she said: "Just a moment—I'll see if he's free."

Marshall watched her as she dialed Richardson's number on the inter-office telephone. She knew everything, of course. She knew how Kingham felt and why he had gone to Mexico and, in all probability, when he was coming back. But if you tried to get any information out of her you would merely cause an embarrassing situation and get nowhere. Nobody ever knew quite what she thought about anything, but even if someone did know, it wouldn't make any difference. She might think you were a hero and Kingham was a louse—but she was paid to keep her mouth shut, and there it was. She said, "Mr. Richardson *is* free."

"Thanks." He hesitated for a moment before leaving. He had the feeling that, in the most muted possible way, she was trying to tell him things. To be careful, perhaps? To watch his step? He knew that.

"Things pretty much the same here as when I went away?" he asked tentatively.

"No big changes," she said. "There's been a certain amount of—reorganization." She gave one of her rare smiles. They had a reorganization every few months, of some kind or another.

"Anything special?"

"Not really. Some go down—some go up. You know how it is."

"Yes." Richardson, for instance, was evidently up a little. You couldn't just knock on his door and stick your head around any more. Somebody had to telephone and see if he was "free." In a world where one man was supposed to be as good as another, little things like that took on an unusual significance.

If Richardson's rating had increased, he showed no obvious sign of it. When Marshall walked in he jumped up and wrung him by the hand, his pale blue eyes bulging with good will.

"Good to see you, Chris. Sit down and relax." He regarded Marshall appreciatively. "My, you certainly look fit—Europe seems to agree with you. Did you have a good flight?"

"Pretty comfortable. I got in last night an hour before schedule. We had a tail wind."

"Is that so? It certainly makes a difference when you get a tail wind." He shook his head in wonderment. "An hour early—can you beat that?"

He couldn't be *that* interested, Marshall thought, wondering why he had mentioned the tail wind in the first place. It was just the sort of tedious conversation one always tried to avoid—flight schedules, hotels, the advantages of the new Oldsmobile over last year's Mercury. And what was Richardson's Christian name? This was no time to sound high hat.

He remembered with relief. "You're looking pretty good yourself, John."

"I get along. Though—this heat . . ." He leaned back in his swivel chair. The superficial courtesies were over; it was time for business. "Miss Curran told you that Mr. Kingham was away?"

"Yes."

"Certainly keeps moving, doesn't he?" said Richardson admiringly. "Has his hand on everything—all over the world. He never seems to rest. I don't think there are many men of our age who'd care to take on his job."

Like hell you don't, thought Marshall. "And when will he be back?"

"Nobody knows exactly. I doubt whether he knows himself. You remember what he's like—finishes what he has to do and then grabs the next plane." He said, "I'm sure he was sorry to have missed you."

Richardson had spoken as if Marshall were making a routine visit of no special significance. It was possible that he knew nothing of the circumstances, and it would be foolish to tell him. Marshall said, "Did he leave any message for me?"

"Yes. He said he looked forward to seeing you when he got back. In the meantime . . ." He pressed a button on the intercom. "Could you bring in those surveys for Mr. Marshall?" Turning back to Marshall, he went on, "There are some market surveys we've had made for various countries. Kingham said he'd like you to go through them and write a report on the prospects for possible trading in the areas concerned. Some of them are pretty exotic, but the boss doesn't believe in missing a trick anywhere if he can help it." The secretary came in and handed a file of reports to Marshall. "Well—there you are. I guess that should keep you busy."

Nice of Kingham to think of something for him to do. "Shall I use my old office? Or is that taken?"

"I'm afraid it is. Rose Bauer's in there."

Good old Rose, he thought, she was up too. "Is she publicity co-ordinator now?"

"Well, not exactly." Richardson was almost apologetic. "That post doesn't exist any more as such." Marshall nodded understandingly. They hadn't wasted any time in throwing that useless department out of the window once they had packed him off to Europe. "She's supervisor of technical advertising."

"She's a fine girl. She'll do a wonderful job." This was to show he wasn't jealous of Rose. Besides, it was true.

"Oh, sure." Richardson darted a glance at his watch. Until this moment he had seemed to have time to burn. Now suddenly he was in a hurry, waiting for Marshall to leave. It was an executive's trick to establish an ascendancy—your time was more valuable than the other man's. He stood up. "If you'll excuse me, Chris, I'm pretty tied up this morning. Perhaps we could have a talk about things later—over a drink or something." Before Marshall could suggest an actual time he went on, "We have managed to find an office for you temporarily. It's three floors down, on the twenty-fourth—you know how crowded we are for space up here." They were almost out of the door now. "Gladys will show you where it is—won't you, Gladys? Well"—he patted Marshall affectionately on the arm and began to move back into the office—"see you, Chris."

The office on the twenty-fourth was small and ill furnished; it had no air conditioning, and its one window looked out on to a ventilation shaft. The rest of the floor was taken by Accountancy and Statistics. Marshall was to share a secretary with one of the junior accountants.

He opened the file and began to go through the market surveys. There were a great many of them and they were extremely detailed —the firm which had made them had plainly been in no mood to save either trouble or expense. Some of them were quite absurdly out of date. There were three pages of optimistic forecasts about the economic future of a country which had now been engaged in civil war for at least six months. Other areas were rendered inoperative by reason of industrial backwardness, currency restrictions, or unfriendly governments. The surveys were, in fact, quite useless and not worth the time and energy required to report on them. Marshall could imagine how they had come to be made. Somebody in one of those grandiose moods which so often took possession of people at management conferences had suggested them. The idea sounded efficient, the sort of project a go-ahead business firm ought to engage in. There would be a persuasive customers' man from the agency—"a complete survey of world markets, Mr. X, specially tailored to your requirements, with all the benefits of our world-wide service"—and Mr. X himself, anxious to be up to the minute, to "think big." And at the end of it the corporation exchanged a check for ten thousand dollars for a sackful of beautifully printed junk.

Mr. X, whoever he was, had by this time long since forgotten all about it. When he got the reports he found them too boring to read and passed them to the man below him, who passed them on down the line, until eventually they ended up in a filing cabinet somewhere. Some men might have thrown them away, but not Kingham. He had thought of a use for them.

It was, Marshall realized, the business equivalent of moving a heap of stones from one spot to another and back again. His report would probably never be read, and if it was read it would be of no value. That Kingham had left instructions for him to do it made the suspicions that had been growing within him all morning crystallize into certainty. He had watched this happen before with others. The offhand treatment, the slight but perceptible change in attitude of subordinates who knew which way the wind was blowing, the withdrawal of prestige symbols such as a comfortable office and a private secretary, the handing out of pointless and unimportant tasks . . .

He picked up the telephone and dialed.

"Rose?"

"Who's that?"

"This is Chris Marshall. I just got back."

"Why, that's wonderful. And how was——"

"Europe was fine." He realized his voice sounded curt, but it was too late to do anything about it. "I'd like to talk to you, Rose. What about meeting me for lunch?"

"Just a minute. I'll look at my book."

Things had certainly changed. Now Rose had got so important that she couldn't remember with whom she was lunching. He waited impatiently. It didn't surprise him when she said, "I'm sorry, Chris. It seems I'm tied up today."

"Tomorrow?" he asked, just to make sure.

"I honestly doubt if I could make it. There's some sort of a conference——"

He put the telephone down. For a few minutes he stared at the papers in front of him. The telephone rang twice, but he ignored it. Then he picked up his jacket from the back of a chair, mopped the sweat from his face, and made his way up to the twenty-seventh.

Rose was dictating letters. When he walked in she nodded to the stenographer, who slipped out and closed the door. He looked round at the office. It seemed larger and lighter than he remembered. There was a bowl of roses, a photograph of Bauer looking like a musician, a couple of prints on the walls. She had moved the desk to a better position. There was a feminine scent about the place.

"You've made it nice in here," he said.

"Thank you very much."

He sat down in the chair the stenographer had left. Neither of them mentioned the fact that he had hung up on her.

"How's Fred?"

She shook her head sadly. "He got fired."

"You don't say?" Suddenly his anger had left him. It was hard to be anything but sympathetic with Rose.

"Yes. He got high one night on tour and gave them a couple of riffs in the middle of Tchaikovsky's Fourth. I guess it had to happen sometime."

"What's he doing now?"

"Looking around. It's not too easy, as you can imagine. . . ."

"I'm sorry to hear that."

"Things could be worse," she said brightly. "About money, I mean. Since I got this job——"

"Sure." He smiled. "You're moving along fast. I should congratulate you."

He said it fondly, without irony. She replied simply, "Thank you. It was very lucky for me, coming when it did. Though of course . . ."

Though of course it wasn't the same as having a husband with sufficient sense to stay sober and keep himself out of trouble, her tone implied. Poor Rose . . . He asked abruptly, "You knew I was coming back?"

"Yes." She looked at him with obvious sincerity. "I was on the level, Chris—about not being able to meet you for lunch."

"Yes, I know that now. I'm sorry." He laughed shortly. "This place doesn't seem to suit me. I haven't been back twenty-four hours and I get delusions of persecution——"

"Who have you met?"

"Richardson." He added after a pause, "He seems to be a big boy now."

"That's right."

"He'll end up with an electric typewriter one of these days if he's not careful."

She frowned. "What's so wrong with that?"

"Nothing, I guess."

"He's got a right to be ambitious, hasn't he? If you want to stand out of it yourself, that's your own affair. But don't blame other people." She added, "I like Richardson."

"Yes, he's a nice guy." After all, he was a good husband and father, kind to animals, paid his club dues on time—what more could you ask? There was nothing wrong with Richardson.

She said hesitantly, "If they *are* putting the freeze on you——"

He sprang on the remark. "You think they are?"

"You should know better than I." She seemed to be wondering

how much to say. "The rumor round here is that Kingham is after your hide for something or other."

"He hasn't heard what I have to say yet." Suddenly his resentment became so strong that he could no longer sit still. He got up and began to walk about the room. "If he goes on like this he's going to get too smart for his own good. He seems to think the International belongs to him."

"I don't know about that. So far as I'm concerned——"

"He's the boss. Okay, I can see how you feel. But he's not God, you know. There are limits to what he can do."

Rose looked doubtful. To her, for all practical purposes, Kingham *was* God. She knew, of course, that there was a Board, and a chairman, and several vice-presidents, but they meant nothing to her; so far as she knew, they had never affected her in any way. Whereas Kingham affected her all the time. Every decision he made, every new idea, every mood and caprice had to be considered and minutely analyzed because of the momentous consequences they might have on her personal life.

That was all very well for Rose. But there had to be somebody who was different, some outpost of independence. Kingham had tried unsuccessfully to remove this outpost by diplomatic measures. What would be his next move. Siege? Open warfare?

"You should watch him," said Rose. "Whatever you think of him, he's no fool. And it looks to me as if he's out to show you what he can do."

"I can do something too, if it comes to that."

"Such as?"

"I can——" He halted, wondering whether he was talking too much, even if this *was* Rose. But she cut in before he had time to say anything more.

"You can go over his head. But I'd think carefully about it first. Maybe that's what he wants you to do."

He sat down again. "Why do you say that?"

"It just occurred to me. He calls you back in a hurry to see him, goes away for a while and leaves you to sit around waiting. Everything's fixed up to annoy you as much as possible. Obviously you'll be tempted to go to somebody high up and complain. Why does he give you the opportunity?"

"You tell me."

"To show that you think you have special privileges because of your family. He may have complained beforehand that you're difficult to handle on that account. This would prove it for him."

He said nothing. The nightmarish quality which had permeated all his experiences since he entered the building that morning was increasing in intensity. He had been away only a few months, but everything was changed. He was suddenly a kind of outlaw, a person from whom things were hidden. He could trust nobody. He had imagined that while he was in Europe he had been forgotten. But it might be that he had been sent away deliberately so that his position might be damaged in his absence, by a word here and there, a shrug of the shoulders when his name was mentioned, a routine reorganization which omitted to take him into account. Then, on his return, he was to be provoked into doing something foolish, to confirm the rumors and present his own head for the chopping block. . . .

"It isn't possible," he said.

"Why not?"

"He's bastard enough to do it, I'll agree. But to take so much trouble——"

"It might be trouble to you. But it would interest him. To Kingham, a person like you presents a special problem. To solve it might become a point of honor."

He thought it over. Bewilderment and disgust were giving way to a cold rage. He wished no harm to anybody. Why wouldn't they leave him alone?

"I don't like that," he said.

"But why should you worry? You never liked this work anyway. If you left——" Like all women, having aroused him, she felt the necessity to calm him down.

"That's not the point."

She looked at him questioningly, but he made no attempt to explain. There was no sense in dragging Rose into it. She had enough problems of her own. Verrier meant nothing to her, and

Paris was a long way away, a strange foreign city you sometimes saw in the movies, full of cafés and boulevards and nude shows and Maurice Chevalier. Nothing serious ever happened there. The things that really mattered were that Richardson had an increase in salary or that Bob Gross had been in trouble with the accountants or that Bernstein had invited Flack up to his house for dinner three times in the last two months. Even for him, it took an effort in this place to remember the apartment in the rue Zurbaran, the hospital, the man lying in a cheap grave in the cemetery at Père Lachaise with an ugly hole in the top of his skull. . . . It took an effort, but it could be done.

He said, as much to himself as to Rose, "I made a promise. . . ."

CHAPTER II

For the next week he arrived at the office punctually at nine and left at five, working, or pretending to work, at his report. He would not give them any opportunity to accuse him of slackness. There was no news of Kingham's return, and after a few days he stopped ringing up to ask. Each day some minor incident reminded him of his own isolation. He knew nobody on the twenty-fourth floor and all his former friends on the twenty-seventh had become unaccountably busy. Evidently the word had got around. The only cheering event was a letter from Jane.

Dear Chris,

I hope things are going well in New York. I was so glad to receive your letter and feel sure you are doing the right thing. Furac sounds quite *unspeakable* (which I had always suspected anyway, from the way Mr. Wilcox talked about him). Gilbertson arrived back from Paris in a very bad temper and even snapped at Miss Carvill-Sykes—vicar's daughter or not! —so that evidently the trip hadn't been a great success as far as he was concerned. I am doing my best to cope with your correspondence unaided (3 letters yesterday!). There is also some personal correspondence, mostly bills. Do you want me to hold onto them or post them to you? I suppose it will rather depend on how soon you are likely to return.

I don't suppose what you are doing now will be easy, but after all you are in the right and that is a good deal. Try not to be too discouraged if you run into difficulties. I am thinking of you all the time and looking forward always to your return. . . .

He smiled. It was like a clear, crisp breeze in this humid atmosphere. It was almost as if she were the older, more responsible one of the two. Each word she wrote, even the forward-sloping, unfeminine shape of her handwriting, reminded him of her presence. Affectionate, yet without possessiveness, irreverent, unafraid. Here at least was someone who could be neither bought nor intimidated. Just as there was no man as dependent as the Wilcoxes, the Richardsons, with their mediocre abilities and large salaries, so there were few people as free as a competent, intelligent secretary earning the equivalent of thirty to forty dollars a week. At that rate she owed nothing to anybody—no gratitude, no loyalty, no respect. She had no obligation to feel part of the system or to fool herself that there was something mystically important about it. To her, Gilbertson, Furac, Kingham, perhaps even the great Bernstein himself, were no more than a group of balding dyspeptic men talking solemnly about markets and trading conditions, dictating pompous letters to each other—playing a ridiculous but also rather pathetic middle-aged game they referred to reverently as Business.

He wrote a reply to the letter, tossed it into his out tray, and wondered what to do. It was several days since he had been up to the twenty-seventh—he had been kept away by an obscure fear of embarrassing people. He decided he might as well try Miss Curran again—she might just possibly have some news.

When the elevator stopped at the twenty-seventh floor there were several people waiting outside the doors. In the middle of them, no more than a yard away, was Furac. For a moment they stood face to face. There was no time, for Marshall at least, to decide on an attitude to take up toward such an unexpected meeting. Furac, though surely he must have at least regarded it as a possibility, seemed equally at a loss. His eyes blinked anxiously; his shoulders wriggled a little. It was easy, seeing his nervousness, to underestimate him, until one remembered the determination and intelligence which lay beneath it. The reminder of his ability was doubly disconcerting when it came.

Furac's lips moved in a thin half-smile. In it there was neither friendship nor enmity, nothing but a desire to escape as quickly as possible from an awkward predicament. Then he was past, shielded once more by the intervening bodies of his companions. The elevator doors closed behind him.

Miss Curran was sitting in the outer office. She swung around from her typewriter and regarded Marshall warily. Before she had time to speak he said, "I want to see Kingham."

He had intended to sound coldly businesslike, with perhaps an undertone of menace. But from her expression he realized that his anger must be a great deal more apparent than he had thought. He tried to tone it down a little.

"He *is* back, isn't he?" he asked.

"Yes."

"I thought you were going to let me know——"

"I said," she corrected him, "that I'd tell him you wanted to see him the moment he got back. And I did. After that it was up to him." Seeing his expression, she added, "I'm sorry, Mr. Marshall——"

"Yes—all right." This wasn't the time to discuss Miss Curran's ethics. "How long has he been here?"

"Since the day before yesterday."

"He's seen Furac?"

"Yes. They had a dinner for him—last night——" She opened a drawer in her desk, picked out a sheet of paper, and handed it to him. It was a list of guests for the dinner. They were all members of the International with one exception.

"Bernstein was there?"

"Yes." She took the list and replaced it in the desk. For her, it had been quite an indiscretion. No doubt she would regret it later.

He looked toward the door of the inner office. "Is he by himself?"

"Yes, but——"

"You tried to keep me out," he said, "but I pushed past you." He walked to the door, knocked lightly, and without waiting for an answer walked in.

Kingham looked even smaller than usual sitting behind the large desk. His chair seemed somehow too high for him; he had to point his toes a little to reach the floor. The sunlight glinted off his spectacles as he looked up. His face showed neither surprise nor annoyance.

"Hello, Chris," he said. Then he frowned. "I don't remember making any appointment——"

"You didn't. But I want to talk to you."

"Yes, of course. There are several matters . . . However, I'm pretty busy right now——"

Marshall advanced into the room. "I'd like to talk to you," he repeated.

Kingham looked at him for a moment. Then he seemed to make up his mind. "Okay," he said. "Sit down. I'll just sign these letters." He went through a pile of letters, made corrections on one or two, signed his name neatly and carefully on the others, and rang for Miss Curran. As she went out with the letters he said: "And cancel that call to Washington. I'll let you know later." He swung around and said, "Now, Chris, what is it that needs telling about in such a hurry?"

"Why did you call me back from Europe?"

Kingham paused before replying. He seemed to be wondering whether it would be beneath his dignity to answer the question at all. "Because I thought it was time," he said eventually. "Next question?"

"Why did you so suddenly think it was time?"

"Chris, I want to remind you of something. I'm the head of this division. I don't have to account to you for the way I run things."

Marshall made a gesture of impatience.

"This is fine. Nobody has to account to anybody for anything. Furac said much the same thing to me in Paris."

"Did he?" Kingham's lips tightened.

"Yes. Hasn't he told you?" Marshall knew he was attacking recklessly, ignoring the conventions, making an amicable settlement of the matter almost out of the question. But his experiences of the past weeks had damaged his self-control. Perhaps that was the object of the technique—a softening-up process designed to destroy a man's judgment. He said, "I hear you had a long talk with him last night."

"So what?" It was difficult to know whether Kingham's rising anger was genuine or simulated. "What business is it of yours who I talk to?" He leaned forward in his chair. "I'm an easy man to get along with, as you know, but you're beginning to try my patience pretty hard. I don't know who the hell you think you are, pushing your way in here when I'm busy——"

Marshall could see the game moving away from him. He counter-attacked desperately. "Don't you know that Furac's a crook? Or don't you care?"

There was a moment's silence. Kingham regarded him impassively, his brow furrowed, his anger seemingly replaced by mystification.

"A crook? What are you talking about?"

"He's cheating his staff—and us too, for that matter. You remember a man called Verrier?"

"This person who shot himself? I gather he was out of his mind."

"That's the story. However, I got talking to his wife——" He opened his wallet and took out two folded sheets of paper. "While I was waiting for you, I prepared a report about him—with figures."

Kingham read it through without any change of expression. Then he put it down on his blotter.

"I should like to check on this," he said.

"Naturally."

"Though I must say, even if it proves to be correct——" He looked up in perplexity. "Is this all? You mean this is what you're getting so steamed up about?"

"Verrier killed himself," said Marshall.

"But not over this. For God's sake, the whole claim can't add up to more than a couple of hundred dollars."

Marshall leaned forward and said earnestly, "But that's the terrible thing about it, don't you see? It means nothing to us, next to nothing to Furac. But to a man like that, it was the difference between life and death." In his agitation he got up from his chair and began to pace the room. "Whether you like it or not, Verrier worked for us. He sold our merchandise and was paid with our money. He hadn't a house or a piece of furniture of his own; when he died he left his wife just enough to pay for his funeral; he was cheated and exploited and underpaid, and he knew it. He protested to us, and nobody took a damn bit of notice. So finally he took a gun and blew his brains out." He halted at the end of the desk, looking down at Kingham. "Now, I contend we have a responsibility here——"

"To do what?"

"To offer compensation, for one thing. To make sure that it isn't happening in other cases, and won't happen again. And to get rid of people like Furac."

Kingham nodded thoughtfully. "You think we should just shoot off our mouths and tell them how to handle things—or else. Is that it?"

"In a case like this—yes."

Kingham said nothing. Instead he lit a cigarette and threw the pack across the desk. Marshall, suddenly self-conscious about his standing position, went back to his chair.

Kingham blew out a cloud of smoke. "I'll tell you something, Chris," he said confidentially. "I was mad with you. The way I saw it was this: I picked you out for a real opportunity, one that most of the boys around here would have given their eyes for. You went off to Europe and what did you do? For the first month or so, so far as I could see—nothing." He cut short Marshall's protest. "Okay, I reminded myself, give him time, you told him to take it slowly at the beginning. He's getting himself settled in, learning to handle the people, and so on. Better that than going off half cocked—at least he isn't annoying the distributors. So I waited. And then—boom! What do I find? Not only have you done nothing useful. Not only have you gone over to Paris without notifying me. But after only three days there you have insulted one of our most important business associates, called him a crook and a racketeer, tried to cross-examine his staff——" He asked reasonably, "Are you really surprised that I recalled you?"

"It might have been a good idea to hear my side——"

"I've heard it now. If I heard Furac first, it's because I've known him a lot longer than you. Like me, he's been in this business for the last twenty years. He's a smart man, and he's done wonderful work for the company. He knows conditions in France like no one else. He's an associate of ours, not an employee. I wouldn't feel like trying to interfere in his relations with his staff."

"So you won't do anything?" Marshall said bitterly. He was not surprised; he had not really expected Kingham to do anything, but nevertheless he felt his heart sinking. There was no prospect now of an easy way out.

"I shall go into the matter—check the facts——"

"And then?"

"Then you'll have to leave it to me." He put his palm down on the report and said, "You've done your part now—you've turned in your report. You can forget it."

Marshall shook his head. "I'm sorry. I can't take it like that."

Kingham looked at him and said softly, "I'm afraid you'll have to, Chris."

"We'll see."

"No." He snapped out the word. "We won't see—we'll have it out right now. I don't give a damn who your father was, you're in my division and under my orders. You have no special privileges."

"I don't want anything for myself——"

"That's not the point. The point is that I'm in charge and you must accept my decision or get out. Is that clear?"

His body was rigid; his face peered forward as if to emphasize the determination behind his words. It occurred to Marshall that Kingham could have stalled had he wanted to. He could have promised an investigation, a discussion with Furac which would drag on and eventually come to nothing. In his position he had so many advantages; he could have won easily enough by guile. He must know that. And his rejection of the easier course could mean only one thing—that he had decided that this was suitable ground for an issue of principle, a test of strength between the two of them. From this moment there was no possibility of compromise.

Nor was there anything further to say at the moment. Without replying to the challenge, he got up and walked out of the room.

CHAPTER III

"I DIDN'T COME to you before," Marshall said to his brother, "because I wanted to do things the right way."

"Uh-huh." Jeff took a cigar out of a box on the sideboard, crackled it against his ear, and cut the end off. "You don't use these, do you?"

"No, thanks."

He lit, puffed, inspected the burning end. It glowed symmetrically; the ritual was completed. "Why don't we go out in the garden?"

Outside, the heat of the day was fading. The trees made long shadows on the lawns; the water from the sprinklers glittered in the last rays of the setting sun. Behind them, through the open upstairs windows, they could hear the voices of the children as they were put to bed. Jeff looked around him and sniffed the scent of the summer evening. He thought of his new Buick and the Dodge station wagon, the lake at the end of the garden where his cabin cruiser rode at its moorings, and sighed with happiness.

"Pretty nice out here," he observed.

"Yes."

"Wonderful relaxation after the city. The way I look at it, even if you only get an hour or so each evening, it's worth it. Gets back your sense of proportion somehow. And as for the kids—— You know, Chris, you ought to settle down." He frowned, to show he wanted to be taken seriously. "No, I mean it. You'd be surprised the difference it would make to you."

"Only a few months ago you were advising me to pack up and go to Europe."

Jeff laughed disarmingly. "Yes, that's right. Well, maybe I was mistaken about that."

"Maybe you're mistaken now."

"I don't know." He was thoughtful again. "I'm a great hand for giving people advice, I guess. When things go pretty well for you, you want them to go well for others too." He would have liked his brother to have a cigar and a wife and a house and three kids and two automobiles and a cabin cruiser. There was, after all, no real difficulty in obtaining them. It seemed mysterious to him that a man could perversely reject happiness when it was so closely within his reach. "But perhaps," he said without any real conviction, "what suits me might not suit you." When Marshall said nothing, he went on, "You had something on your mind?"

"Yes. As I was saying, I thought I ought to take it to Kingham first, because it concerns the International——"

"That's right." Jeff nodded energetically. "Can't be too careful about things like that."

"However, I didn't get anywhere with him, so I thought I'd have a talk with you about it."

"I don't have any authority over Kingham, you know."

"Who has?"

"Only Bernstein. And the Board, officially—but in practice that means Bernstein again."

"But, as a member of the Board, you are in a position to raise any question that's of importance to the company——"

"Yes, I suppose so." He spoke with slight impatience. Like many rather slow-thinking men, he was always in fear of being driven into a corner and disliked talking of hypothetical cases. "But why don't you tell me what it's all about?"

He was, Marshall thought as he told the story, a good listener. He had no temptation to interrupt or to see ahead to a later point in the narrative and lose concentration until it was reached. Thought, for him, was full-time work and he liked to devote all his energies to it. When Marshall had finished, Jeff was silent for a while, puffing at his cigar.

Finally he said, "It seems to me there are two separate issues here. One is Furac and this guy—what was his name?"

"Verrier."

"Right. Maybe there was a racket going on in a small way. The question is whether it's any of our business, and if so, what we ought to do about it. Agreed?"

"I think we *have* to do something."

"Kingham doesn't agree?"

"No."

"The second point concerns your own position. You contend that as soon as you found out about this Kingham called you home, put the freeze on you, and generally kicked you around——"

"That's not so important in itself. But just the same, it shouldn't happen. And it hasn't happened just to me. You knew Wilcox?"

"Just slightly."

"I'm pretty sure the same thing happened to him, for the same reason. You could talk to him——"

"I doubt it." He looked at the end of his cigar regretfully. "Cigars," he observed, "are like a lot of other things. If you want to get the full enjoyment, you have to stop just that little bit too soon." He threw the butt away into some bushes. "No, Wilcox isn't going to be any use to you, I'm afraid. He's left the company."

The announcement was like a sudden withdrawal of support. Marshall was shaken. To some extent, at least, he had been counting on Wilcox.

"When?"

"A few weeks ago. I don't know any details. I just heard. I don't even know where he went."

At least he might be able to make something out of it. "Well, there you are, you see how it is. Why should Wilcox walk out? He was a promising man——"

"Lots of people are promising until somebody decides they're not. Maybe he was dissatisfied. Maybe he had reason, I don't know. But either way, he's gone now and that's it. He wasn't even fired—he walked out."

"He was squeezed out."

"That's possible." Jeff shrugged his great footballer's shoulders. "Don't let's be naïve, Chris. It happens all the time. Sometimes it has to be done that way. A man may be no good. He may be good but his face doesn't fit with the boss. Nobody likes to fire him outright, but he's not going to get anywhere sticking around. If he's smart, he sees it himself. If not, he gets a hint. It may be rough on him, but in a competitive game like ours you have to do it, otherwise you get loaded down with dead wood."

"All right, then." The point was reasonable in general. Nobody could run a business or any other organization efficiently on the basis of absolute fairness. If a man was to be given authority, he must be allowed to choose his subordinates and get rid of others. The methods by which the selection was carried out might vary; the process itself would always be painful and frequently unjust. It was the price of action. "I agree that if Kingham doesn't want somebody, he has a right to squeeze him out. But not simply because he complains about racketeering."

Jeff looked at him with slow disapproval. "It seems to me that there are a lot of assumptions there that you wouldn't like to be asked to prove."

"I can prove that Furac's a crook."

"To the tune of about a hundred and eighty dollars."

"That's all we know about. There may be other things."

"We can only talk about what we know. All the rest doesn't amount to a row of beans." Jeff frowned. "The thing I can't figure out is this. You say you're pretty sure Wilcox must have brought this matter up before?"

"I'm certain. That's why he was moved."

"Then there should be some record. If Kingham concealed his report or destroyed it, that would certainly put him in the wrong. For one thing, he has an obligation on financial matters to notify the accountants." He said dubiously, "I suppose I could raise that point with him. Would you like me to?"

"Yes. Do it whatever way you think best. But I think he should answer—to somebody." An idea came to him. "Would it be worth telling Bernstein?"

Jeff shook his head decisively. "No. He doesn't have anything to do with details of administration. He's too busy buying and selling companies, making stock issues, and so on. You couldn't interest him in a small thing like this. He might even take it the wrong way. And talking of that——" He hesitated. "I suppose you understand that, whichever way this turns out, it isn't going to do any good to your personal position?"

"Yes, of course." Kingham would never forgive him. But that hardly seemed to matter. "Just the same, I'd like you to see him."

Jeff was silent for a little while. Marshall realized that, for all the sympathetic reception Jeff had given to the story, he had little appreciation of the issues at stake. To him, the matter was a small one. Of more importance was the fact that his younger brother had been badly treated, and he felt a family obligation to come to his support, just as he had done when Marshall had been set upon by other boys at school. The obligation was a nuisance but carried a certain satisfaction of its own. Jeff knew that his family had always thought him stupid and unimaginative. In a household dominated by his father, only the flashier virtues had been thought worthy of consideration. But in the long run he had proved them wrong—patience and stability had prevailed. Now his brother had to come and beg for his assistance.

"Okay then," he said heavily. "I'll see what I can do." It was quite dark now, and the lights were on in the house. Paula had come downstairs after bathing the children and was watching television. They could hear the muffled boom of voices, interspersed with an occasional snatch of music. Jeff turned toward the house. "I'll see him tomorrow morning. Now let's go in and see how Paula's getting along."

Inside, Jeff mixed drinks for the three of them and they sat watching television. After a while Marshall grew tired of the program and began to watch Jeff and Paula instead. Their chairs were together, and Paula's hand was resting on her husband's arm. On occasions like this it seemed to give her pleasure to be in physical contact with him, no matter how slight the contact might be. She was like a dog who cannot sleep soundly without one paw on his master's boot.

Whatever Jeff might be to anyone else, to Paula at least he was a personage. She pushed him around in many ways, of course. She was demanding and possessive, not only on her own behalf but also on behalf of the children. She was jealous, too, without any obvious cause. But Jeff did not seem to mind. He had always longed to be loved and respected. As a boy he had seen the love of his mother and the hopes of his father fixed on his younger brother. Even later, when Chris had proved a disappointment, he had only been accepted reluctantly, as a second best—he had worshiped his father and never received anything but indifference in return. But with his marriage to Paula everything had changed. He was suddenly a person of importance. At home his desires were studied, his views treated with as much reverence as if he were Marcus Marshall himself. Each night his self-confidence was replenished; each morning he took it with him to the office like the papers in his brief case. He was able to believe in his own ability and, now that his father was dead, others were prepared to believe in them too.

The corporation, under the direction of Bernstein, had moved into a quieter and more prudent phase. The days of wild, brilliant growth had given way to a process of consolidation. Unprofitable subsidiaries were closed down, the more speculative ventures sold at a loss. Into this atmosphere Jeff had fitted perfectly. His ponderous approach had given him the reputation of being a safe, thoughtful man. Success had come to him as a pleasing surprise; he had accepted it with dignity and a certain complacency.

The program faded out, the announcer came forward, bright-eyed, anxiously seductive, like an old man trying to entice a schoolgirl into a back alley. He was halfway through a commercial about somebody's beer when Jeff snapped off the set.

He yawned and looked at his watch. "Guess it's about time for us working people to get to bed," he said.

CHAPTER IV

The next morning his office seemed even hotter than ever. The electric fan he had obtained with so much difficulty made no noticeable difference; it did no more than move around the same stale, humid air grimed with the smoke of innumerable cigarettes. He tried to concentrate on his report, but work was impossible. Three floors up, Jeff and Kingham were talking about him; relaxed and reasonable, no doubt, in large leather armchairs suitable for men of consequence. Never before had he resented so bitterly his own inferior position. He could not blame anybody else—it had been his own doing. He had defied authority, and authority had struck back by depriving him of the gifts it had to offer—power, prestige, the privilege of access to those higher circles where decisions were made. He had never wanted them before. Now, when something needed to be done, he craved them desperately. This was the result of his policy of detachment—that in a matter of the greatest importance to him he was reduced to relying on Jeff to put his case.

It was nearly twelve o'clock when Jeff finally appeared. He walked into the office, nodded curtly, and seated himself in a chair on the other side of the desk. The expression on his face was somber. Marshall felt his hands grow clammy. Jeff was a man who enjoyed bringing good news. He would almost certainly have been smiling if things had gone well.

"Did you see him?" Marshall asked anxiously.

"Yes."

"Well—how did it go?"

"How did it go?" Jeff's voice rose in indignation. He said hopelessly, "God, Chris, I don't understand you. I really don't."

"What do you mean?"

Marshall was bewildered. However things had gone, he could see no reason for such bitterness against himself. "What happened?"

Jeff ignored the question. "I'm going to speak frankly to you," he said. "I feel I have a right to do that. You'll admit that I've always played square with you, no matter how we might have differed sometimes——"

"Of course."

"And I had the idea that it was the same with you. To my way of thinking, you did some goddamn stupid things, but you were always on the level. It honestly never entered my head that you'd try to put something like this over on me."

"I still don't understand——"

"No?" He looked closely at Marshall for a moment. "You really don't? Then maybe Kingham's right."

"About what?"

Jeff said curtly, "He says you're nuts."

"And you believed him?"

"I might as well. I can't believe you any more." Suddenly he seemed to become aware of what he had said. Half a lifetime of trust had been cut across. As if stretching out a hand in a wild effort to restore it, he said helplessly, "I don't know what to say. I trusted you. I never even bothered to confirm your story."

"For God's sake, what is this all about? My story was true. I can substantiate any part of it."

Jeff shook his head. "You told me you knew nothing about this business until you went to Paris."

"That's so."

"And that Kingham must have heard about it from Wilcox and deliberately concealed it."

"There's no other explanation."

"That's what I told him. He sat there without saying anything and let me accuse him of covering up a fraud. Then he showed me this."

He zipped open his dispatch case and took a memorandum file out of it. He tossed it across the desk. It was in the usual form for internal correspondence, with the names of the department heads to whom it should be circulated on the cover, the memorandum itself bound inside. It was headed: "Financial Arrangements concerning Foreign Agencies." It was dated February of that year.

Marshall looked inside. The memorandum was closely printed and several pages long. He began to skim through. As usual, the style was turgid, the prose almost unreadable, the meaning in many places hard to follow. The first page was concerned mainly with office equipment. He was halfway down page two before he found anything which applied to his own problem.

". . . Notice has also been received that in some cases there is a lack of exact correspondence between sums paid by distributors to employers on account of direct compensation . . . certain complexities of accountancy varying in nature in different territories. . . . Particular taxation systems liable to influence the use of variable ratios between direct compensation and expense accounting . . ." (In other words, thought Marshall, some of the boys would sooner get part of their wages in the form of expenses and avoid tax. Well, okay.)

". . . It is felt that any attempt to enforce a rigid uniformity in this respect would not only create difficulties for the distributors but also put an additional burden on the Finance Department which it is not at present equipped to handle. Also, lacking special knowledge of local conditions, it might be that decisions made in the U.S.A. would be found impossible to implement in certain foreign territories. . . ."

He began to skip. Old familiar phrases appeared. ". . . avoid unnecessary interference . . . excellent relations with foreign associates . . . complete confidence . . . no reason to abandon certain fundamental principles . . .

". . . It is therefore recommended," said the memorandum with sudden brevity, "that the details of implementation of such financial agreements be left, as heretofore, in the hands of the agents concerned."

Marshall looked up, frowning. "Well, so what? This is just a lot of gobbledygook. They put it in general terms, mix it up with a lot of other stuff, make it as difficult to understand as they can, then stick it in the file. It's just a cover-up."

"You can understand it, can't you?"

"Sure, but——"

"The English may not be so good, but it's clear enough to me what it means. They discussed the whole thing in February, and a collective decision was made to do nothing about it."

"Collective, hell! You mean Kingham decided to do nothing about it."

"Others were consulted," said Jeff coldly. He added, "Look on the outside of the folder."

Marshall turned back to the cover sheet. On it were the names of most of the department heads in the International. The memorandum had been widely circulated. Opposite each name were the scribbled initials of the person concerned, and in the space for comments, always the single word: "Agreed."

The last signature on the list was his own.

It seemed a long time before they spoke again. Marshall looked down at the sheet of paper on which was written, as clearly as if it had been expressed in words, his own defeat. The pain was violent, sickening, but not unfamiliar. He remembered the school examinations failed because of laziness and overconfidence, the voice of Mayer saying: "Have you considered any alternative occupation?" In each case the possibility of failure had been contemplated beforehand yet never fully believed. It was unthinkable, it couldn't happen. You would fall down dead, the world would explode, you would wake up and find you had been dreaming. But when the time came, nothing like that occurred to let you out. You had to stand there and face the moment, dumb, suffering, letting it hit you. It couldn't last forever. Every second took it a little farther away.

"Well?" said Jeff finally.

"I don't know——" He tried hopelessly to arrange his thoughts, to think of a new approach.

"That's your signature? You're not trying to tell me he forged it?"

"Of course not." The sickening truth was that there was no need for forgery, as Kingham probably knew. Marshall had always regarded the endless circulation of memoranda as mere bureaucratic stupidity. But perhaps he had underrated his enemies. Perhaps this was a deliberate method of securing assent to dubious propositions, by sandwiching them in between a mass of verbiage. He explained weakly, "I must have signed it without reading it very carefully. There are so many of these darned things—you get half a dozen on your desk at the same time. You know how it is."

He looked up, hoping for some sign of understanding or sympathy, but Jeff was untouched. Plainly, this excuse meant nothing to him. It occurred to Marshall that his brother was probably the only man in the organization who went through all the memoranda before signing them.

"I can't say I do. It seems to me there isn't much point in circulating things unless people read them."

At least, thought Marshall, he believed the excuse even if he was unable to understand it. It was more acceptable to Jeff to think of him as a careless incompetent than as a liar. More plausible, too.

Though he was now without any real hope, he felt the necessity to try again, to salvage something from the wreckage.

"Okay, I was sloppy. I should have read it, I know. But that doesn't alter the facts about Verrier——"

Jeff interrupted him impatiently. "Chris, be your age. This stuff about Verrier is dead, stone cold dead—you must see that. It never amounted to much anyway. Even last night I was doubtful whether you could make it stick."

"You didn't say so."

"I didn't want to hurt your feelings. And I thought you had a point of view. But it so happens that Kingham's one of the best men we've got, as far as efficiency goes. Whether he's in the right or in the wrong, nobody's going to be fighting for the chance to slap him down over a matter of a hundred and eighty dollars."

"I keep telling you, it's not the amount of money that matters. It's the principle——"

"I heard you. And I was prepared to buy that—last night. Now" —he pointed to the file on the desk—"it's just ridiculous."

"I don't think so."

"If you can't see that——"

"Listen, Jeff," he said desperately. "I want you, for my sake, to try to understand about this. The point is that, even if I had read that memorandum in February, I should still probably have signed it. It would have looked to me, as it looked to all the others, like the sensible thing to do. But since then I've seen the people, I know what it really means. You can kill a man with a signature, Jeff."

Jeff looked at him with some disgust. He was being melodramatic.

"I don't think this is getting us anywhere."

"Let's forget about ourselves for a moment. You're mad at me, I know, and I sympathize. But this isn't about me. The fact that I've made a fool of myself shouldn't mean that a man like Verrier should have to suffer."

Like someone teaching a lesson to a child, Jeff said, "But it does. That's what responsibility means. You always thought I wasn't very smart, but at least I have brains enough to know that." He leaned forward, attacking. "You took the attitude that business was a kid's game, not big enough for somebody of your intelligence. It had to be like that, if fools like me could succeed in it. You couldn't bother your head with a lot of routine jobs, like reading reports and attending conferences. The reports were badly written; at the conferences everybody talked too much, they hadn't got your incisive brain, they couldn't express their ideas—isn't that so?"

"Yes." His head was aching; his unhappiness was so great that he felt no resentment against Jeff. "Yes, I said all those things. It was tactless, I suppose."

"You're damn right it was tactless. It doesn't matter so much with me. I know you and I make allowances. But other people take it differently."

"You mean Kingham?"

"Not just Kingham. You've made plenty of people sore, talking like that."

It was like being back at school. The same thing had happened there. Innocently he had opened his mouth too wide, spoken his thought aloud, questioned authority; and suddenly found himself, to his utter astonishment, suspect and unpopular. It had never occurred to him that his opinions would cause such general hostility. He had always imagined that the great majority, secure in their own world, would regard him with tolerance, as a licensed eccentric. It was always a shock to him to discover how superficial that tolerance was, to have his own familiar world turned upside down and suddenly filled with strange and menacing faces.

All these years, he realized now, Jeff had been defending him, making excuses for him. He said unhappily, "I'm afraid I put you on the spot."

"You surely did." The recollection was painful. It would remain so for a long time. "I had to apologize to Kingham."

"I'm sorry. I mean it—I can't tell you how sorry I am."

"Okay—well—it's done now, let's forget it." He meant, Let's say no more about it. Neither of them would ever forget it. Jeff hesitated. There was another awkward question to dispose of. "The important thing is, what happens now?"

"To me?"

"That's right. You appreciate, don't you, that you can't go on just as if nothing had happened?"

"I suppose not." He waited. When his brother said nothing, he went on with a touch of irony, "Well, come on. You've got some ideas, I imagine. You discussed it with Kingham, didn't you?"

"Yes, I did. Do you object?"

"I'm in no position to object to anything. What's your proposition?"

Jeff settled back in his chair. He was on more comfortable ground now, dealing with what was essentially an administrative problem. "In the first place, you obviously won't want to go on working in the International. Correct?"

Marshall almost smiled. Such crude, pathetic courtesy, the pretense that the choice was his. But it was kindly meant. "Correct," he said.

"On the other hand, it would be a pity if you decided to leave the company altogether. After all, you have a special interest in it, just as I have. . . ."

Jeff was almost coaxing. Marshall was aware that his brother was anxious for him to stay on, in spite of everything. Why? Family loyalty? Or was it, perhaps, the block of shares he held, which indirectly strengthened Jeff's own position?

"I don't know——" he said indifferently.

"If you do want to stay, I'm sure I could fix something for you."

"Such as?"

"I'm not sure yet. Something in Domestic Sales, probably."

"In New York?"

Jeff was doubtful. "I'm not so sure about that. We've a pretty full team here and I wouldn't like to break it up. Maybe, when we have a move sometime, you could come in——"

"From where?"

"I can't tell you right away." He became vague. "Chicago—Kansas City—New Orleans—somewhere like that."

It was, Marshall realized, too much to expect that they would not punish him in some way. A job out of New York would be obvious to everyone as a demotion.

"I'd sooner stay here."

Jeff frowned. "Maybe. But as it happens, there's nothing free." With a trace of exasperation he added, "I'm doing my very best for you, Chris——"

"Okay, okay." Arguing at such a hopeless disadvantage was tiring him out. He knew that Jeff was trying to restrain himself from saying that the whole affair was his own fault and that he was in no position to pick and choose—he ought to be very grateful that someone was taking the trouble to help at all. "Whatever you say."

"That's the boy." Now that Jeff had his way, his joviality returned. "You'll probably enjoy it, you know. You'll have more freedom out there, be able to develop your own ideas. In the New York office we're too close on top of each other. Everybody's driving himself at ninety miles an hour to push ahead of the next man.

It has to be like that, otherwise we go soft. But just the same, it's a strain." He smiled ruefully. "It's a rat race."

Marshall nodded. Jeff was a great man for seeing the advantages of the inevitable. He was reminded of a similar conversation after Kingham had offered him the job in London. He wondered how Jeff would feel if it was proposed that he, too, needed a rest from the rat race, in New Orleans or Kansas City.

"When do I start?" he asked.

"I can't say exactly. I shall have to make some arrangements first. A week or two—something like that."

"I have some affairs in Europe that I want to tie up——"

"Yes, of course—I imagined you would have. That was another thing I talked over with Kingham." Jeff hesitated and then said delicately, "Between ourselves, he was a little against it. He was all for"—he searched for a tactful word—"for making a clean break as far as Europe was concerned. But I didn't think that was reasonable. After all, I reminded him, you were called over here without any expectation of its being permanent. You were bound to have personal affairs to settle. And also, I wouldn't be able to find anything for you to do in the next week or two anyway. So he finally agreed."

"That was generous of him."

Jeff missed the sarcasm. There was something on his mind and he liked to think of one thing at a time. "There was one stipulation he made, though."

"What was that?"

"On the whole, I think it's reasonable, considering what's happened." Nevertheless, he was awkward. "He wanted me to make it clear to you that you are no longer accredited by the company and have no authority to engage in any business dealings over there. He doesn't want you to make any contact with our representatives in the area."

"Anything else?"

"No. That was all."

There was a silence. Marshall tossed the pencil he was holding onto the blotting pad. Unconsciously, throughout the conversation he had been doodling on the thick white paper, drawing wild, bizarre shapes whose meaning was obscure even to himself. As so often in times of crises, they had formed themselves into a pattern of interlocking shadows of increasing darkness and complexity. He saw his brother's disapproving glance and wanted to explain that it was an unconscious activity, a sort of nervous spasm; he wasn't as frivolous as he appeared.

Instead he said, "Well, there we are. Everything seems to be settled." And after a pause, partly because it was expected and partly because he really did feel under an obligation, "Thanks for everything."

Jeff smiled as he rose from his seat, a hearty, big-brother smile. "Forget it," he said.

PART V

CHAPTER I

There was nobody to meet him this time, no bright scrubbed young man in a double-breasted blue suit with a triangle of white handkerchief showing at the breast pocket; no hired limousine. That, at least, was something. He sat in a corner seat in the airport bus, looking out at the characterless suburbs of north-west London. The semi-detached houses stretched for miles along the arterial road in a belt of uniform, featureless gentility. Between the housing developments were model factories, equally prim and house-proud, manufacturers of vacuum cleaners, razor blades, lip-stick; each with its piece of lawn, its ornamental flower beds. Most of them were closed today—it was Saturday morning.

At Waterloo he took a taxi and drove to the flat. When he opened the door he noticed that there was no heap of letters behind it. Nor was there that curious, still, dusty smell which speaks of closed windows and lack of habitation. He put down his suit-cases and went into the living room.

The room was unusually tidy. There was a fire in the grate and Jane was sitting beside it in a high-backed chair, reading. When he came in, she carefully marked her place, put the book down on the radio, and then stood up.

"Jane—darling!"

Instead of moving toward him, she stood there, unusually shy, waiting for him to make the first move. "Surprised to see me?"

"Why, yes——" He went up to her and took her in his arms. Even as he was kissing her, she seemed a little more reserved than usual.

"You didn't mind?"

"Why should I?" He looked round at the room. The furniture was polished, the carpet newly swept, the books on their shelves dusted and placed in alphabetical order. "This is wonderful. The old place never looked like this in its life. You must have been working——"

"When I got your cable I thought it would be nice to have things ready for you." She added with disapproval: "The place was in a dreadful mess."

"I left in rather a hurry. I wrote a message for the daily woman——"

"She obviously hadn't bothered her head. I wondered what to do and then decided I couldn't just leave it; it would be very cheerless for you when you got back——"

He smiled at her affectionately. "It was very thoughtful of you."

"There wasn't much to do when you come down to it." She paused and then said rather awkwardly, "Well, that's all really. I think I ought to go now——"

"Go?" he said, puzzled. "Why? Have you got a date or something?"

"Not exactly. But you'll want to get settled in. I should only be in the way."

He put his arms round her shoulders. "Now why would I ever think you were in the way?"

"You might." She was very serious. "While I was sitting here waiting I wondered whether perhaps it wasn't a mistake. I was only intending to be friendly, but I thought you might see it differently." She added with emphasis, "I can't bear women who *impose* themselves on men."

A thought occurred to him. "How long were you waiting?"

"Oh, not so very long. An hour or two."

He said apologetically, "The plane was a little late. I'm sorry about that. Waiting for people is a little like lying awake at night. After a time the craziest thoughts come into your mind."

"This isn't crazy," she persisted. "I'm serious. I still think——"

"It's always crazy when you start thinking about 'men' and 'women' in quotes. This is you and me—an entirely different matter. It never occurred to me that you were imposing on me—and furthermore, I wouldn't mind if you did."

She began to relax. "You're very nice to me. Nobody was ever as nice to me as you are."

"Perhaps nobody was in love with you before."

"They said they were. Perhaps they even meant it. It's not always easy to tell, is it—even with yourself?" She went on, "That was what I was worried about. When you've been apart for a while you get things more in perspective. This would have been a good moment for you to change the tempo, to start off on a different footing if you wanted to. And by being here waiting for you, I was spoiling it for you." She smiled precariously. "That was what I was afraid of."

"You were silly, weren't you?"

"Was I? I hope so." She walked over to the sofa and sat down, closing the subject. "Now tell me about New York."

In a second the feeling of unreasonable happiness, of homecoming, was gone. Love was like a sort of sleep in which you could immerse yourself for a time, forgetting your troubles in vague, irresponsible dreams. But always in the morning there remained the business of living.

"It was a flop," he said painfully. "They beat me."

Her face fell. "But, darling, how? What happened?"

"The worst thing was, it was my own fault. I ran right into it. . . ."

As he told the story he found that it was not quite so bad as he had expected. Perhaps there was a relief in unburdening himself to her. Or perhaps it was simply a fatigue of emotion. You could not stimulate a nerve at maximum intensity forever.

At the end she said, "You say what really finished you was the fact that you had put your signature on the report?"

"In a way, yes."

"That sounds absurd to me." She had a feminine scorn for formalities. "Why, half the time businessmen sign things without reading them. It was just bad luck."

"No." He was ready for this one. It was too easy—dangerously easy. "I won't accept that. Whenever I flopped out before, there was always somebody to say, 'Bad luck.'" He turned to her desperately. "Don't you see that I'd sooner be anything—stupid, ridiculous, ineffective—anything but unlucky? That's the one thing you can't beat."

She said gently, in an attempt at consolation, "You mustn't make too much of this. It isn't the earth——"

"It mattered a lot to me. More than I would have thought. Not just because of Verrier, though that was important. But because I'd gone on for years saying to myself that this was the kind of thing I could do if I had to. Then, when it came to the point, I was useless. I let everybody down, Madame Verrier, myself, you——"

"In a way it was my fault. It was I who persuaded you——"

"You gave me a chance and I made a mess of it. You can't blame yourself."

She was silent for a while, no longer looking at him. It was as if her thoughts were turned inward, searching her mind for a decision on a problem which was worrying her. Eventually she said, "Have you made any plans?"

"I shall have to be back in New York fairly soon. There are various things to arrange here. I have to see about disposing of the flat, for one thing. And I left some stuff at the office——"

She pointed to a large package in one corner of the room. "I brought everything of yours over here."

"Then you knew I wasn't coming back?"

"Gilbertson told me. From the way he said it, I guessed you must have run into trouble over there. Naturally I asked who would be succeeding you. He looked very pleased and said, so far as he knew, nobody. The job hadn't ever served very much purpose anyway. He made it pretty clear that, so far as he was concerned, you didn't exist any more."

"Did he advise you not to see me when I came over?"

"Not in so many words. He just said you wouldn't be coming near the office and that presumably none of us would be seeing you again. He isn't fool enough to try to tell me what to do out of office hours."

"No." He looked at her loyal, stubborn little face. "I can see that."

"The next morning when I came in, your room had been completely cleared. The desk drawers were empty, and Travers moved in."

He frowned. There had been nothing of any significance in the desk, but even so he was affronted by this invasion of his privacy. So far as Gilbertson was concerned, she had said, he no longer existed. . . . Suddenly he thought of another aspect of the matter. "But what about you? Are you working for Travers now?"

"No. I've been promoted," she explained. "Miss Barraclough gave notice while you were away—she's going to get married. Mr. Gilbertson asked me to work for him."

He felt unreasonably that in some way she had betrayed him. "And you agreed?"

"Why not?" Seeing the reproach in his eyes, she reminded him, "I'm a working girl, you know. I can't be too particular."

"I suppose not."

He struggled to be understanding. It was the same with everybody—Jeff, Richardson, Rose, Gilbertson, even Jane—they had a job to hold down and they couldn't be too particular. Only he had thought of himself as able to afford a romantic gesture—and where had it got him? But he must be a good loser, he remembered. The British were said to admire good losers.

"Well, there it is," he said with as much cheerful gallantry as he could muster. "I did my best, but it wasn't good enough. There's no use crying about it."

"You're going to leave it there?"

"More or less. There's Madame Verrier, of course. I'll have to make some sort of personal settlement with her. Maybe I can manage to fool her into thinking the money comes from the company."

"That's not very satisfactory, is it?"

"Of course it isn't. But what else can I do? I've tried to think of some other way of going about it, but so far as I can see there isn't any. I'm at a dead end."

She was silent for a moment, then said, "Is this thing so very important to you?"

"You know it is. I'd do anything——"

"Anything?"

"Well, you know what I mean—anything within reason." He

looked at her questioningly. "Why? What is it? What are you getting at?"

She paused again, then said with obvious reluctance, "There's something I haven't told you."

"What's that?"

"You said you didn't know where Wilcox was." He nodded. "Well, he's in London. He wants to meet you."

Astonishment held him silent for a moment. Then he felt a surge of hope. Perhaps this was a break. Perhaps he was in the game again.

"I met him a few days ago," Jane went on. "Or rather, he met me. He was waiting for me at the Bond Street tube station when I went home from the office. It was quite a surprise."

"I can imagine."

"He said he wanted to talk about something important and had I time for a drink. Naturally I was curious, so I went. He told me that he'd left the company about a month ago."

"Yes," said Marshall. "I heard that in New York. But nobody seemed to know where he'd gone. It certainly never occurred to me that he would have come back here. Who's he working for now?"

"I don't know," she said. "He didn't say and I didn't ask him." She added a little oddly, "Himself, perhaps."

"What did he want?"

"I told you. He wanted to get in touch with you. He picked on me as the best way of doing it."

"He knew I was coming back to London?"

"Yes. But he didn't know when."

"So you told him?"

She shook her head.

Puzzled, he asked, "But why not? I'd like to meet Wilcox."

"I'm not so sure," she said doubtfully.

"Why not?" He looked at her with concern. "What's worrying you? You talk as though there was something wrong with him."

It was as though she found it difficult to put her feelings into words. "I didn't like his attitude——"

"What about his attitude?"

"Well, it was too—personal, somehow. He wants to get his own back on the company for what they did to him. He has a grievance."

"I can understand that."

"Oh, so can I. But—just the same—as you know, I'm not very attracted to people with grievances. And he drank too much."

"Well, maybe." She was being a little intolerant, he thought. Surely it was possible to sympathize with Wilcox, even if he was hitting the bottle a little. "What else did he tell you?"

"Not a lot." She made a grimace. "He was talking big—about what he was going to do to various people, and so on. But all very vague—you know how drunks are. I don't know how much it really meant."

"You weren't impressed?"

"No."

"You think he's just a soak?"

"Not quite. But—well—I suppose it was a shock to me. I hadn't seen him since he was working here. I wouldn't say he was ever my type—he was shallow and pleased with himself and he often irritated me—but at least he had vitality. That was how I saw him, anyway."

"And now?"

"Now I can see how precarious it was. It all depended on everybody else thinking he was a coming young man. Once that was knocked away, he just fell to pieces. He hasn't any normal, decent ambitions any more. All he wants is trouble."

"What sort of trouble?"

Once again she did not answer him. She said, "You really want to meet him?"

"What can I lose?"

"A lot, I think." She added obscurely, "We might all lose a lot."

"What's that—woman's instinct?" He smiled, but she did not smile back. "I wish you'd explain."

"No," she said definitely. "He can do the explaining." From her attitude it was plain that Wilcox had said more to her than she was prepared to repeat. She opened her bag and took out a slip of paper. "This is the telephone number he gave me."

CHAPTER II

It was a Museum number. He picked up the telephone and called it. A sharp female voice said, "Drax Hotel."

"I'd like to speak to Mr. Wilcox."

"Staying in the hotel?"

"I've no idea. I presume so——"

"You don't know his room number?"

"No."

"One moment, please."

There was silence for several minutes, then Wilcox's voice.

"Hullo—Marshall?"

"Yes."

"How are you?"

"Pretty good, thanks."

"I hoped you'd be calling." His eagerness was obvious even over the telephone. "Are you in London for long?"

"Not very long."

"Why don't we have a drink together? Can you find your way around here?"

"Tonight?"

"The sooner the better. There's something important I want to discuss with you."

"Okay." Wilcox sounded sober enough at the moment. His voice was a little nervous and aggressive, but that was nothing new. It had never been very easy to make satisfactory contact with him.

Marshall wondered whether everybody found him difficult—or was it just himself? Even now, when they were both allies in misfortune, there was no real feeling of sympathy—only an artificial good-fellowship thinly disguising suspicion. "I have a dinner engagement," he said, "but I can come along afterward. Will nine o'clock suit you?"

"Fine. See you then."

After dinner he took Jane home and then directed his taxi to Bloomsbury. The Drax Hotel was a very large building with a multitude of tiny windows and a façade which seemed to have been made out of enormous slices of some patent non-fattening biscuit—a long-discredited experiment in synthetic construction. A large yellow sign above the main entrance announced: ONE PRICE: BED AND BREAKFAST 25/-. There were indications that this figure had been changed on several occasions to keep abreast of inflation.

There was a crowd at the reception desk. Marshall found himself jostling for position with individuals more accustomed than he was to the struggle for existence in cheap hotels. There were notices everywhere: "The Management regrets that it can take no responsibility for valuables left in rooms." "Guests are respectfully reminded that all accommodation must be paid for in advance." Guests were also respectfully told that rooms had to be vacated by noon on the day of departure, that breakfast would under no circumstances be served after 10 A.M., that no alcohol could be consumed in the main lounge.

At last he reached the front of the queue. A young man in a shiny black suit regarded him with undisguised hostility.

"Yes?" he asked sharply.

"I've come to see a Mr. Wilcox."

"Initial?"

"M., I think."

"We may have several Wilcoxes, you understand." He picked a series of cards out of his filing system and flipped through them. "M. F. Wilcox, 513."

"Thank you. Do you suppose——"

The receptionist had already turned his attention to the next person in line. He looked back at Marshall with a frown.

"Yes, what is it?"

"I'd like to speak to him."

By way of reply the man pointed silently to two telephone booths in a corner of the hall. One was marked "Internal," the other "External." There were people waiting outside each one. Nothing, it seemed, was easy at the Drax. He walked to the lift and pressed the button for the fifth floor.

There was a long way to go down a dark corridor floored with linoleum. He knocked at 513. Wilcox opened the door almost immediately.

"I couldn't get to the internal telephone," Marshall explained, "so I came up."

"Sure. Come right in." The room was small and ill furnished. There was a bed, a wardrobe, a couple of cheap modern chairs, and a dressing table. The window looked out on to the gray blank wall of a block of offices.

Marshall sat down on one of the chairs. Wilcox regarded him for a moment without speaking.

"A drink?" he said anxiously, as if he were afraid of a refusal. It occurred to Marshall that Wilcox was already showing signs of an alcoholic's oversensitivity—he didn't like people to see him drinking alone.

"Thanks."

Wilcox took a bottle of scotch out of the wardrobe. On the writing table there was a carafe of water and two glasses. There was no ice.

"Plenty of water for me."

They sat opposite each other. Wilcox took a large gulp of his drink and gave again his brisk, uncertain smile, the smile of a man with something to sell. His lightweight American suit had a crumpled appearance. The hotel valeting service was not very good, perhaps. Marshall wondered why he had been so insistent that they should meet here. To demonstrate his poverty and attract sympathy? But he had never thought of Wilcox as that kind of man. He was the type, surely, who would try to keep up an appearance of prosperity to the last. He had been brought up in a world where appeals to sympathy paid few dividends.

For a little while neither of them spoke. Wilcox seemed to be wondering how best to make his approach. Finally he said, "So they fixed you up too, uh?"

Marshall hesitated. "You might call it that."

"What else is there to call it?" Like all salesmen, he was more confident once he had started talking. "Of course I don't know all the details, but I have one or two connections in New York who keep me informed. . . . I believe you were asking after me?"

"Yes. They told me you'd quit."

"That's right. I walked out on them," he said with satisfaction. "I was smart enough for that, at any rate." He took another drink and said, "It didn't take me long to realize that Kingham had played me for a sucker."

"Oh?"

"Yes. When he transferred me he gave me a lot of stuff about the big opportunities there were in the Domestic Division. When I got there, I found there wasn't a damned thing. They'd only taken me to oblige Kingham. They were just looking for a nice suitable opportunity to get rid of me. But I didn't wait that long." He offered Marshall a cigarette. As he leaned forward to light it, he said, "It could happen to you, you know."

Marshall was noncommittal. "It's possible."

"Brother or no brother."

"I'm not counting on that."

"No?" said Wilcox skeptically. Suddenly he laughed. "Kingham must have been sore about you. He certainly never thought of you as an eager beaver. I'll be honest with you—it surprised me too." The laugh died. He had never really thought it very funny. It was all part of a build-up. A curious build-up—mainly man-to-man, confidential, both-in-the-same-spot, why-don't-we-take-our-hair-down-and-get-together—but shot through all the time with these hostile, needling remarks. Suddenly Marshall knew that Wilcox hated him, had always hated him.

"You told me over the phone you wanted to discuss something," he said.

"Yes." Wilcox paused for a moment, then said, "I was interested to know how serious you were."

He frowned. Hadn't Jane said something rather similar? "About what?"

"This whole affair."

"Of course I'm serious."

"You mightn't be. You might be just playing at it. After all, nobody enjoys being beaten——"

"It isn't just a question of"—the words were distasteful to him—"being beaten." Yet he had to admit to himself that to some extent it was. As time went on it became increasingly difficult to distinguish between the claims of abstract justice and personal pride. He said, "There's such a thing as a matter of principle. Verrier was just a little man——"

"Sure." As Wilcox lifted his drink his hand trembled a little. "We're all little men—Verrier—me—you too—— The hell with us."

Marshall waited for him to say something more, but he simply emptied his glass and stared in front of him, shaking his head gloomily. Surely there was going to be more to it than this; he had not been invited simply to take part in a crying jag?

"Jane told me you had some sort of a proposition," he said.

Wilcox nodded solemnly. But instead of answering he asked, "Has it occurred to you to wonder why I came back to Europe?"

"Up to a point. I presumed it was your own business——"

Wilcox went on as if he had not spoken. "I came here at great personal sacrifice—and expense too, if it comes to that. I had jobs offered to me in the United States—plenty of jobs. I turned them down. I came here—on my own money——" Was it, perhaps, Marshall wondered momentarily, no more than an elaborate prelude to a request for a loan? Wilcox, not yet too far gone in whisky to observe the expression on his face, waved a hand impatiently. "But that's not the point. I came back because I was mad at the way I'd been treated—I wasn't prepared to just let it go. Also, I was convinced that there was something wrong."

"In what way?"

Wilcox flopped back in his chair. "Well," he said, "when you look at it, there was always something phony about this particular deal.

So much fuss and trouble over a few hundred dollars. Didn't that occur to you?"

"Why, yes. In a way that was one of the worst features——"

"Oh, sure. But why is Kingham prepared to put himself in the wrong over so little? Just obstinacy?" He shook his head. "He's not that obstinate."

"Furac——"

"Exactly. The important thing is to lay off Furac. Furac is a genius. Everybody should be kind to him at all costs. And, after all, when you consider the business situation, you can see their point of view. In England and Germany and Scandinavia we can hardly break even. But in France we can sell all we want—at our own price. How do you explain that?"

"I don't know. It was one of the things I couldn't understand. I asked Gilbertson——"

"Yes. So did I. And I couldn't get any sense out of him." Wilcox said triumphantly, "Now I know why. I discovered recently that those instruments we sell in France don't stay there very long. They're re-exported."

"Where to?"

Wilcox hesitated. It was as if at the last moment he was reluctant to part with his secret. Finally he said, "Eastern Germany."

There was a long silence.

Wilcox threw away his half-smoked cigarette and lit another. The air was heavy with smoke. They could hear movements through the thin wall separating them from the next room. A motor bicycle coughed its way noisily up Southampton Row. Marshall said, "I take it you have some proof of this?"

"Of course." Wilcox regarded him with slight amusement. Then he walked toward the bed and picked up the telephone.

"Five-fifteen," he said.

A moment later Marshall could hear the telephone ring in the next room—the wall was little more than a plywood partition.

"Okay, honey," Wilcox said into the telephone, "you can come in now."

CHAPTER III

SHE WAS much the same as he had remembered her from their meeting in Paris. If anything, her face was a little paler, her expression even less trusting. Wilcox closed the door and showed her to a chair with exaggerated courtliness, like a lawyer with a star witness. He himself sat down on the bed.

"You've met Louise Verrier before, I think."

"Yes." To her, Marshall said, "I was planning to visit you in Paris in a few days' time. Though not with very good news, I'm afraid."

She was not surprised. "I did not expect it. Mr. Wilcox told me you had been unsuccessful."

"I'm afraid so. I can assure you," Marshall said earnestly, "that I tried my very best——"

"Yes." Her acknowledgment was perfunctory. She had never, at the best of times, been a very gracious person. "Thank you so much."

"Louise understands," Wilcox cut in. "I explained the position to her." He touched her reassuringly on the shoulder. His attitude was curiously proprietary—did the adjacent rooms have any special significance? "As I told her, this is a tough fight. You have to use everything you've got, otherwise you don't stand a chance. Isn't that so?" He looked challengingly at Marshall, as if trying to lead him toward some sort of admission. When he received no answer he went on, "It was Louise who put me onto this. I found that she had, without knowing it, a piece of very valuable information."

"What was that?"

In a dull voice, as if repeating a lesson, Louise said, "It was after you left. They sent André's clothes and belongings back in a parcel from the hospital. In his wallet I found a bill from a hotel in Zurich, made out to someone called Girard. I couldn't understand it because we knew nobody called Girard, and so far as I knew André had never been to Zurich. I checked on the date and found that it was at a time when he had told me he was going to Bordeaux." She said dispassionately, "Naturally I thought at first it was a woman. . . . But the hotel was most expensive, far more than he could ever have afforded, and there was a charge of sixty Swiss francs for dinner. Across it, in André's handwriting, was scribbled—'Wenner.' I thought about it for a while, but I still couldn't think of an explanation. So when Mr. Wilcox came I showed it to him."

"It didn't make much sense to me either, at first," said Wilcox, "but I thought it worth while going to Zurich to find out. We took a photograph of Verrier with us, and the hotel people identified him straightaway as Girard. So then we made some inquiries about Wenner."

"He was an agent?"

Wilcox nodded. "It was too easy really. One of our boys from the American consulate told me over a few drinks that they'd been watching him for years on account of this kind of thing, but they couldn't get the Swiss to co-operate." He explained cheerfully, "He told me it's a pretty well-known game. Quite a lot of prohibited materials are going across that way. You pass it through several different companies. Most of them have big-sounding names, but they're just dummies when you come down to it. They change the packing and labels and hand it over to an exporting agency with connections in Switzerland. Of course if it comes out—you're horrified. You didn't know a thing about that."

"And Verrier?"

"You have to have *some* direct connection—to make arrangements about advance shipments, methods of payment, and so on. You can do it yourself—or you may think it safer, for routine messages anyway, to use a runner."

"So Verrier was the runner?"

"He must have been."

"And did he know——"

"I am sure he knew," Louise broke in. "I noticed he grew more depressed after each time he went away. He was brooding about it." She added with conviction, "That was why he killed himself."

Wilcox said, "It sounds reasonable, doesn't it? After all, he was that kind of person——"

"Was he?" Marshall asked, almost to himself. "I never knew him."

So this, he thought, was Verrier, the little man, the victim . . . He looked up and saw that Wilcox was holding out a slip of paper toward him.

"The hotel bill." When Marshall had looked at it, Wilcox said, "Are you convinced?"

"I suppose so."

"Good," he said with satisfaction. The first phase of his project had been accomplished. "The next thing is—are you prepared to do something about it?"

Marshall frowned. There was something rather odd in the way Wilcox had expressed himself. "But this is your discovery—don't you want to handle it yourself?"

Wilcox shook his head. "It wouldn't be too easy for me," he explained. "For one thing, I've left the company. An affair like this has to be handled at top level, and I haven't the contacts." He seemed to realize himself that this was a lame excuse. "Also, there's something else——"

"What?" Marshall was immediately wary.

"You'll notice that this hotel bill connects Wenner with Verrier, not Furac. That was the whole point of sending Verrier. Furac will obviously say that he knows nothing about the deals, that Verrier was fixing them himself on a commission basis or something. Everybody else who's been implicated will want to blame Verrier too, especially since he's dead. They might easily get away with it."

Marshall thought for a moment. "Maybe," he agreed. "But that's a risk we have to take. There seems to be no alternative."

"There is," Wilcox said, leaning forward. When Marshall made no reply, he went on, "On the second of every month a letter comes through from Paris to Gilbertson marked 'Private and Confidential.' Nobody else has ever looked at one of those letters and nobody knows where they're filed. It's reasonable to suppose that they contain details about trading in France which Gilbertson doesn't want anyone else to see." He paused. "I'd very much like to have a look at one of those reports."

"Well, so would I, but——"

"Next Friday," went on Wilcox, "is the second of the month. The mail arrives at nine-thirty and Gilbertson doesn't get in until ten. It would be very easy for somebody with access to the correspondence to remove that letter." He said deliberately, "And Jane Lancing is now Gilbertson's secretary."

Marshall recoiled. "Oh no, for God's sake——"

Wilcox shrugged his shoulders. "That's your proof. It's not the nicest way to get it, I'll agree, but it's the only way. After all," he said persuasively, "you've got to remember how serious this is. These people are practically traitors. Do you suppose the FBI would hesitate to open this mail?"

"I'm not the FBI."

"No. But you have certain duties as a citizen."

He was repelled by Wilcox's obvious insincerity. "Don't let's get too damn virtuous about it."

"All right." The appeal to patriotism, Wilcox realized, had been a mistake. "Then don't do it," he said. "Hold onto your virginity. Let them beat you again."

There was a silence. Marshall could feel the tension as Wilcox waited for him to speak. Madame Verrier looked at him with a detached, almost contemptuous interest. Eventually he said, "Did you speak to Jane about this the night you met her outside the subway?"

"Yes."

So that was why she had seemed to be holding something back. "What did she say?"

"She wouldn't do it."

"Well, then——"

"Not for me, that is." He added significantly, "But she'd do it for you."

"Did she say so?"

"No. But I could tell."

He knew now why Wilcox needed him so badly. He said, partly to gain time, partly because he needed to know, "Tell me something. What are you hoping to get out of this?"

"Nothing unreasonable." He said with sudden passion, "All I want is to be back where I was before this thing began—with a good job, some prospects, money in the bank. Why, I've spent two thousand dollars already on this trip alone——"

"I'll cover that."

"I don't want it from you. I want it from the company. Can't you understand that?"

"Yes."

In this, at least, he realized, Wilcox was sincere—he wanted more than money. It was something harder to get than money, something that required more than a signature on the bottom of a check. A form of rough justice—that right should prevail and the wicked be defeated. It was what he himself wanted too, to be justified, to taste victory, just this once. But there was a price to pay. He knew in his heart that Wilcox was correct—if he asked her, Jane would take the letter. But he could not bring himself to take the step.

"I don't know," he said after a little thought. "I'm not sure that I'm justified——"

"Now don't get things out of proportion," said Wilcox with obvious anxiety. "After all, it's only a letter——"

"No, it's not just a letter." He was not certain whether he would do it or not, but at least he wouldn't fool himself. It might be necessary perhaps. He could not persuade himself it was unimportant.

"I agree that nobody likes to open another man's mail. But surely, in the circumstances——"

Marshall looked at him. Was it any use to try to explain? Wilcox had been educated in the same school as the rest of them. When you had a chance, you took it. When you gained an advantage, you exploited it. When you scored a victory, you looked around for a way to extend it. There was no other law. The only difference was that Wilcox was down while the others were up.

He said slowly: "This isn't simply a question of opening mail.

Gilbertson treated me as his friend. He entertained me at his house. Now I'm asked to steal his private correspondence and use it as evidence to destroy him. Worse still, I'm to use somebody else——" He stopped, unable to speak to Wilcox of his feelings for Jane. But the question was insistent within him. Was he prepared to make use of her love for him to corrupt her loyalty, to persuade her to violate a trust? Could the circumstances justify that? So far, his hands were clean. It was the advantage he had over Furac, Gilbertson, Kingham, all of them. It was not an easy thing to throw it away. If he refused, he could tell himself that he had retained his integrity. But what else would he retain?

He got up from his chair. He had a sudden conviction that it would be impossible to make any sane decision in this small fetid room. He needed to make contact with the world outside, to talk to ordinary people who led sensible, balanced lives, free of ambition and bitterness and revenge. From them he might be able to absorb some fragment of simple knowledge, some sense of the prosaic decencies of life. It might become plain to him what was right and virtuous; he might be able to recognize his own motives, to distinguish scruples from cowardice, a genuine desire for justice from mere pugnacity.

"I can't make up my mind just now," he said. "I'll let you know tomorrow."

CHAPTER IV

WHEN HE LEFT THE HOTEL he began to walk in what he vaguely presumed was the right direction. The fresh air cleared his head without giving him any clue to the solution of his problems.

There was, it seemed to him, no solution which did not involve some form of debasement. They said power corrupted. If that was all, it would not matter; he had little desire for power. But there was more to it than that. He realized now that a sacrifice of integrity could be demanded not merely by ambition but by even the simplest and most well-meaning course of effective action. If he was to defeat corruption he must be prepared, to some degree at any rate, to become corrupt himself, to cheat and steal and exploit the affection of those who cared for him. Yet the alternative was to refuse all action, to do nothing and be nothing, to accept a life of idleness and futility. Was there much virtue in that?

He passed through streets he didn't know, narrow clefts between lines of seedy houses, coffee bars, Indian restaurants, bookshops overflowing onto the pavement. Every so often the sound of jazz would come bursting out of a basement—Nick's Club—Late-night Jiving—Skiffle Alley—the buildings above seemed to shiver and vibrate, but resignedly, like an old person with an uncontrollable tremor in one limb. Outside the doors the fat, corseted prostitutes stood and gossiped, the barrow boys shouted the price of oranges, the three-card men sold packets which might contain pound notes for half-a-crown a time. On a corner an old woman peddled wilted violets out of a basket.

This was not New York, where a simple exercise in mathematics could always tell you where you were and how far from home. Sometimes the streets here curved almost imperceptibly, so that you started going south and came out facing west; sometimes they ended unexpectedly against a blank wall or in a large deserted square, as a river might suddenly widen into a lake with islands and half a dozen confusing exits. He was lost. He could ask someone—they were always ready to tell you the way—but somehow he could not bring himself to do so. They seemed so utterly occupied in their own pursuits. He felt that if he spoke they would not hear him; they might pass by, unconscious of his existence, leaving him even more alone than before.

He halted on a corner, a little tired from so much walking, uncertain which way to go. Someone opened the door of a public house. Inside he saw a long bar, bright lights, a haze of smoke. Bursts of conversation and laughter came to him through the open door. It sounded warm and companionable—he felt a longing for human society. People walked into these places, ordered a glass of beer or spirits, got talking to others, and made friends; for a time, at least, they had a place in life, they were no longer alone. On impulse he walked in to the bar and ordered a whisky. It tasted sickly and lukewarm. Did one give a tip to the barman in a place like this? he wondered. Americans were always in trouble abroad—either they gave too much, in an effort to be popular, or else they turned morbidly suspicious and got into arguments about pennies.

A small man in a greasy hat and a threadbare overcoat stood beside him at the bar. He took his face out of a pint glass and said, "American?"

"Yes."

"You haven't much of an accent." It was presumably intended to be a compliment.

"I was educated partly over here."

"Ah!" Everything was clear now. "I had a cousin who married a GI. Went to live in Chicago. You been there?"

"Once or twice."

"Finkel, his name was. I don't suppose you've ever run across him?"

"I'm afraid not."

"We used to pull her leg about it. Mrs. Finkel." He laughed reminiscently. It was obviously a treasured family joke. "But not in any unpleasant way, mind you. What I say is, we're all brothers under the skin, no matter who our fathers may be. Isn't that right?"

It was always the same, he thought. You had the idea that it would be nice to talk to somebody, and then when it happened they bored you to death. It was like those animated conversations the French and Italians went in for. If you didn't understand them they sounded vivacious and exciting and you envied them. When it came down to it they were probably just discussing the stock market or the price of vegetables.

"I said to her, 'You watch out you don't get mixed up with any of them gangsters out there——' "

Now he was stuck with this little guy. But you couldn't be rude and walk out on him. Perhaps buy him a drink and then say you had to be somewhere in a hurry. . . .

"What are you drinking?"

The little man looked distastefully at his glass. "I was having mild-and-bitter—but it's poor stuff here." He repeated his eager, shifty smile. It was worth a try-on. "To be sociable, I'll have the same as you."

"Two large whiskies."

The barman put the drinks in front of them.

"Well," said the little man, "here's to the Star-Spangled Banner."

When they put their glasses down, Marshall saw the barman regarding them sardonically. Another American sucker taken for a free drink. So much for life, for the good, simple, human folks with their instinctive courtesy and sense of values. So much for the good-fellowship of the English pub. It had been a mistake to come into the place at all.

"Going already?" said the little man with obvious disappointment.

"I'm afraid so." He tossed a ten-shilling note on the counter. "Have another one on me."

By the time he got back to the flat it was almost midnight. But the thought of going to bed was intolerable to him; certainly there would be no chance of sleep for the next hour or two. On an impulse he picked up the phone and asked for his mother's number. While he waited he poured himself a drink but didn't finish it; the taste reminded him of his experience in the bar. He chain-smoked cigarettes and tried to get his ideas into perspective. But the same propositions, the same alternatives presented themselves. There was nothing further to argue about with himself. He needed some new internal voice, beyond argument, to give him the conviction of what he must do.

The telephone rang.

"Is that you, Mother?"

"Yes, dear. Is everything all right?"

"Yes, fine. I just thought I'd like to speak to you, that's all."

"That was very sweet of you, dear." She was pleased, but obviously puzzled. "It's good to hear your voice. How are things in London?"

"Pretty much the same."

"When will you be coming back home?"

"I'm not sure."

"Jeff said——"

The mention of his brother's name made him irritable. It was a reminder of the bad days in New York. "Never mind about Jeff."

"I think he was only trying to be helpful. He's anxious that you shouldn't get involved in any more trouble——"

"Oh, is he?" Had Jeff known? he suddenly wondered. Had they all known about Furac and Wenner and the rest of it when he was allowing them to walk all over him in New York? God, if they had . . .

There must have been something odd about his tone of voice. His mother said, "Chris, are you *sure* everything's all right?"

"Why do you keep asking that?"

"I don't know. You sound so strange——"

"Strange?"

"Yes. Not like yourself at all." He waited for her to say more, but she said, "I can't explain on the telephone. Come and see me as soon as you get back, won't you?"

"Of course."

There was nothing more to say, except how was Jeff and how was Paula and the children, and was Virgie's rheumatism acting up again? He hadn't made the call for that. He wondered, when it came down to it, why he *had* made it. Some vague instinctive hope of support, perhaps an absurd reversion to the days when he had clutched at his mother's hand in a crowd for fear of being swept away.

As if she had read his thought, she said, "Chris darling."

"Yes."

"Don't worry too much about what happened in New York. Jeff told me all about it." Trust Jeff, he thought. "I know it must have been terrible for you——"

"I'm over it now."

"That's good." Vaguely she said, "After all, success isn't everything——"

She continued talking, trying to reassure him with platitudes of which he heard nothing. He had heard them so often, the excuses, the consolations for failure. He remembered Madame Verrier talking of her husband. He remembered her voice, a mixture of pity and contempt. "André was a failure. And when a man is a failure, failure is the most important thing about him. To love him, you have to love that."

He was there now. He had reached the end point of the reaction, the stage when judgment had grown tired and one emotional truth was stronger than a whole world of logic. He was in the grip of inevitability, of the thing that must be done.

He waited impatiently for his mother to ring off. As soon as she had done so, he picked up the telephone again and dialed Jane's number. It was late, but he had no doubt that she would answer.

CHAPTER V

"So THIS is where you live?"

"Yes."

Wilcox walked over to the window and looked out at the view over St. James's Square. "Better than the Drax."

"Yes." Marshall wanted to forget the Drax. "Why don't you move somewhere else?"

"It's cheap."

"Send the bill to me. I'm financing the operation from now on." Before Wilcox could say anything, he went on, "And you don't have to feel indebted. I shall get it back from the company."

"What about Louise?"

"Take her with you. Unless she's in a hurry to go back to Paris."

"I think she'd rather stay here—for the moment——"

"That's fine." So his suspicions had been correct—Wilcox was playing around with her. Marshall was, if anything, pleased at the discovery. From this point onward Wilcox was likely to be more of a liability than an asset—his drunken quarrelsome presence would be an embarrassment in New York. If he could be persuaded to stay in Europe with his mistress on a generous expense account, that would be an ideal arrangement.

Wilcox looked at his watch. "How soon will Jane be here?"

"Soon, I hope. She should have arrived at the office now. The first thing she does is to sort the mail. There may be nothing from Paris, of course, though she tells me it's pretty well invariable. If the letter's there she'll get out as soon as she can and bring it to us here."

"Supposing it isn't?"

"She'll get through on the telephone."

"In that case, if she doesn't telephone within five or ten minutes, we know she's got it."

"Not necessarily. Sometimes the mail comes late. Or she may have difficulty getting privacy for the call. We shall have to be patient."

It was curious how, once the decision had been taken, his relations with Wilcox had changed. Now he was in charge. Wilcox did not resent his leadership; indeed, he seemed actually to welcome it as a relief from responsibility. It was as if the effort of having carried the project so far had exhausted him. The more Marshall saw of him, the more obvious it became that Wilcox could have gone no farther without help. That night at the Drax he had emptied his pockets and thrown everything he had left onto the board.

Now he had the air, not of the initiator of the scheme, but of a nervous and not exceptionally reliable supporter. Looking at the tremulous, nicotine-stained fingers, the slightly bloodshot eyes, Marshall knew he was committed, if successful, to restoring Wilcox to a place of responsibility in the company equivalent to the one he had held. In fairness, he was entitled to it. Who could tell whether his present state was a consequence of the treatment he had received or whether it would have been inevitable anyway? You had to give him the benefit of the doubt—he might improve when his grievance was removed. If he didn't, that would be too bad. No firm could be expected to carry him forever.

"You think we can rely on her?"

"Yes."

"So do I." Wilcox clenched his hands together. "She's a wonderful girl. I have the greatest confidence—— She'll fix it all right, don't worry."

To whom was he talking, thought Marshall—himself? Some imaginary prospect? That was the way it was if you were a salesman. Selling wasn't just talking to a man about a thing you wanted to buy, it was a state of mind, a form of prayer. "Sell yourself first. Be convinced. Believe in yourself—and believe in the product. Then you can start talking." Being convinced could become a sort of habit, an end in itself, so that the object of your convictions could be changed conveniently from day to day as circumstances demanded. Marshall had always been a little baffled by salesmen—he tended to overestimate their transient enthusiasms. They stalked their objectives with the ferocious intensity of a kitten attacking a ball of wool—but, like the kitten, they were easily distracted.

Wilcox went on, "Did she make much difficulty about doing it?"

Marshall shook his head. He did not want to discuss Jane with Wilcox. She had made what Wilcox would have considered no difficulty at all. She had required no persuasion. But that did not mean that she was in favor of the act. It meant simply that she knew he was likely to ask her and had decided beforehand what her answer would be. It had not occurred to her to bargain with her acquiescence. She had not waited to be coaxed or bribed or reassured. She had simply said, "You want me to do it?"

"I don't want to put pressure on you. Only if you feel justified——"

"No," she had said decisively. "That's not for me—I don't know anything about justification. I don't know about law or politics or anything like that. I wouldn't do it for anyone else. If I do it," she had said, echoing Wilcox's words, "I'll do it for you. But you'll have to ask me."

He was ashamed of his attempt to retreat from responsibility, to involve her in his decision.

"I'm asking you," he had said.

He heard footsteps on the stairs which he recognized as hers. A moment later she walked into the room. She was wearing her neat secretary's clothes, the black skirt, the white crisply laundered blouse—it was the way he had first seen her. She was carrying the leather hold-all she usually took to the office. Without a word she picked an envelope out of her handbag and handed it to him.

He looked at the Paris stamp, the label "Personal and Confidential." He had imagined the situation and had known it must be like this, but even so, it seemed a terrible thing to open another man's private correspondence. This, more than cruelty or jobbery or fraud, was a breach of all the conventions, a resort to the law of the jungle.

Wilcox was watching him intently but, with unusual tact, said nothing. Marshall hesitated slightly, holding onto the moment, the last seconds of a life which would never return to him. At least, he thought, he owed it this much, to remember exactly how it ended. Then he tore across the flap of the envelope.

Now he was a professional, like the others. He had lost something, it was true, but he consoled himself that the loss was inevitable. This was merely the final stage in a process of growing up which had taken away from him, one after the other, his childhood hopes, his confidence in his artistic genius, his respect for his father, his belief in God. Now his personal honor had been discarded, like an old handsome suitcase, admirable in its way, but too heavy for a fast flight.

He read the letter and passed it over. On Wilcox's face anxiety turned to relief, then to triumph.

"This is it, all right."

"Yes."

"Just what we want. He mentions Wenner's name three times—did you notice? That should take some explaining——"

Excitement had made him voluble. Marshall heard the sound of his voice without listening to the words. He asked himself, what did he feel? This was a big moment, after all—but he seemed to feel nothing. He had the means to win now, the weapon of destruction. It had been necessary and he did not regret it. Yet when Wilcox returned the letter to him he had to brace himself to touch it.

He felt an absolute necessity to get rid of Wilcox as soon as possible.

"I think the first thing we must do," he said, "is to make some copies of this as quickly as possible. Then we can put the original away in a safe-deposit." He took the cover off the portable typewriter on the desk. "Jane could do that now. The other thing is to notify Madame Verrier——"

"She's back at the hotel," said Wilcox. "I can ring her there."

As he moved toward the telephone Marshall said, "I thought you might prefer to tell her personally. . . ."

Wilcox put the telephone down. He looked from Marshall to Jane and said easily, "Okay, I can take a hint. We can talk about the details later. I'll ring you from my new hotel." He picked up his hat and nodded to Jane. "You did a wonderful job, honey." She said nothing. "See you."

When he had gone she said without expression, "I'll do those copies for you now."

"There's no hurry. I only said that to get rid of Wilcox."

"Oh, I see." She looked down at the letter lying on the desk where he had dropped it. "Well, that's it, isn't it? You've got what you needed. Everything's wonderful." With a rather forced cheerfulness she asked, "What will you do now?"

"Go back to New York. With this, they'll have to take notice of me."

"And Madame Verrier will get her money and Wilcox will get his job back—— Do you think it will do him any good, in the end?"

"He'll have his chance. He may be able to straighten himself out once this is over." He said impatiently, "Let's forget about Wilcox for the moment."

"All right." She picked up her hold-all from the floor and began to fumble in it for a packet of cigarettes. The bag was bulging with assorted objects—shoes, boxes of face powder, a tin of coffee, a brush and comb. "I had to bring all my stuff from the office," she explained. "I can hardly go back there."

"Of course not. But don't worry about that——"

"I wasn't worrying. I was tired of Gilbertson anyway." She lit her cigarette and sat down. "Don't look so solemn," she said. "You're wearing a face like a funeral."

"I hated myself for asking you to do this," he said unhappily.

"You mustn't let it get you down." She was determinedly cheerful. "I didn't enjoy it much myself. In fact, I felt worse about it than almost anything I've ever done. But it's done now—no use worrying about it any more."

"I *used* you," he said bitterly. It was, he remembered, the one fault he had never been able to forgive his father. It was just possible to accept the others—the lies, the tricks, the bluster and bragging, the bogus good-fellowship. Only this had seemed to him unforgivable—that love and loyalty should be treated as expendable assets, to be cashed as the occasion demanded.

She took his hand in hers, squeezing it gently in an effort at consolation. Her fingers were small, the nails neat and sensible. She wore a small ring, an onyx in the center of a circle of tiny diamonds. The onyx was chipped, the setting a little out of date. "Of course you used me," she said. "We always use the people who are fond of us. We're right to do so."

"No——" he protested.

"Yes. Because they ask for it. They want it. It gives them the sense of being needed." She looked up at him, as if perplexed by his simplicity. "Surely you understand that?"

He knew that she was wrong—his sense of having betrayed her remained. He said, excusing himself, "It had to be done. There was no other way. You do see that, don't you? With this letter we can't lose. It means the end of Furac—and Kingham as well, for that matter. We can wrap up the whole affair——"

"And then?"

Then, he thought, he would really have earned his freedom. He would be able to escape at last from those constant personal struggles, the detestable expedients. For five years he had stayed with the organization as a man might cling to a stick for fear of being unable to walk without it. When this affair was concluded he would have discharged all obligations, to himself or others. He could carry on alone. "That'll be the end as far as I'm concerned," he said. "I've had enough of them all. I shall walk out."

"Ahead of the game?" she said with slight irony.

"Yes. I suppose that's what I mean."

"And do what?"

"I'm not sure. I'll think of something." Perhaps he might go back to Paris and try painting again. Perhaps—— Now there seemed to be a hundred possibilities. "But first we'll take it easy for a while—go away for a holiday——"

"We?"

"Yes." He stopped walking and looked at her. "I want you to marry me, Jane."

There was a silence. She regarded him gravely and then shook her head. "No."

Her reply astonished him. It had never occurred to him that there was any chance of a refusal. "Why not?"

"Because—well——" She seemed to search desperately for some way of expressing herself. "Because I don't really know what sort of a person you are."

"But you must know me pretty well by now——"

"No, I don't really. Sometimes I haven't the least idea of how you're thinking or why you do things. Though I've grown to like you very much and I suppose I can even say that I'm in love with you, the idea of marriage frightens me somehow. You're still a foreigner to me in some ways, and I have a feeling that in America you might seem even more so."

"America isn't so different from here."

"Isn't it?" she said unbelievingly.

"No. People are pretty much the same wherever you go."

"I don't even believe that," she said sadly. "You see how it is, we disagree already."

"You said you were in love with me," he pointed out. He was almost pleading—the idea of going back home without her was unthinkable. "That must mean something. Why don't you give yourself some time to think about it? Come over with me when I go to New York. You can see how things are over there. If it doesn't work out, you can either get a job in the States or come back to England, whichever suits you." When she hesitated, he said, "For God's sake, what can you lose?"

"Nothing I haven't as good as lost already, I suppose," she admitted.

"So there you are. You can have a good time; get around. We could go and stay with my mother in Connecticut. She'd love to have you."

She laughed. "Getting the once-over from Mom. It sounds frightening. What is she like?"

"It's difficult for me to say." He became hesitant. How to describe his mother? He said inadequately, "I think she should appeal to you. She's very unpossessive. When I was younger I used to resent that sometimes. I wanted her to be more dependent on me. If she had been, of course, I should have spent my time struggling to get free."

"Yes, of course." A man never changed, she thought, in his attitude toward women—mother, mistress, wife, it was always the same. She asked, "Does she live alone?"

"Yes, except for an old colored couple and a local girl——"

She laughed. "In one of the big white colonial houses made of timber, with a paddock and a little lake——"

"Something like that. How did you know?"

"I go to the pictures. But it's no use trying to persuade me that those houses really exist. I'm fully prepared to find you're lying. When I get there I shall find it's just a tin shanty on the wrong side of the tracks. That's what happens to young girls who marry Americans."

He smiled. "So you'll come—if only to show me up?"

"All right."

He put his arms around her and was just about to kiss her when the telephone rang.

"Damn!" He picked up the receiver. "Who is it?"

"Mr. Marshall?" It was a girl's voice. "One moment, please." There was a click. "You're through now, Mr. Gilbertson."

"Is that you Marshall?" The well-known, languid voice carried more authority on the telephone when one couldn't actually see him. Marshall felt a spasm of nausea.

"Yes. How are you?"

"Excellent, thank you." There was a slight pause. The voice went on, bland as ever, "Excuse my asking, but you don't have my secretary with you by any chance, do you?"

He felt himself blushing. He was a child again, caught in the act of some petty but humiliating crime. He tried to answer casually. "Yes, she's here."

"Would you mind asking her to come to the phone?"

He hesitated. He had not fully prepared himself for this situation.

He glanced at Jane's face—her eyes were bright with alarm. "I'm sorry, that's not possible."

"Why not?" Gilbertson's voice was suddenly curt, military. "Is she afraid to speak to me?"

"If you have anything to say, you can say it to me. She acted under my instructions."

"She did *what*—under your instructions?"

"You must know, or you wouldn't have called me up."

"Naturally I know. I just wondered," said Gilbertson contemptuously, "whether you would have the courage to admit it. You told her to steal my confidential correspondence?"

"One letter only."

"On what authority?" When Marshall did not reply he went on, "Does Miss Lancing realize I can prosecute her for theft?"

"She realizes you won't." Marshall made an effort to pull himself together. He was getting the worst of this. "My recommendation is that you forget about your secretary's position and think about your own."

"Meaning what?"

"For God's sake, you don't want me to talk about it on the telephone, do you?"

There was quite a long silence. He could imagine Gilbertson at the other end of the line struggling to control his anger, to remember his wife, his country house, his son who in a year or two would be going up to Oxford. When he spoke at last, it was obvious that self-discipline had triumphed.

"Perhaps," he said with only slight distaste, "the best thing would be for us to meet and discuss the matter."

"If you like. Though I wouldn't like you to think that you can influence me in any way——"

"Perhaps not. But at least you'll be able to give me an explanation of your behavior. I think I'm entitled to that."

He would have to meet Gilbertson, if only because the prospect was so repellent to him; it was necessary to prove his own courage and determination before facing the storm which awaited him in New York.

"All right, I'll meet you. When will be convenient?"

"Not today, I'm afraid. I'm extremely busy." Not too busy for this, surely. But time was needed. Time to ring Furac, Kingham, to give the advance news of the attack, the fall of the first outpost, to confer on methods of defense. "Tomorrow I'm free."

"That's Saturday," said Marshall.

"Yes. Could you manage to come out to my place? We can talk in peace there."

He was about to insist that Gilbertson come and see him. Then he rejected the idea. The strength was his, and he must be generous. The least he could do was to allow his opponent the choice of ground.

"Very well. I'll come out tomorrow evening."

"We could manage," said Gilbertson with obvious reluctance, "to give you some dinner."

"No, thanks." He was definite. The thought of a meal with the Gilbertsons under present circumstances was unbearable. "I'll come out afterward."

Gilbertson did not press the invitation.

"Good. There's an excellent train from Waterloo at eight o'clock. Will that be convenient?"

"Yes—fine."

"I'll arrange to have you met at the station. . . ."

CHAPTER VI

THE LITTLE STATION was almost deserted when he got off the train. Down at the other end of the platform there was a woman waiting. As she approached him in the gathering twilight he saw that it was Mrs. Gilbertson.

"Charles asked me to apologize for him," she said. "He would have come himself but he had to go over and see one of our neighbors. Some argument about a fence and some cows."

"You shouldn't have bothered. I could have got a taxi."

"I doubt it. We have only one and he's usually drunk on Saturday nights." She gave her nervous, abrupt laugh. He suspected that the drunken taxi driver was a source of satisfaction rather than annoyance to her; these bucolic inconveniences made her feel closer to the realities of country life. "What a pity," she said rapidly as they got into the car, "that you can't stay over the weekend. Perhaps another time . . ."

"I'm afraid I shall be going back very soon."

"Yes, of course." The invitation, he realized, had not been seriously meant. It was just the sort of thing one always said, the reflex of a hostess. How much had Gilbertson told her? he wondered. He noticed no difference in her manner from the last time they had met—if anything, it was a little less formal, because now he was no longer a stranger. But that might mean nothing with people of this kind. She might be hating him, despising him, fearing him. He would not know.

They drove in silence for some time. Occasionally he glanced at her face. It was tense and strained, but that might be due to the effort of guiding the big car down the narrow country lanes. She drove erratically, crouching over the wheel and occasionally having trouble with the gears. Eventually, as if feeling her social obligations again, she said:

"I don't think you met either of my children when you visited us before."

"No. They were at school."

"James is away at some camp or other, playing at soldiers. But Gillian's home from school." She made a harassed gesture. "Now, of course, we haven't the remotest idea what to do with her."

"Has she no ideas herself?"

"Well, you know what girls are at that age—heads full of nonsense. They all want to be fashion models."

She stopped the car in front of the house. There was a young girl standing on the terrace, fresh and attractive in a shirt and tan-colored slacks.

"This is Mr. Marshall, dear."

"How do you do, Mr. Marshall." She shook hands dutifully, but her eyes were impatient. Parents were exasperating. They insisted on keeping you hanging about to meet their friends, people you didn't care about and who couldn't possibly care about you—business friends, Americans, usually about a hundred years old and as dull as ditchwater. She had done her bit. Then she turned back to her mother.

"Mummy," she said eagerly, "the Dawsons just rang up. They're going to a dance in Guildford. Can I go with them?"

"Well, I don't know——"

"Oh, Mummy, *please* . . ."

She stood there, fidgeting impatiently. Plainly, both Marshall and her mother existed in her mind merely as obstacles to her pleasure. Marshall remembered the old rule that to establish ascendancy one should always seem to be in more of a hurry than the other fellow. The young did it without effort or intention. Who has less time to spare than a girl of seventeen waiting to go out on a date?"

"Have you asked your father?"

"He's not back yet. I said I thought it would be all right."

"Well, I suppose so. But you can't go in those clothes."

"I can change in a second." She was already halfway up the stairs.

"Well, don't be too late. . . ." Mrs. Gilbertson looked apologetically at Marshall. "They're always chasing off here and there."

He smiled back, the sort of smile that older people gave. But the smile was false, and he was aware of a stab of wounded vanity because the girl had so obviously found him uninteresting. Could he really seem so old to her? he asked himself. He wanted to tell her that at least he was on her side. To him, too, most of the pretensions of adult life appeared as nothing better than an elaborate fraud. The young were right, he thought, in their instinctive distrust of authority. They watched the antics of their elders like savages confronted with the white man's magic—powerless, bored, suspicious without knowing why. Well, soon they would know why, as he did now. In time they would become part of the fraud themselves.

"You'll have a drink?" said Mrs. Gilbertson.

Always the drink, the scotch, the glass of sherry, the apéritif, the martini (very, very dry, you said, and the barman understood—he gave you straight gin with a twist of lemon floating in it). Nothing could be done without a drink, without the spurious air of friendliness that went with it. He accepted because he was afraid to alarm her; everybody knew that Americans drank all the time, and Mrs. Gilbertson might read something sinister into his refusal. And, indeed, his acceptance seemed to reassure her. She knew something was wrong, but it could not be as bad as all that if you could sit in friendly conversation over a drink on the terrace on a summer evening. She talked about her children. The boy was clever, he had won a scholarship, but shy and slow to make friends. Gillian was popular but scatterbrained. She had almost too many friends. Some of the boys were much older than she was. . . .

"So long as they don't get drunk and go driving around in cars . . . That's what worries me most. But she's a sensible girl at heart," she added with more faith than conviction. "It's no use denying it, children are a great responsibility—as well as a great expense." She had not talked of her children so much on his previous visit. Was this, he wondered, a roundabout way of appealing for sympathy, of throwing herself on his mercy? "You're not married, Mr. Marshall?"

"No."

"No, of course not." It was as if somehow she had held an irrational hope that he might be. "I remember you told us . . ."

Gilbertson came round the side of the house. He was dressed in the dilapidated tweeds he affected for weekends. What would happen, Marshall wondered, when they wore out completely? He could hardly wear new ones. Perhaps he arranged for them to be broken in by the gardener.

"Sorry I couldn't meet you, Marshall. I got caught up in an argument with a farmer——" He went into some detail about a minor boundary dispute which had been brought to a head by the incursion of a Jersey cow into his kitchen garden. It was a dull story, and even Gilbertson himself seemed to get bored with it after a while. But his code of manners obviously demanded that some pretense of general conversation should be made, even on an occasion like this. It would have been hard to say which of the three was the most ill at ease. Eventually Gilbertson said, "So there we are. Not that I suppose I shall be able to get a penny out of him when it comes down to it. . . ." He seemed suddenly weary of this pantomime of normal behavior. It was impossible for him to keep the anxiety out of his eyes, the deepened furrows of his face. "But perhaps we'd better get down to business. Would you like to come into my study?"

The study was quite a small room, rather dark and smelling of dust. In one corner there was a set of golf clubs, in another a pair of fishing rods. On the bookshelves were mainly sets of bound volumes—*Country Life, Chambers' Encyclopaedia* (1935), the *Waverley Novels*. Gilbertson cleared the front of the desk and then half sat, half leaned against it. He motioned Marshall to a leather club chair. The chair was deep, and when he sat down he found Gilbertson towering almost directly above him, looking down at him with his melancholy bloodhound face. Always before, he had thought of Gilbertson almost as a caricature, a man whose every action carried a slight touch of exaggeration and absurdity. But now he was no longer ridiculous; in this moment of crisis he had acquired a sort of desperate dignity, an air bordering on menace.

They regarded each other in silence for a little while. Then Gilbertson said curtly:

"How is Miss Lancing?"

"Fine, thanks."

"I hope you're looking after her properly. She's deserved well of you." He added sourly, "I imagine the rates of pay are pretty high for work of that kind?"

Now that they were alone, it was evidently permissible to be offensive. Marshall could not help feeling sympathy for him. It was always a terrible thing to find oneself betrayed. He said with careful moderation, "Is that why you asked me to come here—to make cracks about Miss Lancing?"

Gilbertson shook his head, then half closed his eyes like a man who had felt a spasm of physical pain. "I trusted her," he said.

"I'm sorry." Marshall looked away. "Believe me, I'm sorry it had to be done."

"Is that considered enough?"

"I believe my action was justified by what I found in the letter," said Marshall stubbornly.

"Do you? I'm afraid you wouldn't find many people in this country to agree with you. By British law nobody has a right to open confidential letters—not even the police——"

"I know, I know," Marshall said wearily. "But let's be realistic. I've got the letter now, and you can't do a thing about it. You have to face the present situation." To save Gilbertson the indignity of asking, he added, "I should tell you that I know all about Furac's methods of doing business. We have a good deal of other information——"

"We?"

"Myself and Wilcox. Wilcox went to Zurich and made inquiries."

"I see." Gilbertson was silent for a moment. "Have you spoken to your superiors in New York about this?"

"Not yet."

"But you propose to do so, I take it?"

"Naturally."

"Did they know you were making these—investigations?"

"No. In fact, they've been doing their best to keep me in the States. But you know all this," he said impatiently. "There's a telephone line to New York. You must have spoken to Kingham yesterday."

After a moment's hesitation Gilbertson said, "We had a short conversation. He used some harsh words about you, as you can imagine."

"And what instructions did he give you?"

Marshall was ashamed as soon as he had spoken. It was a cheap taunt, but Gilbertson took no offense. He appeared to regard it rather as a fortunate opening for something he had to say.

"I'm interested," he said, "that you should put it like that. It confirms my suspicion that you have an oversimplified approach to this very complex situation." He spoke coldly and slightly patronizingly, master to pupil. "Please try to realize that I am not a puppet of Mr. Kingham's. Nor," he added, "have I the slightest desire to become involved in any of your faction fights in New York."

"Do you really think this is just a personal feud between myself and Kingham?"

"In that direction," said Gilbertson with feeling, "nothing would surprise me."

"I can assure you it isn't. And I'm afraid it's impossible for you to shrug your way out of it. This letter definitely shows you to be involved——"

"Have I denied it?" His voice held more exasperation than guilt. "Certainly I knew of these transactions. But I don't take responsibility for them. Why should I? They weren't my idea."

"Whose idea were they then?"

"Your father's."

Gilbertson was regarding him closely for his reaction. This, no doubt, was a shot he had been saving up. Don't fire till you see the whites of their eyes—then give it to them. . . . But he had misjudged his effect. Marshall was neither disconcerted nor even, on reflection, particularly surprised. He had not thought of his father as the initiator of the scheme, but once it was suggested to him, he was only too ready to believe it.

"That sounds plausible," he said. He felt the necessity to make his position clearer. "I should perhaps inform you that I have no great admiration for my father. So far as I was concerned——" He stopped himself. His family problems were no concern of Gilbertson's. "How did it start?" he asked.

Gilbertson levered himself off the desk, walked around it, and sat down in the chair behind. It was as if he had abandoned his first idea of dominating Marshall and was now prepared to try reason and explanation.

"It was after the war," he said, "that I first met him. I was trying to build up a business again. It wasn't easy—my old office had been destroyed by bombs and I'd been in the Far East for several years. But the people I used to know before I joined the Army were very helpful and I picked up a few small agencies, enough to pay my rent, but that was about all. Then one day your father walked in. He'd heard of me from a friend of mine in New York and he was looking for a distributor in England. We met a few times and he took a fancy to me. That was how he put it, anyway. He liked to think of himself as having an instinctive judgment of men. He was the sort of person——"

Marshall cut in, "I know what sort of a person he was."

There had been no pain, or practically none, on hearing that his father was dishonest. But this description of his petty vanities aroused a trace of some old, unsuspected loyalty. You could never completely eradicate the emotions of your youth. They remained within you like the germs of a forgotten sickness, dormant, walled off, yet still carrying a primitive flicker of life, ready to awake and return to the attack if the opportunity arose.

Gilbertson was saying, ". . . and, as you can imagine, the agency was attractive to me. We did very well at first. European industry hadn't had time to change over to peacetime production and we had a clear field. In fact, we did so well that I hadn't really time for the other agencies, and when your father suggested I should give them up I agreed. That made me dependent on Marshall's, of course, but it was obviously a decision one had to take sometime and I wasn't too worried. But a year later we ran into trouble. The wheels were beginning to turn again in Europe. And their costs were lower than ours. They were prepared to do anything to get back into the market again. They cut down the price until we couldn't get anywhere near them. It seemed as if the only sensible thing for Marshall's to do was to pull out of the European market altogether. I wouldn't have been surprised. After all, they were making plenty at home and in other parts of the world. But your father wouldn't give up. Not because he gave a damn about me but because he'd gone into Europe against the advice of his Board. It seems they'd told him this would happen and he wouldn't take any notice. He was determined not to be proved wrong. He came over here and told me that he was going to find a way of making the European area pay—somehow. And he did. He found Furac."

He paused, remembering, and then went on, "Perhaps you can imagine the awkwardness of my own position when he told me what he was proposing to do. I was tied to him completely by this time and he knew it. If he withdrew the agency I was broke. You may think I should have done the big thing and told him to go to hell, but I didn't. It was an underhand proposition and I didn't like it, but I had my wife and children to think of. If it had been a British regulation we were breaking, I should probably have acted differently, but the way I looked at it, this was an American law and, if the Americans wanted to get around it, it was up to them. I wasn't the keeper of your father's conscience."

"So it didn't worry you?"

He said sharply, "I told you I didn't like it. But I don't feel ashamed." He showed his long teeth in the trace of a smile. "Not nearly so much as you do, I should imagine, for stealing my correspondence." He went on before Marshall had time to protest, "And don't tell me this might make all the difference in the next war. I know a great deal more about war than you do. I gave up six years of my life to the last one—while you people were making money."

"We fought too, you know."

"Eventually. Eventually. But please don't think I resent your good fortune. I'm just trying to point out your approach to this question is to some extent a function of your income. You can indulge in moral attitudes which I can't afford."

"That doesn't make the attitudes wrong."

Gilbertson did not reply. Suddenly Marshall grew impatient. This was getting them nowhere. "Hell," he said, "I can see your point of view. I'm not blaming you for what you did. But that's not the point. I just can't leave things to go on as they are."

Gilbertson hesitated for a moment, as if wondering whether, in spite of his inner convictions, there might be something to be gained from making one last attempt. When he spoke, the sour, contemptuous note had left his voice; he had decided to throw away the advantage given to him by Marshall's theft of the letter.

"Why not?" he said. "After all, who's losing by this? Ask yourself that." He leaned forward. "Marshall, I think I can talk sensibly to you. Many of your countrymen, if you don't mind my saying so, have a tendency to wrap up the facts of life in a cocoon of pompous verbiage and idealistic fluff. It's a vice of conquering nations—we went in for it a great deal in the days of Victoria. But when you're up against it you have to look at things as they are. Supposing some of these instruments *are* getting to Russia or China or wherever it is. Is that going to start a war? Is it going to affect the result of a war if one does start? Does it, in fact, make a damn bit of difference to the balance of power in the world? You know as well as I do that at any moment there might be a diplomatic shuffle or a lessening in tension or whatever they call it, and these things would be taken off the prohibited list. It just doesn't make sense."

"Not to us, maybe. But it's not for us to decide. If it's the law——"

"Your law—not mine."

"Sure. So it's for me to carry it out." When Gilbertson said nothing he added, "Believe me, I wish this didn't have to happen. I can see it means a great deal to you."

"It's my livelihood. Naturally"—he picked his words carefully; even now it would never do to sound melodramatic—"I'm deeply involved. I've spent twenty-five years trying to get back into the world I was born into. . . ."

In Marshall, sympathy struggled with incomprehension. This futile, obsessive attempt to put the clock back . . . Gilbertson was a man of intelligence and ability, in spite of his affectations. How could he fail to realize the unreality of his ambition?

"Do you really think it was worth it?"

"My dear boy," said Gilbertson pityingly, "you don't do things because you think they are worth it. You don't estimate profit and loss in these matters. The future's a mystery—life is a jump in the dark. You jump in the direction you do, not because it's the sensible thing, but because you must. If you break your neck as a consequence, there's nothing to be done about it." It came to Marshall that Gilbertson knew perfectly well that his own ambitions were impractical and, to others, absurd. To him, it was Marshall who was childish in his demand for common sense in a world which had never been even remotely sensible. "Now it's your turn to jump. Do so by all means. But don't think that things will turn out as you expect. They never do."

There was a silence. Outside now it was quite dark. They could hear the sound of a train in the distance, puffing its way across the green fields toward the south coast. Gilbertson gave the impression of searching his mind for some other avenue of persuasion worth exploring. Finally he seemed to decide that there was none.

"You're quite determined to go ahead with this?" he said.

"Yes."

"Then there's no point in wasting time." He got up from his seat. He had retained his dignity, if nothing else. From now on, for him, there was no security in possessions, no pride of ownership, no confidence in the future; he had lost, but at least he had not abased himself unnecessarily. "No doubt you'd like to get back to London."

As they went into the hall, Mrs. Gilbertson came out of the drawing room. She was carrying a pair of spectacles in one hand and a book in the other. Marshall suddenly had a picture of her sitting alone, pretending to read, as she waited for the sound of their footsteps.

"All finished?" she said anxiously.

"Yes," said Gilbertson.

It was dark in the hall. She snapped on the light and looked at their faces. Then something seemed to happen quite suddenly to her personality. She was no longer awkward and self-conscious, tortured by the desire to be correct. It was as if despair had made her drunk.

"And what are you going to do, Mr. Marshall?" she asked.

He had been asked this question so often before, sometimes with impatience, more often with a lukewarm, perfunctory interest, but never, until now, with fear. Always in the past the question had meant what was he going to do with himself? Now he disposed of the lives of others.

Before he could think of a tactful answer Gilbertson cut in, "I think Mr. Marshall's in rather a hurry for his train, Hilda. I can explain to you later——"

"There are plenty of trains," she said. Then she turned to Marshall. "Before you go I'd like to be sure you understand the situation. My husband may not have made it entirely clear to you because——" She hesitated. "Because he's too proud—he doesn't like to make a scene. And no more do I, but then somebody has to, don't they, if they see their whole life going——"

"Hilda!"

"Please let me speak." Her eyes were still on Marshall. "I don't understand you people. You come here, expecting to be liked—you visit our houses, we behave to you as we would toward anyone else, and then——" The tears were beginning to run down her cheeks. She was almost incoherent with grief. "I want you to know what you're doing to us. My husband and I had to start again from nothing at the end of the war. Gradually we built up something for ourselves—now you want to take it away again. Your father made him do it—do you know that? You don't suppose he wanted to, do you? But he hadn't any choice. And now you come here, sitting in judgment on him——" She shouted at him, "Who do you think you are, for heaven's sake?"

He felt no resentment toward her, only pity. He would have liked to promise her hope, but there was no turning back now. He had paid for his victory with Jane's honor and his own—it was not thinkable that at this stage he should change his mind and refuse it. Somebody must suffer. If you accepted action, you accepted with it suffering, corruption, betrayal, shame. You did not will them, except in so far as you willed the thing that caused them. For the first time he felt for his father the faint stirrings of understanding, almost of sympathy.

"I'm sorry," he said.

She looked at him as Madame Verrier had looked at him in the hospital corridor on the night of her husband's death.

"You're sorry," she said bitterly. Then, quite quietly: "I've finished what I had to say. You can leave now—go and catch your train. I never want to set eyes on you again."

She turned around and went back into the drawing room, slamming the door behind her. It was just possible to hear her sobbing from behind the door. Gilbertson made as if to follow her and then changed his mind. His face wore the baffled, weary expression of a man growing old in a world he has ceased to understand.

"It's best to leave her for the moment," he said. "I'll drive you down to the station."

PART VI

CHAPTER I

He looked at his face closely in the mirror fixed behind the door of his cabin. It seemed to him that a man ought to do this periodically, just as he ought to review his financial position, estimating profit and loss, capital expended, reserves for the future. A face, of course, could never be as encouraging as a balance sheet. You never made a profit, you never grew richer—the triumph lay in keeping down the inevitable drain on your resources, in postponing for as long as possible the day when you looked and saw that you had nothing left.

In his early twenties there had been little enough to read. Youth, in those days, was like an enormous fortune which you spent freely since you could not imagine that any extravagance could diminish it. But recently, each year, his face had begun to tell him something. He could see, not exactly wrinkles—it was not as bad as that yet—but a slight coarsening of the skin on close inspection, a darkening of the beard area, a fixity of the creases of expression. By most standards he looked young for his age (and why not? He had been rich and idle and cared for; he had never worked very hard or had great responsibilities; he was no more than a moderate drinker) and yet, when he looked at himself very closely, in this particular light, the secret was out. He was no longer a young man.

And so what? Did he have to be young, if it came to that? There were plenty of his friends in their late twenties who were fathers of families, were putting on weight and growing bald and had accepted readily—indeed almost eagerly—a comfortable, canasta-playing, carpet-slipper life-in-death. They were not discontented; they did not watch the years going by with an uneasiness which at any moment might mount into panic. They had decided on the future they wanted; they had set a course and were sailing it, would go on sailing it with all the skill and strength they could muster. The end was decided. Only the means remained as a preoccupation.

When you are moving in the right direction, he thought, time is not too important. Life is really too long for most of us, anyway—it gives us a plentiful margin to realize what gifts we have. If we are making any progress at all we shall get there in the end. But what of the man who is making no progress, who has not even decided on a course, who may be drifting, for all he knows, in the wrong direction, toward disaster? Who sees the years of decision passing by him, knowing that a day will soon come when he is too old, not so much to accomplish something new as to have the mental resilience to attempt it?

He snapped off the cabin light. In the twilight his own image looked more reassuring. He was once again as most people must see him, a youngish man of pleasant, prosperous appearance on whom so far life had sat lightly—a man of fortunate background and considerable opportunity. This insistent conviction that time was running out and that he must decide to set the course of his life before it was too late—this was his own secret. Only Jane knew him well enough to share it.

The engines had quietened as the ship reduced speed. They must be moving into the channel at the mouth of the Hudson. When he went up on deck he found that most of the passengers had moved forward to the bow, eager to catch their first sight of Manhattan. There were a great many unfamiliar faces, an unusual amount of noise, a profusion of children. In these last few hours the barriers between first class and tourist had been relaxed.

He found Jane standing at the rail. She squeezed to one side to make room for him. There was land on either side now. The ship had been delayed by storms and it was already dark—the lights were glittering on Long Island and the Jersey shore. Apartment and office buildings, ugly and featureless in the daylight, were converted by darkness into a row of glittering jewels, rendered doubly brilliant by their reflections in the dark mirror of the waterfront. Car headlights streamed along the parkways like tracer bullets.

"Can we see it?" said Jane.

"Manhattan? Not yet. In a moment or two——"

Over the whole harbor there was hanging a shimmering incandescent glow from some source as yet unseen. Then the ship veered slightly, the channel curved, a tongue of land moved away on the starboard bow, and there it was; very small at first, the brilliant focal point of the glow which lit the sky, then gradually discernible as a mass of separate units. A red searchlight stabbed intermittently at the clouds with enormous urgency.

"There it is," he said.

She squeezed his hand and said nothing. The traffic in the channel was increasing. They heard the loud, hollow boom of a siren.

"What's that?"

"The Staten Island ferry."

He looked across the water at the people leaning against the rail of the ferryboat and knew he was home. Until that moment Manhattan had been a façade, a view, a picture postcard. Now it was the old, familiar, teeming ant heap, the home of express elevators and up-to-the-minute air-conditioned funeral parlors and the hamburger with the college education. Not to speak of Miss Rheingold and nobody (but nobody) underselling Gimbels. . . .

The buildings of Wall Street were discernible now.

"This beats getting in by plane," said Marshall. "You get the sense of an event."

"Even for you?"

"Yes, even for me." He waved a hand at the familiar yet ever-startling skyline. "What do you think of it?"

"It's amazing, of course." Her voice was tentative, as if she had difficulty in interpreting her own feelings. "But—at the same time—intimidating——"

"Because it's so big?"

"Not only that. It's not a friendly approach; somehow it's indifferent. You can come if you like or you can stay away. It doesn't seem to care."

He tightened his grip on her hand. She was right, of course. Manhattan, he thought, was like a wealthy and fashionable woman waiting to have a photograph taken. It was used to being rich and important and admired; it quite enjoyed showing off but in a casual, almost contemptuous way. At heart it was totally preoccupied with itself.

"But then," she added, "I'm a foreigner. After all, why should it speak to me? It doesn't know me. Perhaps with you it's different."

He shook his head. "It's the same with everybody. You have to take it as you find it."

Shortly afterward they docked at the Cunard pier. They had just finished with the immigration authorities when Marshall saw a tall, bulky figure striding toward him across the lounge.

"Jeff!"

"Hello, boy! Is this a surprise!" As hearty as usual, thought Marshall, perhaps even more than usual. And what the hell was Jeff doing here anyway? He had deliberately told no one when he was coming or by which route. Had the company resorted to using detectives? It was by no means impossible.

Jane was standing behind him. "Jane, this is my brother Jeff. Jane Lancing."

"Glad to meet you, Miss Lancing."

"How do you do." She smiled. "You're just exactly as I imagined you." She explained, "Chris has told me a lot about you."

"Nothing bad, I hope." He laughed, too loudly. His uncertainty was obvious. Evidently nobody had told him anything at all about Miss Lancing. The detective agency had slipped up on that one. He turned back to Marshall.

"Well, you're certainly looking fit, Chris."

"Thanks."

"Did you have a good crossing? Plenty of sun—good food—that's the way to do it." They began to move with the crowd toward the gangway. "And you, Miss Lancing—you enjoyed your trip? Fine, fine. Believe me, if I had my way I'd travel everywhere by sea. You get some time to think; you can get your problems into perspective. Don't you think so, Chris?"

"It's a point of view," said Marshall absently. His cabin steward had collected his suitcases and was signaling to him. "If you don't mind, I'd better just make arrangements about the baggage."

"Don't worry about a thing." Jeff put a reassuring arm around his shoulder. "Just relax. There's a guy I know who manages shipments for us and he's promised to fix it so that you won't have any unnecessary delays. He knows the customs boys and they're prepared to do him a little favor now and then. . . . So we should be able to whip you through pretty fast. Then I've got a car waiting outside to take you to your hotel——"

"Jane will be coming with us. She's also staying at the Plaza."

"Well, that's wonderful—wonderful." His eyes searched Marshall's face for some clue to the situation but found none. He turned to Jane. "Are you staying long in New York, Miss Lancing?"

"I'm not sure."

"You're from London?"

Marshall cut in restlessly, "You know, I think we ought to be getting off the boat." He smiled. "You two can play Twenty Questions later."

For all Jeff's influence, it took them over half an hour to get through customs. Down the street a company limousine was waiting.

"Do you always do things in such style?" said Jane admiringly.

"By no means. In fact, this is quite unusual." Marshall looked pointedly at his brother. "Isn't that so, Jeff?"

"Well, I don't know." Jeff wriggled in his seat. "After all, you don't come back from Europe every day."

"That's true."

The car pulled up at the Fifty-ninth Street entrance to the hotel, and he was really home. Even the doorman recognized him—or pretended to. After they had registered, Jane said, "If you'll excuse me, I'm tired. I'll go straight to bed."

"Sleep well," said Marshall. "I'll see you in the morning."

When they had seen her into the elevator, Jeff said, "Are you in a hurry to go to bed?"

"Not particularly."

"I thought we might have a little talk——"

"Sure. Why not come up to my room? I'll tell room service to send up a bottle of scotch——"

"I think you'll find that's been done." Jeff's voice showed embarrassment. It had seemed a good idea at the time, but now he was not so sure.

"Well——" Marshall looked at him with amusement. "We'd better go up right away and see what else Santa Claus has brought."

Up in the room there were two bottles of scotch, some soda, and a bowl of ice. Marshall poured out the drinks. There was a short silence.

Eventually Jeff said, "Seems a nice girl."

"Jane? Yes—she's a very nice girl."

"You met her on the boat?"

"No, I met her in London." It was time to put Jeff out of his misery. "She used to work for Gilbertson." After a slight pause to let Jeff take in the implications of this, he added, "We're thinking of getting married."

"Married!" Astonishment was mixed with something like relief. So far Jeff had given the impression of improvising, without confidence, in a situation which was strange to him and more than a little distasteful. But now at last he felt firm ground beneath his feet. He knew how to act when people got married. "Well, congratulations! I'm delighted. But why so secretive? Why didn't you let me know earlier? I was talking to her as if she was someone you'd just met casually. I didn't know she was liable to become one of the family." He shook his head ruefully. "Hell, what she must think of me——"

"I shouldn't worry about that."

"It's all very well for you to say, but you don't understand women like I do. These things matter to them. For God's sake, you never even wrote or anything! Does Mother know?"

"No," said Marshall. "Nobody knows. Anyway, it's not definite yet—that's really the reason I didn't write to you. Jane has to look around here, meet Mother, see if she likes America, and so on. She has to get herself adjusted. After all, we haven't known each other so very long."

"Oh, sure—I understand."

"So if you don't mind, I'd rather you didn't mention it to anyone."

"Don't worry about that. I'll be as tight as a clam." He became solemn. "Chris, I'm sure she's a wonderful girl and you'll be very happy."

"You hardly know her," Marshall pointed out.

"No, but I know you. You've taken plenty of time to make your choice, but now you have, I'm confident that it'll be a good one. And, as you know, it's always been my conviction that what you really needed to stabilize you and give you a sense of purpose was a wife—the right kind of wife. Why, I remember the last time we spoke together——"

Marshall ceased to listen. He was accustomed to Jeff, on occasions like this, saying with an air of discovery all the correct, conventional things that had been said a million times before. He not only failed to add to one's enjoyment of an experience by talking about it—he managed positively to destroy it. In his hands marriage became no longer an adventure but a sound measure of mental and physical hygiene, an expression of conformity with the collective outlook of Nice Girls and Regular Guys, a vote of confidence in the American way of life. Behind all his genuine good will there was an unmistakable note of satisfaction. He was going to be proved right after all. Chris would soon forget all his egghead nonsense and settle down like anyone else—some people just matured late, that was all.

The flow dried up momentarily. Jeff paused and then said, "Of course this explains a lot. I was wondering why you stopped over in England so long."

"Were you?" Marshall looked at him without expression. The courtesies were over now—they were moving toward business.

"Why, yes. You were expected back sooner."

"So everyone was anxious about me?" It was impossible to refrain from teasing him a little, if only as a reprisal for being so dull.

"Well, not exactly anxious——"

Marshall smiled maliciously. "That's the way it looks. The company pulling wires at Cunard to find out which sailing I was coming on. Calling up all the hotels to check my booking. Little presents in my room. And you—down to meet me at the dock in a big black Cadillac. . . . Quite touching, it was. Especially since by rights I ought to be in the doghouse for overstaying my leave."

"Hell," said Jeff awkwardly, "if I'd known you'd take it like this—— I mean—well, if a man can't meet his own brother off the boat without arousing a lot of suspicions——"

Jeff made a halfhearted attempt to take offense. But his uneasiness was too great to make it convincing, even to himself. Marshall got up and poured more whisky into his glass. He looked at the sulky, anxious face and said, "Poor Jeff. They certainly give you some lousy jobs, don't they?"

He replied weakly, "I don't get you."

"You shouldn't let them do it, you know. After all, you don't have to do what Kingham tells you." Marshall's voice hardened. It was the thought of Kingham which made the difference. It was possible to play it almost as a game up to a certain point. A vicious, dangerous game, of course, one in which he had to make certain of winning, but nevertheless something without too much passion —he could, for instance, spare a little time to amuse himself with Jeff. But with the mention of Kingham his hands began to tremble and there was no possibility of taking a light, civilized attitude any more. There was something almost frightening to him in the realization of how much he hated Kingham. With sudden viciousness he said, "Why don't you try telling him to do his own dirty work?"

"Honest, Chris, I don't know what's got into you," Jeff said plaintively.

"You know damn well what's got into me. You can't be as dumb as that. The last time we spoke together I was right on the bottom —a piece of nothing. Remember? You were practically doing me a favor saving my job for me. And then what happens? I go back to Europe and I do everything wrong. I stay too long, I talk to all the people I was told to avoid as if they had smallpox, I notify nobody of my movements—and what do I get? Practically a ticker-tape reception. Do you think I don't know why?"

Jeff's face had become contorted into a characteristic expression.

His brow was wrinkled, his eyes slightly narrowed, as if he were suffering from some internal pain which he was too manly to complain about in words. Ever since childhood it had been his way of reacting to a situation which he had discovered himself incapable of handling.

"I can imagine just how it happened," said Marshall. "Kingham came to you and said, 'Jeff, my boy, I want to confide in you. The truth is, I'm very worried about your brother. He's been talking to some very peculiar people in Europe and they've filled him up with all sorts of crazy ideas. Now I'm fond of Chris and I don't want him to do anything foolish. For the sake of the organization, I think somebody ought to meet him the moment he arrives in New York and straighten him out a little. As you can imagine, it's difficult for me, in my position, but you, as his brother——' " He stopped for a moment. "Wasn't that it?"

Sulkily Jeff replied, "Well, if it was, I can't see anything so terrible in that."

"Not so far as I'm concerned. But it doesn't look so good for you, if that's the sort of job they hand you." The wrinkles on Jeff's forehead deepened, as if his initial agony had suddenly become intensified. Really, thought Marshall, there was no satisfaction in this—it was like hitting a man who lay helpless on the ropes, silently pleading with his eyes for mercy. In a softer voice he asked, "How much did Kingham tell you—about this particular episode, I mean?"

"He wasn't very definite. Naturally I asked him, but he didn't seem to want to say too much. He said there was a certain suspicion that some of the French consignments might have fallen into the wrong hands."

"I see." Marshall hesitated. The question now was, what to do with Jeff? Throw him out with an offensive message to take back to Kingham, use him as the first show of strength? He deserved it for allowing himself to be placed in such a humiliating position, and yet . . . For all his weakness and stupidity, for all his pompous moralizing, he was essentially a decent, kindly man who would sooner do good than harm if it was not too costly or dangerous. And they were, after all, brothers. In the moment that Marshall made his decision he suddenly knew that it was not only the right one, it was also the wisest.

"I'd better let you have the whole story," he said.

As he told it he watched Jeff's face with considerable care. It was important to know how far the knowledge went. He had never really thought it possible that Jeff was in on the secret, and now he was certain. His brother's astonishment was genuine enough. They had told him nothing. He was just the office boy, to be fed with as much information as was suitable for him to hear.

"But that's terrible—terrible," he stammered. "Hell, it really is." He looked up pleadingly. "Can you be certain? I mean—have you any proof?"

"Yes." Marshall hesitated, but there was no point in turning back now. "We have a letter."

"Can I see it?"

Marshall opened his brief case and took out a sheet of paper. "This is a photostat."

Jeff rubbed his fingers on the stiff texture of the paper. For a moment he did not look at what was printed on it. Reproachfully he said, "You could have trusted me with the original."

Marshall said nothing. The original letter was in the file with the photostats and he could just as easily have handed it to his brother to read. There was, he knew well, no danger that Jeff would steal it or destroy it. Then why the photostat? He could find no very clear reason in his own mind. A month ago, he thought with shame, he would not have done it. Now distrust was becoming a habit.

"Read it," he said sharply.

Jeff read through the letter.

"How did you get this?" he said.

It was something you couldn't be delicate about, and certainly it would be a mistake to strike an apologetic note. Marshall realized that this was one of the things he would have to face all through the struggle—that, once he produced the letter, his moral initiative was gone. He no longer represented virtue against evil. The best way was to attack. It was necessary, and he had done it. They could think what they liked.

"I stole it," he said. The effort was painful, but he would make it more painful still. He would leave no secret vulnerable point for his enemies to attack. "Or, to be more accurate, I got Jane to steal it for me. She was Gilbertson's secretary."

He waited, searching Jeff's face for any sign of censure or protest, ready to hit back immediately with every weapon at his command. But Jeff merely said, "So she comes into this too?"

"Yes."

So far as one could see, Jane's involvement made little impact on Jeff. The enormity of the main situation filled his mind to the exclusion of any side issues. He ran a hand over his forehead. "Christ, I don't know what to say," he said. And then, in a voice reminiscent of the days when they had got into scrapes together as children: "What are we going to do, Chris?"

His helplessness was complete. He had given up any claim to leadership. The claim had never been convincing anyway. "You don't have to do anything," said Marshall. "This is my affair."

"Well, yes." There was relief in Jeff's eyes. "But in a way it affects both of us." He said incredulously, "You say it was Dad who started this?"

"Gilbertson said so, and I've no reason to disbelieve him."

"He might have just said it as a get-out for himself."

"I don't think so."

"I just can't believe Dad would do a thing like that."

"Can't you?" said Marshall indifferently. "To me it seems just the sort of thing he would have done."

With a flash of resentment Jeff said, "You always hated him."

"No." Somehow it was very important that he should be clear on this point. He said, "It's not as simple as that. At first I admired him, I was proud of him. Then I found he was a liar and a cheat and I despised him—I despised myself, too, for having been taken in by him." He struggled to explain. "It wasn't him I hated—it was what he did——"

"That's the same thing."

"No, it isn't. I used to think so, but it isn't. It's not always easy to do things the way you want to do them." Who was he now to condemn the old man? He too had betrayed a trust and pleaded the justification of events. If his father had lived he could have gone to him now and said, "I am grown up at last, I am a man as you are, you can talk to me and I will understand." But the time for that had long since gone. He heard Jeff saying:

"You sound as if you were making excuses for him."

He smiled. Jeff, the believer, would not find it easy to reconcile himself to the betrayal of his faith. It was to those who expected nothing that forgiveness came most easily.

"Why not? He probably thought at the time that the law was stupid and couldn't see why he should sacrifice his business to it. He had a point of view."

"I can't see it."

Marshall stopped himself from saying anything more. You could not explain a thing like that to Jeff, who lived in a world where everything was black or white. The two brothers sat for a moment in silence. Then Jeff said, "Are you going to see Kingham?"

"No." He had thought about this on the boat. "I'm not interested in Kingham."

Jeff said resentfully, "He put me in a hell of a spot. Asking me to come and meet you like this. Not even telling——" He squared his great shoulders. "I think I'm going to go and ask him for an explanation——"

Marshall shook his head. "I wouldn't." He had no faith in Jeff's ability to cope with Kingham. Even with all the cards in his hand he was certain to be outmaneuvered in some way. No, the way to handle Kingham was not to give him a chance of a straight fight at all. "I should leave Kingham right out of it." He said carefully, "This is an important matter. It needs to be taken right up to the top."

Jeff ran a finger around the inside of his collar. "Bernstein?" he said.

"Who else?"

"Do you think he knows——" Jeff stopped, frowning at the possible implications of the question.

"If he doesn't, it's certainly time he heard."

"I guess so," said Jeff unhappily. He was silent for a moment. "And what about you?"

Marshall pretended to misunderstand the question. "I plan to stay in New York for two or three days—show Jane the sights and so on. Then we both might go out to Falls Ridge. Mother's at home, I suppose?"

"Oh, sure. She'll be there," said Jeff abstractedly. He put his question again, more specifically this time: "What I really meant was—aren't you coming with me to see Bernstein?"

Marshall shook his head. He hardly knew Bernstein; he had no personal feelings about him one way or the other. But when you were in a strong position it was always worth while emphasizing it from the very beginning. "This time people are coming to see me."

CHAPTER II

He woke up next morning with a feeling of unusual contentment. It was good to be off the ship, to sleep on a bed of adequate size, even to hear the traffic rumbling and hooting below the window. It was pleasant to be finished with waiting. The meeting with Jeff had gone well last night; the right atmosphere had been established from the start. It had really been a mistake on their part, he decided, thinking it over, to send Jeff at all. Kingham had shown his anxiety without gaining any compensating advantage.

After a while the telephone rang. It was Jane.

"Are you up yet?" she asked.

"Just thinking about it."

"I awoke at seven o'clock and I haven't been able to get to sleep since. Everything's far too noisy and exciting. And now I'm hungry. What about some breakfast?"

"I'll meet you down in the restaurant in half an hour."

He bathed and dressed hurriedly. When he got to the restaurant she had not yet arrived. The sunshine was streaming through the windows—an exhilarating change after the rain of London and the surly dullness of the North Atlantic. He ordered a large orange juice, bacon and eggs, and coffee.

Shortly afterward Jane came down to join him. When she had ordered breakfast he said, "Did they give you a good room?"

"Wonderful, thanks. But enormously expensive, I'm sure."

"Well, of course," he said cheerfully. "It's all part of the plan. I'm trying to spoil you so that you won't want to go home."

"Ah, very crafty—I hadn't thought of that." She smiled at him. "You're looking very pleased with yourself today. Any special reason?"

"Not exactly. I guess I'm much more glad to be back than I thought I would be." He could not be certain what the difference was this time, but there *was* a difference. For some reason New York appeared to him as an easier, more amiable place. It was as if it accepted him as a man of its own kind. Why was that? he wondered. Was it because for the first time he entered it as a person of consequence? Was his sense of well-being due to nothing more than the knowledge that, a few blocks away, men who had once ignored his very existence were now waiting anxiously on his word?

The idea repelled him. He hastened to change the subject.

"I rang up Falls Ridge this morning," he said. "Mother's looking forward to seeing us on Saturday. That gives us two or three days here. I imagine you'd like to have a quick look around Manhattan."

"Yes, of course——"

"We could go up the Empire State, spend an evening in the Village, hear some real jazz——"

"Won't it be boring for you?"

"No." He went on thoughtfully, "It's difficult to explain. I don't approve of New York. Nobody does. Everyone agrees it's noisy and dirty and hot and crowded and ridiculously expensive. And yet . . ."

"I know," she said. "Places get a claim on you in some way. I was born in a little town near Stoke-on-Trent—a dreadful place. Nothing to be said for it at all. Not so long ago I went back there and walked along the street where my parents' house was. It looked very small and old and ugly. Nobody on the street knew me any more. But somehow it almost frightened me. It was as if it could draw me in and take hold of me, put me back where I was as a child—and this time it would see that I wouldn't break away again." She spoke with unusual intensity. "Nothing else is quite as real as the things which happened to you as a child."

He looked at her, thinking how right she had been in London

when she had said they knew so little of each other. To know people it was not enough to know them alone—you had to know also their home, their family, the whole pattern of influences which had made them what they were. Otherwise they were like a phrase read out of context. They might mean anything—or nothing.

He spread some marmalade on a piece of toast. "I spoke to Jeff last night."

"Yes? What happened?"

He gave her an account of their conversation. She listened attentively but somehow without animation. It was as if other matters were uppermost in her mind. He found himself cutting the story short for fear of boring her. At the end he said, "So, as you see, that leaves the next move to them."

After a slight pause she said, "Supposing they do nothing?"

"They daren't. I can pull the company to pieces tomorrow, and they know it. They have to come to me."

"What's the advantage of doing it this way?"

"It's better psychologically." He hesitated. It was not too easy to explain. It was one of those things one instinctively knew. "It emphasizes the strength of my position."

She sighed rather impatiently. "I suppose you must be right. Personally, I wouldn't have the patience. I hate the whole business so much that I'd want to get it over. I'd probably burst into Bernstein's office tomorrow morning, have a tremendous fight with him, and settle everything there and then. Then I'd rush out and take a deep breath and think: Now I can start living!" She smiled at him. "Don't you feel like that at all?"

He thought about it and then shook his head. "It would be a mistake. I know just how you feel. I hate all these politics just as much as you do——"

She looked at him doubtfully. "Do you?"

"Well, of course."

"It just occurred to me," she said, "that perhaps you were rather enjoying it."

There was a moment's awkwardness between them. He found it difficult to meet her eyes.

"It's not a question of enjoying it," he said. "This is a job I have to do. It's important, not only to me, but to a lot of other people. Surely you can understand that."

She said, as if she had made an accusation which he had refused to answer, "I understand perfectly."

"Very well then." She had a way, he thought, of questioning everything. Nothing could be accepted, every attitude and enthusiasm was automatically suspect. It was one of the things which had attracted him to her in the first place, this stern independence and refusal to take anything for granted. But it was slightly disconcerting to see it applied to himself. "I have to do it my own way," he said stiffly.

"Well, of course, if that's how you feel about it," she said. "I only said——"

"It wasn't just what you said." What else was it? Something about her voice, the lift of her eyebrows when asking a question? "You must understand that this is going to be a difficult time for me," he said in a slightly aggrieved voice. "I shall need all the support I can get."

"Yes, I know." She smiled at him and touched his hand. "I didn't mean to sound disloyal." She picked up her handbag and pushed back her chair. "Now I'm ready to go and have a look at Fifth Avenue."

It was two days before Jeff telephoned.

"Is that you, Chris?"

"Yes."

"I only just got to see Bernie this morning. He's been out of town. I've just come from talking to him now——"

"How did it go?"

"Well . . ." He sounded a little dubious, as if he could not be sure how it had gone till he received an opinion on it. "Listen, I can't talk about this over the telephone——"

"Then come over to the hotel."

"No, that's not too good either." Had they told him to keep away? Marshall wondered. "I tell you what. You're spending the weekend at Falls Ridge, aren't you?"

"Yes."

"Then why don't you and Jane drive over to my place for supper Saturday evening? Paula would love to meet her, and you and I could have a little talk about things. How about that?"

"Fine. I'll see you then. Give my love to Paula and the kids," he added as an afterthought.

It was the usual Saturday-morning crowd, he thought as he packed his car into the northbound procession on the Merritt Parkway. Mom and Dad in the front seat, the kids in the back, shouting, making faces, smearing the windows; teen-agers in secondhand convertibles, the radio going full volume. America was having fun.

He said to Jane, "I hope you'll like Falls Ridge."

"I hope so."

"It's a little phony in some ways—but it has a sort of charm. Just like my mother herself, really." After a slight pause he continued, "I should explain that she's from the South—they export charm just like Detroit exports automobiles. She likes to run the house as if it were a broken-down cotton plantation with the mortgage liable to run out at any moment. In fact, she has plenty of money. It's a sort of game——"

"It sounds as if she just likes to pretend. That's not the same as being a phony."

"Perhaps not." He laughed. "It used to annoy my father. He thought it was bad for business."

She was the one person, he thought, who had finally beaten his father. She had employed a technique which the old man was simply not equipped to understand. She would smile gently and agree—and do nothing. Shouting, blustering, threats had no effect on her. Sometimes she would appear to make an attempt to carry out his wishes, but always in the end, almost imperceptibly, her good intentions would lapse, and they were back where they started. Gradually his father had become baffled. In his family affairs (in contrast with his business dealings) he usually felt that he had right on his side, but he had consistently failed to impose his moral convictions on his wife. Eventually he had accepted defeat. "It's essential," he had once said to Marshall with unusual resignation, "not to waste your strength against something you can't beat. Your mother has a unique talent for putting other people in the wrong."

At Falls Ridge everything was much as usual. The dirt road was a little more overgrown, the house still needed painting. Virgie was waiting for them on the porch, toothless, grinning, shy in the presence of the strange foreign woman. His mother came in from the garden, pulling off a pair of thick leather gloves.

"I was trying to tidy up the rosebushes," she explained. "Virgie says they're a disgrace. But it's hopeless—the place has become a wilderness. At one time we used to have two men to handle that garden. And now look at it. There was a young man came up here the other day who wanted to lease part of it from me—that piece down by the highway where the fruit trees are. He wanted to put up a gas station. Imagine—a gas station . . ."

"Mother, this is Jane Lancing."

She smiled sweetly at Jane. "My dear, I'm so glad to meet you. And so pretty—why didn't you tell me she was so pretty, Chris?" She turned back to Jane. "These two boys of mine, they tell me nothing. I have to find out everything for myself. Well, as I was saying, this person came to my door and offered me ten thousand dollars to build a gas station. 'Young man,' I said to him——"

She led them into the house, still talking. Marshall and Virgie carried the suitcases up to the bedrooms. Later Marshall came down and found his mother alone.

"Jane's up in her room," she said. "She wanted to unpack for this evening."

He sat down and lit a cigarette. "Do you like her?"

"She seems like a very sweet girl."

"We're thinking of getting married," he said abruptly. His mother nodded, showing mild interest. In spite of his knowledge of her, he was a little piqued at her lack of reaction. "You don't seem very surprised."

"Naturally, since you'd brought her all this way, I assumed something of the kind," she said. "Besides, I could tell by the way you looked at her. . . ."

"It's not definite yet. She wanted to come over here and see how she liked it before making up her mind." When his mother said nothing, he added, on the defensive, "It's reasonable, after all. She's never been to America before——"

"Perhaps things are different nowadays," Mrs. Marshall said vaguely. "I remember when I married your father we never thought of where we were going to live. My parents were against it, of course—they said he was unstable," she went on, wandering effortlessly into reminiscence, "and of course they were right. He *was* unstable. But then he was living in an unstable world, and it suited him. It's never possible to give anybody advice about the future." She reflected for a moment. "Perhaps it's you that she hasn't quite made up her mind about."

"Well—maybe—I don't know——"

She made one of her sudden butterfly changes of subject. "Why did you call me up that night from London?"

Should he tell her? he wondered. But the effort of explaining it all was too great. Nor had he sufficient confidence in her ability to respond. It was only too likely that her mind would wander while he was talking and he would find at the end that she had understood only half of what he had said. "It was just an impulse," he said. "Nothing in particular."

He suddenly realized that she did not believe him. Yet at the same time she accepted the lie she apparently did not resent it. Her expression seemed to imply that she was used to being shut out of other people's lives and regarded it as a reasonable price to pay for maintaining the privacy of her own.

"Ah well," she said. "I expect you're old enough . . ." Her relief was apparent. She had offered contact and it had been refused. There was nothing more she was obliged to do. She was silent for a moment and then said, "Do you mind fish?"

"Fish?"

"Yes, for lunch." She said earnestly, "I eat practically nothing else now."

"Why?"

At last he felt that her attention was really concentrated on something. "For my blood cholesterol. Do you know it's up to two hundred and sixty?"

"Is that bad?"

"Bad? It's terrible. Dr. Aronson says that if you get over two-seventy you might just as well go out and shoot yourself. It seems that I was slowly poisoning myself with all those eggs. So now it's fish, fish, fish—nearly all the time. Virgie can't stand the stuff," she added with quiet satisfaction.

That evening Marshall and Jane drove over to see Jeff.

"Paula, I want you to meet Jane Lancing."

"Glad to know you, Jane. Jeff's been talking about nothing else ever since he met you off the boat. How do you like America?"

"Give her a chance, honey," said Jeff, "she's only just arrived——"

"So far I think it's wonderful. But then, as your husband says——"

Since Marshall last visited the house a square brick extension had been added to one side of it. It was rare that Jeff and Paula left the place alone for very long. There was usually something new whenever he visited them—a car, a color television set, a baby, a piece of domestic equipment. They liked to be asked to show them off. (They would show them off anyway, but it was more fun for them to be asked.) "I see you have some new construction over there, Jeff."

"Oh sure." Jeff's face lit up with simple pleasure. "I forgot you didn't know about it. We've extended the kitchen—it was kind of unsatisfactory. And there's a room up above for the boys, where they can racket around without getting in Paula's hair all the time. We've got electric heating up there—wonderful system, it runs around under the floor somewhere——"

"Why don't you show Chris around," Paula suggested, "while Jane and I go and take a look at the baby?"

"Sure, sure." As they walked away there was a sound of crashing glass. Two small boys came running around the side of the house, one behind the other, the larger slashing purposefully at the smaller with a baseball bat. "Paul! Paul!" Jeff cried plaintively. "Son, you mustn't do that. Now listen here——" The boys disappeared in the distance. Jeff said, "That kid's becoming quite a worry to me. The psychiatrist says he has cross dominance—his right hand doesn't work with his left eye or something, so he gets all mixed up. No wonder he raises hell all the time. Paula worries a lot, but the way I look at it, we shall just have to be extra understanding——"

Marshall said, "Did you speak to Bernstein?"

Jeff blinked, as if he had received a sharp blow between the eyes. "Yes." He hesitated. "He was pretty mad," he said solemnly.

"Because I didn't approach him direct?"

Jeff nodded, retaining his funereal face. Obviously Mr. Bernstein's indignation had impressed him. "You're certain this is the right way to do it?" he asked.

Marshall did not answer the question. "Did he look surprised? Do you think it was news to him?"

"Oh, sure. He looked very shocked."

Marshall tried to control his exasperation. It was, of course, impossible to hope for any valuable impression on such a matter from Jeff. Any child could deceive him. That had always been one of the drawbacks of playing it this way. He had thrown away the advantage of surprise. He might never know how much Bernstein himself was aware of what was going on. Curiously enough, he knew very little about the man. Bernstein was too high, too remote to be appreciated as a person by anybody as junior as himself.

"How smart is he?" he asked.

"Bernie?" Jeff laughed shortly. "Hell, he's president of the corporation. That doesn't make him exactly a dope——"

"If he's smart," said Marshall, "surely he must have known——"

"Not necessarily. It's pretty far away from his direct responsibility."

Marshall nodded. Perhaps that was true. Perhaps Bernstein had vaguely suspected and done nothing. Perhaps it didn't matter very much anyway. After a while one grew weary of trying to apportion guilt.

Jeff said, a little breathless at his own courage, "I told Bernie that something would have to be done. I said that otherwise I couldn't carry on with the company——"

"If something isn't done there won't *be* any company," said Marshall. "But leave it to me. I'll fix it. You won't have to resign."

"Yes, but how? I mean, I have to know——"

"For God's sake, Jeff. I said leave it to me."

Jeff became agitated.

"But I want to know you're not going to do anything wild. I've been thinking about this. Whatever you do, you can't get the stuff back from the Reds. It has to be stopped, of course, but who gains from making a song and dance about it?"

"You think I haven't thought about that too?" He felt a disinclination to discuss anything in detail at the moment. There was no way in which Jeff was competent to help, and he was liable to get frightened and raise difficulties. Marshall repeated, "I said leave it to me."

There was a silence. They were standing outside the new wing, but Jeff had completely forgotten about showing it to him. Eventually he shook his head and said solemnly, "I notice a big change in you, Chris."

"Yes?"

"You must know it yourself." He looked at Marshall with concern and a certain bewilderment. It was like his children. He went on thinking he had them taped, they respected him and looked up to him, and then suddenly he had lost them—they were out of control. "What happened?" he asked.

What happened? thought Marshall. Perhaps it was quite simple. "I got tired of being beaten."

"By whom?"

"By everybody. I was beaten by my father, by Kingham, by Gilbertson, by Furac, by Bernstein—even by you. Up to a point I tried to pretend it didn't matter, they weren't worth the trouble of fighting." He smiled sourly. "Then I got tired. I said to myself, 'Just this once I would win.' "

Could it be true, he wondered, that this was all there was left? What had happened to all the rest, to the fight for justice, the championship of the small man crushed by the machine, the hatred of lying and cheap swindling and hypocrisy? Had that all really gone, been lost in the heat and the sweat, the bitter expedients of the battle? He heard Jeff saying anxiously, "And what happens afterward?"

"I don't know." He had instinctively refrained from planning too far ahead. There were too many variable factors to make it worth while. When the time came he would know what to do. "It depends on how things pan out. I won't rock the boat too much if they're prepared to be reasonable. But there are going to be some changes." After a pause he said, "That should be good for you. You're the one person who's definitely in the clear over this business. You'll be in a strong position from now on."

Jeff shook his head dubiously. "I don't know. It ought to be like that, maybe, but—you see, Chris," he said confidentially, "my job looks good on paper and it carries a high salary but—well, I don't know why, but somehow it doesn't seem to have the weight it should."

You mean, thought Marshall, you don't have the weight. Only physically. Behind those footballer's muscles of yours lurks a wretched, frightened little boy.

"You have to make them take notice of you," he said. "Tread on their toes and wait for them to apologize." That was a thing his father used to say. And then laugh triumphantly when he saw the disgust on the face of his younger son. "Make it so that it's less trouble for them to agree with you than to fight you."

"I've tried sometimes." Jeff made a helpless motion of his head. "I guess you have to be born to it, though. And it's not so easy when you're on your own." He added tentatively, "Now, if the two of us could work together——"

Marshall shook his head.

"No? But why not, Chris?" Jeff said eagerly. "I've been thinking about this. Between us, we can really amount to something. We have the shareholding and the background. And this present business gives us something to push with. Just now you can ask for what you want from Bernie, and he has to give it to you. If Kingham leaves the International——"

"He'll have to."

"Well, then——" Jeff looked at him. "Who comes in in his place?"

"I hadn't thought of that. I don't know. Maybe Richardson, Livera—someone like that."

"Why not you?"

Marshall laughed. "Can you see them offering it to me?"

"They might," said Jeff knowingly. "This business makes you

important. It might be considered policy to offer you something." Before Marshall could protest, he went on, "Hell, Chris, why not? You're as good as Richardson or Livera, you know you are——"

Marshall shook his head. It was the sort of stupid, half-smart idea that you had to expect from a person like Jeff. It took for granted that everyone wanted the same things he wanted himself and would use the same methods to get them. "I'm not interested," he said. "All I care about is to fix this one thing. After that I'm getting out."

Jeff was bewildered. "But, Chris, why? At a time like this——"

"This is the right time. I'd have got out before but I'd had too many failures—I couldn't bring myself to admit to another one. But when this is over I shall have done something. I shan't owe any more obligations to myself or anybody else. From then on I can do as I please."

Was that it? Something like that, anyway. You got so that you were too busy to remember why you were doing things; just doing them took everything you had. Plans were things that never worked out; the best ones were those you made up afterward, like those caricatures he had drawn so long ago in the conference room the day they fixed Wilcox. You drew the picture first—then you put a name to it. . . .

He turned away abruptly. "Let's go back and talk to the girls," he said.

When they were driving back to his mother's house he said to Jane, "What do you think of them?" Seeing her hesitate, he added, "You can be as frank as you like."

"I wasn't being delicate. I found it difficult to answer because I honestly don't know. They don't seem real to me somehow."

"Neither of them?"

"The whole household. It's just the Young Executive Family Group, isn't it? Everything so shiny and glossy and prosperous. It's like some ghastly advertisement. You know what I mean."

He was suddenly, surprisingly, defending his brother.

"It's always the same when you first visit a foreign country. A lot of the people seem like something out of a comic strip. Stage Americans or Englishmen or Irishmen or whatever it is." He searched for an example. "Gilbertson, for instance. He was never a real person to me somehow. Not until recently, that is." He said, hoping it was true, "You'll soon get used to the people over here. . . ."

When they arrived home he was surprised to find his mother downstairs. Usually she went to bed early.

"Did you enjoy yourselves?"

"Yes—very well."

"Any news from Jeff and Paula?"

"Not really."

"Well, *I* have some news," she said. "You'll never guess who called me up while you were out."

"Who?"

She shot an unusually acute glance at him. "Mr. Bernstein. Now wasn't that surprising? I haven't heard from him in years. He asked if he could come to dinner tomorrow night."

CHAPTER III

WITH SOME DIFFICULTY Bernstein steered the big black Continental off the highway and onto the road leading to the house. It was a long time since he had been there and the road seemed much narrower nowadays. Or perhaps his car had grown wider. He had never been very happy with the Continental. It was altogether too long and low and powerful; he was a nervous driver and didn't have any use for three-hundred (or was it four?) horsepower, but, after all, a man owed something to his position.

He stopped the car in front of the house. Even that looked smaller, he thought, than it had when Marcus Marshall was alive. Or then again, perhaps it was he who had grown bigger. Like an actor about to go on the stage for the first time in an unfamiliar part, he took a deep breath, swallowed, moistened his lips, and took a quick glance at himself in the rear-view mirror. He was not dissatisfied with what he saw. Time and the painstaking effort of forty years had managed finally to give him the sort of appearance he considered appropriate to his achievements and ambitions. The face was sallow and fine-drawn, the mouth humorous and sensitive, the silky hair now almost completely white. Though never handsome, he had succeeded in becoming distinguished in a casual, unpretentious way. He had always resisted any temptation to flamboyance. Restraint was implicit in everything he did, in the clothes he wore, the unobtrusive signet ring on his little finger, the gray worsted suit tailored so delicately to conceal the tiny residue of paunch which even the most rigid dieting could never entirely eradicate. The total effect was as he had always wished it to be, complete and satisfying, a cover picture from *Time*.

He saw Mrs. Marshall coming out of the house and extricated himself from the car. It was bound to be a slightly embarrassing moment. He had neglected her since the old man died—there had been so many other important things. . . . But she would play along, he consoled himself, whatever she might think about him. By now she must surely be accustomed to the realities of business.

He went straight into his prepared entrance, taking both her hands in his. "Mary!" He looked into her face with an expression of delighted wonderment. "You haven't changed a bit."

"I should have," she said. "It's quite a time since we met."

"It certainly is." He contrived to suggest that circumstances completely beyond his control had kept them apart. "And nobody regrets it more than I do. Still, I always say, the best friends are those you don't have to see all the time—isn't that so?" He turned away. "And, Chris—I suppose I can call you Chris?"

"Sure."

"We're pretty old acquaintances, after all. In fact, you may not know this, but your father wanted me to be your godfather. It's the truth. Even when I pointed out to him that I was a Jew he couldn't see why not." He chuckled. "Theology was never his strong suit."

Marshall smiled thinly. He was trying to get used to the idea of Bernstein at close quarters. So far, apart from a few vague childhood memories, he had seen him only as a shadowy, remote personage, a maker of after-dinner speeches, a collection of photographs for the house journal. He strove to eradicate from his mind any traces of awe which might remain as a result of those earlier impressions. Bernstein was simply a man, a man his father had made and whom his mother principally remembered because he played such a bad game of bridge. All the rest was an act, just as his present performance was an act. Though, he admitted, you couldn't help admiring it purely as a demonstration of technique. The family stuff, the semi-paternal manner, the references, so lightly dropped, to old times. And the Jewishness, not concealed, but not pushed in your face either. . . .

He was at work on Jane now. "Don't be afraid, Miss Lancing. I'm not going to ask you what you think of America. When I first came to New York from Hamburg with my father I was nine years old and couldn't speak a word of English. And within twenty-four hours three people asked me what I thought of America. I got so that I was afraid to go out of the house." Swinging back to Mrs. Marshall, he said, "It's wonderful here, Mary. You haven't changed a thing."

"We let the tennis court go," said Mrs. Marshall, literal as ever. "No one wanted to play on it any more."

"Yes, that's right." Bernstein look around vaguely. Plainly his memories of Falls Ridge were not as detailed as all that. "But the essentials haven't changed. The atmosphere of the place——"

"It's a nice house," she said shortly. She loved it too much to listen to insincerity about it. "Now let's go inside and have a drink before dinner." She looked aggressively at Bernstein. "I hope you like fish."

During dinner he laughed and joked, paid compliments, told stories, and commented appropriately on the food and wine. He seemed determined to make the party a success. Marshall wondered whether he was especially anxious on this occasion. Very probably he was always the same, one of those men who, whatever the nature of the social gathering, always felt the responsibilities of a host. But what sort of person was he? What lay beneath the big handshake, the phony bonhomie? He had come a long way. There must be something which had carried him along—something which would need watching.

When the meal was over, Mrs. Marshall said, "Jane and I are going to have our coffee outside. Bring it out into the garden, will you, Virgie? The two men can stay in here." She smiled maliciously at Bernstein. "It's all right, Alfred, you don't have to pretend—I didn't really think you came to see me. If you like cigars there are some on the sideboard. I don't know whether they're fit to smoke or not—we've had them ever since Marcus died. . . . Come and join us when you've finished talking."

The two of them were left alone. Bernstein examined one of

the cigars, shook his head, and dropped it back in the box. He lit a cigarette instead and then said with surprising directness, "Well, here I am, Chris."

Marshall was slightly disconcerted. While he was trying to think of the right thing to say, Bernstein went on, "Your brother told me you had a problem you wanted to discuss with me." An acid note appeared in his voice. "Though why you didn't do me the courtesy of walking into my office when you were in New York, I'm not very clear."

Marshall shook his head. "I tried it that way once before."

"With Kingham?"

"Yes." The memory of his humiliation succeeded, as always, in rousing his anger against not only Kingham but all of them. "He kept me waiting for two weeks before he'd even speak to me."

"Perhaps you should have come to me."

"You wouldn't have listened to me either."

"I'm listening to you now."

"Because you have to. And that was why I wanted you to come here—to make the position quite clear to everybody. You aren't doing me a favor by listening to me. There isn't any question of saying, 'Thanks a lot, Chris. Nice of you to call around. I'll certainly see the matter gets looked into. Now you just go along and have a nice vacation and forget all about it.' "

Bernstein pursed his lips with the expression of a man who was used to keeping his temper however trying the circumstances. "Why not take the chip off your shoulder," he said, "and get down to business?"

"All right—just so long as we know where we stand." He paused for a moment. "Jeff gave you the story?"

"Yes." He said heavily, "Naturally it came as a great shock to me."

"Did it?"

Bernstein looked up sharply. He had almost forgotten what it was like to have his word questioned. "You don't believe me?"

"How should I know?"

"Would it be of any help to you," said Bernstein with considerable deliberation, "if I swore to you that I knew nothing about it?"

"Not much, I'm afraid." Marshall forced himself to be crude about it. He was afraid that if the discussion was allowed to proceed on a polite, gentlemanly plane Bernstein would use his advantages of age and position and experience to establish an ascendancy over him. "After all," he said, "if you were prepared to do it, you'd be equally prepared to lie about it, wouldn't you?"

"Listen here, Chris." An exasperated note crept into his voice. The façade of self-control was beginning to crack. "I'm a man twice your age and I've come a long way to see you. For that reason alone I guess I'm entitled to some consideration."

"Consideration?" said Marshall. "Who ever gave me consideration? Kingham——"

"Yes, I know about Kingham." Bernstein threw his cigarette butt, half smoked, into the fireplace. "And I'm sorry if you were badly treated. From what I hear, he has a tendency to play God occasionally——"

"But you never did anything about it?"

"You have to allow a man some latitude as the head of a department. You can't always be breathing down his neck—especially if he's turning in good results. Hell, I'm only one man, I can't watch everything, you know."

His voice was almost plaintive. It was the voice of a man who had managed for some years now to believe in his own pretense of being in control of the situation. You had a system of management, a chain of command, and it was supposed to work like a piece of machinery. The first queasy sense of impotence which took hold of you when you first assumed power became gradually no more than an amusing memory as you got used to your position. You began to think that you were really in charge. You had all the symbols and paraphernalia to support you and give you confidence—the limousines and private planes, the suites at Claridges and the Waldorf and the Georges Cinq, the secretaries, the penthouse apartments, the offices high, high up in the air, fifty floors above the street where ordinary people walked and lived and suffered. . . .

It was a good life. And then, to spoil it all, something happened to show you that it was a fraud. You were not in charge at all. Had you really seriously thought you were in control of all those millions of dollars, the shareholders, employees, the unions, the agents and distributors, the government departments, the foreign branches in countries whose language you didn't understand, whose customs were a mystery to you? High up in your eagle's nest, in your mountain fastness, you formulated policies that meant nothing, made plans that were never carried out. And all the time the organization moved, amoeboid, like a stream of lava, in whatever direction chance and circumstance might decree. . . . He repeated, "It's impossible to keep track of everything."

"Well, there it is," said Marshall. "If you don't interfere, one of these days somebody else will have to." He looked at Bernstein unsympathetically. "Have you spoken to Kingham?"

"No. I thought it best to see you first." He explained, "This is going to be an awkward business to handle. No use going off half cocked." The old soothing phrases of management came comfortingly to mind, giving him a feeling that as soon as he had mentioned them some preliminary step had been taken. "We must get together—exchange ideas—formulate a policy——"

"What sort of a policy?"

"Ah well, of course," said Bernstein cautiously, "that's the point, isn't it?" He hesitated for a moment and then said, feeling his ground, "Am I right in supposing that, if we can clear the matter up within the organization, it will be good enough for you?"

"Yes. I don't see much advantage in making it public——"

"Neither do I. Especially since it would ruin us all financially—you included. Now," he said, "I haven't had too much time to work out all the details, but there are certain obvious steps we shall have to take. For a start, all sales of instruments abroad will have to be checked, to make sure that none are going to questionable sources. Agreed?"

"Of course." Marshall waited for a moment. "What else?"

Bernstein lit another cigarette and puffed hard at it several times, as if to extract wisdom from it. "Then," he said, "there's the Paris agency. I don't know quite what we should do about that. So far as I can gather, they've been doing hardly any legitimate business at all. And this man Furac——"

"Furac," said Marshall definitely, "has to go."

"Well, maybe. But we shall need to go cautiously. We have a contract with him, you understand."

"I don't give a damn about his contract."

Bernstein nodded. "Yes, I can see your point," he said reasonably. "If you feel as strongly about it as that——"

"I do."

"Okay then—I'll have a word with the lawyers. I don't know the terms of his contract, but it's possible we may be able to shake free of him without too much trouble." He touched Marshall paternally on the shoulder. "Don't worry about that. Just leave it to me."

It seemed to Marshall that all his life men in influential positions had been putting their hands on his shoulder and telling him to leave it to them, they would look after his interests for him. It was a confidence trick which was extraordinarily difficult to resist. But this time he was prepared for it. "So long as something gets done," he said.

"I promise you that." Bernstein had the air of a man making an important concession. It occurred to Marshall that he had already decided to get rid of Furac but, according to the general principles of bargaining, was making a favor of it.

"Then that takes care of Furac," he said. He moved out of shoulder-patting range. "What about Kingham?"

"Kingham?" An expression of pain passed over Bernstein's face. It was as if this was a problem he had hoped might in some way be avoided. "Well—obviously I shall have to discuss the whole question with him——"

"What is there to discuss? He knew what was going on."

Bernstein held up his hand. "Oh, now, let's be reasonable. I know you don't like the man, but we have no evidence that he was personally concerned."

"Of course he was," said Marshall. "Every time anybody asked a question about the French business Kingham tried to fire him or push him off to California or something." He glared at Bernstein. "What's the matter? Are you afraid of him?"

Bernstein swallowed. By God, thought Marshall, you learn something every minute; he *is* afraid of him—but right now he is even more afraid of me. Otherwise he would simply walk out—he wouldn't stand for this.

The same idea seemed to occur to Bernstein. He adopted the tone of a man at the end of his patience. "Listen, Chris," he said. "I've done my best to keep my temper with you—under considerable provocation—but if you speak to me like that I'm going to walk right out of here."

He had succeeded in making Marshall feel slightly ashamed. "Hell, I'm sorry," he said. And then irritation rose in him again. "But what else do you expect? I know damn well you won't shift Kingham unless you have to."

"Kingham's one of the best men we have," said Bernstein stubbornly. "Even if he was in on this, you've got to admit there were extenuating circumstances."

"You mean my father?"

"Yes. He started the whole thing, after all. Kingham was a young man at the time. Your father was pushing him along. When the International was formed, your father handed it over to him. You know what the old man was like——"

"Yes, I know," said Marshall. He felt suddenly tired. "If Kingham had complained he would have been fired." He shrugged his shoulders. "So it seems he's just out of luck. Now he's going to get fired for not complaining."

"Chris, I don't think you quite understand. It's not so easy with a man in his position——"

"I don't care whether it's easy or not. You've got to get him out."

There was a long silence. Bernstein regarded him with dark speculative eyes, like a dealer preparing to put a final price on a piece of merchandise.

"Can I ask you something?" he said.

"Sure."

"Why is it so important to you that Kingham should go? Is it just a matter of personal dislike?"

"Of course not."

"Then why make such an issue of it?"

"Surely that should be obvious."

Once again Bernstein was silent, as if contemplating a whole series of possibilities. "Supposing I refuse?" he said.

"Let's stop pretending. You can't refuse." He felt a certain pity for Bernstein. It was tough on a man who had worked his way up from a tenement in Brooklyn to become a respected public figure, president of the Chamber of Commerce, a sound Republican. "I have only to drop two sentences to the newspapers and they'll fry you."

"I didn't know anything about this."

"Do you suppose that's going to make any difference?"

"It wouldn't only harm me, you know. You may not care about your father's reputation, but what about your mother and your brother—and yourself, for that matter? After all, you're a fairly large shareholder——"

"You think perhaps I wouldn't do it?" Marshall smiled at him. "But you daren't take a chance on it, dare you?" He had suddenly had enough of the situation. Blackmail was no fun, even in a good cause. "Well, what are you going to do?"

"It's impossible to make a decision on the spot about a matter like this," said Bernstein. He made a feeble attempt to regain his executive manner. "I shall have to consider——"

He could have his face-saver, thought Marshall. He was entitled to that, at least. "All right," he said. "How long would you like? Till Tuesday morning—eleven o'clock?" He patted Bernstein gently on the shoulder. It was his turn now. "I'll come into your office this time."

Sometime later, when he was alone with Jane, she said, "How did it go?"

"Not so bad." Virgie had left a tray on the table with drinks. He put some ice into a glass and poured scotch over it. "A drink?"

"No, thanks."

He came back and sat beside her. She was wearing a plain black dress with very little jewelry. Her dark hair was swept neatly behind her ears. Her body was like a small, tight, perfectly proportioned machine—he could imagine it in ten years' time, hardly changed.

He said, "You look beautiful tonight."

She shook her head. "I'm not beautiful." It was a statement of fact. Her attraction was not beauty. It was somehow too trim and compact. She would never have the compelling, irresponsible brilliance of his mother, for instance. But there was an unimpassioned strength in her which his mother had never had. She was dependable, he thought.

"My mother's crazy about you," he said.

"I like her too." She said seriously, "We were talking quite a lot this evening. You know, she's not nearly so scatterbrained as she likes to pretend. It's a sort of defense—she's afraid of being committed. Don't you think so?"

"Committed to what?"

"Anything. Anybody. Perhaps once she committed herself too much and got hurt, I don't know." She looked at him thoughtfully. "I can understand her. The more you feel, the more careful you have to be. There comes a time when there's no turning back."

"You mean marriage?"

"It happens before marriage. It happens in your mind. And not only with marriage either. With everything important, there's a point of no return. The difficulty is to know when you've reached it."

In some way he could not explain, her manner made him feel uneasy, as if there were some particular and slightly disturbing implication behind her remarks. To change the subject he said, "How did you like Bernstein?"

"All right," she said indifferently. "I'm really not very sure. A lot depends on whether he's a nice old man or just acting the part, doesn't it? If he were an Englishman I think I should know. But here conditions are so different. I might take something as a sign of insincerity which is just a normal way of behavior." She paused for a moment. "Do you trust him?"

"God, no." He spoke casually, as if it were a matter of no particular importance. "But if you're only going to do business with people you can trust, where are you going to get?" He added, "The important thing is that I'm in the stronger position."

"He's going to do what you want?"

"Yes. He stalled, of course. But that's just routine. I made it clear that he hadn't any choice."

She frowned. "He's going to hate you for this, isn't he?"

"Maybe," he said uncomfortably. "But I can't help it, can I? Perhaps he may even respect me for getting tough with him. But in any case I never got anywhere by being nice to people. I can't lose much by trying it the other way."

"No?" She looked at him dubiously, then said, "When will it be finished?"

"Tuesday morning. I have a meeting with Bernstein in his office. Once we've agreed about Kingham, the rest shouldn't be too difficult."

"Who will replace Kingham?"

"I don't know." His laugh was slightly forced. "Jeff was trying to persuade me to put in for it."

She looked at him steadily. "Are you interested?"

"Of course not. In any case, can you imagine them suggesting such a thing?"

It was ridiculous, of course. And yet Jeff had seemed very serious about it, almost as if he had received some sort of hint. And Bernstein had asked very deliberately why it was so important that Kingham should go, as if he suspected that Marshall had some particular reason for wanting him removed. Was it possible that they had decided that this was the motive behind his actions, the price he intended to demand for silence?

Jane seemed to be following his thoughts.

"It would be a good way to keep you quiet," she said. She added without expression, "You ought to be prepared——"

"I told you—long ago in London—I don't want to stay. Not under any circumstances."

"That was some time ago," she said seriously. "Don't think you have to stick to it. You can change your mind if you want to."

"Do you want me to?"

"That's nothing to do with it. It's your own decision."

"I know that," he said sharply. "And I'm going to make it. But I want your opinion. I have a right to know."

"Very well, then I'll tell you. I've always been behind you so far. Right from the very beginning I thought you were right to go on with this, and even later when it meant that—that dreadful business with the letter, I told myself that it was necessary, one had to make sacrifices, there was something worth while at the end of it. But now I begin to wonder." He said nothing. It would have been foolish to pretend he didn't understand. It was what he had thought himself. "As time goes on, it seems to me, you begin to care less and less about anything but just winning. If you go on much longer there'll be nothing else." She said urgently, "You still have time—if you can go out now they'll remember afterward that there was one man they couldn't buy with money or power or anything else they had to offer. But if you stay"—there was something close to despair in her voice—"then it was all for nothing."

There was a long silence. Then he went up to her and kissed her. "Don't worry," he said. "I'm not going to stay."

CHAPTER IV

THIS WAS unknown country. Here the carpets were thick and pastel-shaded, the secretaries soft of voice, the doors closed automatically with a sigh, faint as the breath of a patient under heavy anesthesia. In the reception room there were only the deepest of chairs, the glossiest of magazines. Here a man might wait for hours, inhaling the scented air, soothing his ears with the silence, his eyes with the sumptuous charms of the receptionist. On the walls he would see no advertising slogans, no vulgar photographs of factories, no ill-painted oil paintings of bespectacled tycoons. A Degas reproduction, a bowl of roses, an enigmatic piece of pottery, part man, part fish, part interplanetary rocket, and that was all. Here a man might wait all afternoon and in the end be sent home, without resentment. To have been admitted to Mr. Bernstein's personal waiting room was an achievement in itself.

Marshall did not have to wait very long. There had to be some delay, he recognized, otherwise the whole act would fall to pieces; it was like the ritual coffee drinking which always precedes the discussion of business in Arab countries. Even if a man was tired of it himself, he had to keep it up, if only to retain the respect of his servants.

"Mr. Bernstein will see you now." The girl smiled at him, the doll-like smile of an air hostess, a ballerina. A few moments later he was in Bernstein's office. The door hissed gently shut behind him.

Bernstein was sitting behind the desk. In a chair to the left of him was a man Marshall had never seen before. He was fat and middle-aged, with a domed, balding head and practically no neck. His eyes bulged slightly; his face was gray and expressionless, frog-like.

"This is Mr. Flack, Chris, from the Legal Department. I don't believe you two have met before." As they shook hands Bernstein said, "I hope you don't mind Mr. Flack being present?"

"If *you* don't mind, I don't."

"Good. So far he's the only person I've consulted about this—unfortunate affair. I thought it essential to have a legal opinion before making any move at all. But Flack and I both feel very strongly that the fewer people who know about it, the better. We shall have to be very careful to prevent any leakage. Don't you agree?"

"Up to a point," said Marshall. "Until you've told me what you're going to do."

"You don't need to worry about that." Bernstein paused and then said, "You'll be glad to hear that we've considered your proposals and decided to accept them."

He gave the announcement as much weight as it would carry, perhaps rather more. Certainly it fell flat. Marshall crossed his legs and nodded amiably. Flack exchanged glances with Bernstein and picked up a file from the table beside his chair.

"We can break out of our contract with Furac without much difficulty," he said in a flat, nasal, indifferent voice. "There is a provision for unilateral termination on the payment of certain agreed sums, worked out on a basis of annual average turnover. It shouldn't even cost too much. There was only another two years to run anyhow."

Marshall frowned. "We have to compensate him?"

"Surely. He may have broken his contract by selling to unauthorized people, but that doesn't help us. We're in no position to take him to law." In a slightly patronizing tone he added, "You must see that."

"Yes, but——" He stopped, unable to express what he had to say. The protest in his heart was too simple, too juvenile to be expressed in the world of half-lights and expedients in which all management was carried on. It was useless here to talk of justice, of reward for virtue and punishment for evil. When so many lives were interlocked there were no simple moral decisions any longer, only decisions of policy—and even those were mostly improvisations, an attempt to keep the ship afloat at any cost.

"And Kingham?" he asked bitterly. "Is he to be compensated too?"

Flack nodded. "We can't just fire him out of hand."

"Why not?"

"Because he might make trouble."

"How? He couldn't damage the company without damaging himself."

Bernstein leaned forward over the desk, the elder statesman. "Chris," he said seriously, "let me give you a word of advice. In this life it never pays to squeeze a man too hard. He's liable to get desperate and then you never know what he's going to do. If Kingham had been easier on you he wouldn't be in the trouble he's in today." He sat back and continued on a more reflective note. It was not enough to do what had to be done. It must also be enshrined as policy. "Now, I've come round to agree with you that he ought to go. He's a fine man in his way, but—well, between ourselves, quite apart from this, he's been worrying us a little lately. You see, for a really big post you need something more than a good administrator—you need a really *big* man—you know what I mean? Someone who can keep his head and always remember that he's a member of the team. In an outfit like this we all have to pull together; when somebody gets out of step you begin to notice it." He went on confidentially, "Just recently some of us have been getting a little worried about Kingham. He's shown a tendency to behave as if the International belonged to him. Isn't that so, Sidney?"

"That's right," said Flack in the same nasal, colorless voice.

"So you see——" said Bernstein. Marshall nodded wearily. He understood—now he was a person of experience. He knew all about men who weren't shaping up to the job, who were a little short on drive or background, who got out of step. First Wilcox, then himself, now it was Kingham's turn. But Kingham would not get hurt as much as some. It was a useful insurance to know where the body was buried. . . .

"We reckon," Bernstein was saying, "that it would be a good thing to have some new blood in there. But it can't be done just like that. Kingham's very popular with the Board."

"That's your problem," said Marshall, "handling the Board."

"I can handle them," said Bernstein, "so long as Kingham goes quietly and doesn't start looking for trouble."

"So you want to buy him? Is that it?"

"We have to buy him." Bernstein looked down at the pencil he was absent-mindedly playing with. "We squeeze him a bit as well, of course. We make him realize that this is a generous offer, considering the circumstances."

There was a silence. Then Marshall said, "How much?"

"Can't you leave that to us?"

"I want to know."

"I haven't decided yet. It has to be carefully worked out." He was speaking now with more confidence, the confidence of an expert on his own subject. "If we give too much he'll think we're scared of him. If we give too little he may think it worth while to fight. I'd suggest," he said thoughtfully, "something around a hundred thousand."

"Christ!" His outrage at the magnitude of the sum reminded him that he had already accepted, almost without protest, the advisability of paying Kingham *something*. He said, "That sounds a hell of a lot to me."

"It's not much to keep the company clean. And I have to get it passed by the Board, remember—not you."

"Can you do that?"

"I think so." It was against his practice to commit himself in advance, but his voice carried conviction. This was the sort of thing he was good at. Not the rough-and-tumble of the arena, but the quiet whisperings over drinks in select bars, the gentle flatteries, the final unobtrusive triumph in the conference room. "If you'll leave it to me . . . ?"

Marshall hesitated. But why not? If Kingham was to be bought, did it really matter for how much? "All right," he said.

"Good." Bernstein relaxed. The most difficult problem of all had been dealt with. "Now, there are one or two other people we have to think about." He looked down at a piece of paper on the blotter of his desk. There was a list of names. "Gilbertson."

It was partly a statement, partly a query. Plainly Gilbertson was neither here nor there to Bernstein. He had never met the man and Gilbertson was not a vital part of the machinery of the organization. If it would give Marshall any satisfaction to ruin him, that was all right with everybody present. It occurred to Marshall that for the first time he was being offered a man's life to do with as he pleased. This was not like Furac or Kingham—the situation had demanded that they should be dealt with, and he was no more than its agent. Here there was a choice, a personal choice. He had but to say the word and everything that Gilbertson valued—the house in Sussex, the small farm, the clubs, the whole elaborate charade of his existence—would be blown to pieces as if by a charge of dynamite. He contemplated the possibility with fascination mixed with horror. He looked at Bernstein impatiently waiting for his answer, and Flack, who gave the appearance of being more than usually bored by the whole proceedings. At least, he thought defensively, I have the imagination to take it seriously, I have the grace to be ashamed.

"Gilbertson can stay," he said.

Bernstein regarded him with approval. "It would certainly save a lot of trouble. We don't want to have to rebuild the whole European organization from zero." He looked down again at the list of names. "Wilcox? Now you've seen him recently, I believe?"

"Yes. He wants his job back—or its equivalent. And some expenses."

"That shouldn't be too difficult."

Flack looked up sharply. He was a man who prided himself on speaking only when he had something to say. "I've never met this man Wilcox. Is he any good?"

It was necessary to be fair to Wilcox, even though one didn't like him—perhaps even more so because of that. And yet the truth was the truth. They would find out soon enough.

"Not much at the moment," Marshall said reluctantly. "He's drinking pretty heavily. But he's been under a big strain, remember. He may straighten out when he gets back."

"I certainly hope so," said Flack. "We can't afford to carry drunks."

Marshall glared at him angrily. He was beginning to dislike Flack. For a lawyer called in to give advice, he took too much on himself. "We've carried worse than drunks for plenty of time," he said. "In any case, you know damn well we've got to take him back, drunk or sober. So what's the use of arguing about it?"

Bernstein looked from one to the other with a sort of complacent interest. He was not too displeased to see Flack snubbed and Marshall lose his temper. On general principles it was a good thing to have subordinates who were at each other's throats. "All right," he said, "that takes care of Wilcox. Now—is that everybody?"

"There is someone else," said Marshall. "Madame Verrier."

"Madame who?"

Marshall broke into laughter. It was funny, he told himself. It had to be funny, otherwise . . . Bernstein and Flack were not faking—they had genuinely no idea who she was. They looked at him in perplexity.

"What's the joke?" asked Bernstein.

"Nothing. You wouldn't understand." He controlled himself. "She was the wife of a man who killed himself in Paris. Do you remember?"

"Oh yes—yes." A vague memory seemed to return to him. "You think she needs squaring too?"

"Yes."

Bernstein sighed impatiently. "Well, what does *she* want?"

"Money. What else is there?"

"How much?"

"I don't know." When it came to matters of this kind, he realized, he was an amateur. The two professionals regarded him disparagingly. He took refuge in sarcasm. "Not so much that she thinks we're scared of her, and not so little that she'll go looking for trouble. You know what I mean?"

Flack said dispassionately to Bernstein, "Don't forget, she's a Frenchwoman. Whatever you offer her, she'll ask for fifty per cent more, on principle."

Bernstein tapped his teeth with the pencil. "Five thousand?"

"That sounds about right."

"After all, Verrier was only——"

"Yes," said Marshall, "he was only a little crook."

He heard the bitterness in his voice and wondered against whom it was directed. Bernstein? Himself? The situation seemed designed to destroy all moral attitudes. It had led him, step by step, into positions where no clear-cut stand could ever be taken. The problems were so complex that it was no longer a question of a correct solution—but of *any* solution. Some decision had to be taken in a hurry to stave off disaster. An end had to be attained. If it could be attained only by bribery, by treachery, by blackmail, then they had to be accepted.

Bernstein ignored his last remark. He made a tick on his piece of paper and said, "That seems to take care of most of our outstanding problems." He smiled at the other two, the smile of a man who has turned yet another awkward corner in a harassing career. Then he glanced at his watch. "It's getting very near one o'clock——"

Almost as if this were a prearranged signal, Flack squeezed himself out of his chair. "Do you need me any more just at the moment, Bernie? I made an appointment with Kelsey from the Patent Office——"

"Sure." Bernstein sprang cheerfully to his feet. "Don't let me hold you up. Good of you to come along at all at such short notice—I know how tied up you are." When he had ushered Flack out of the room he turned to Marshall and smiled indulgently. "Now," he said, "I think we've earned a drink. Anything else we can talk about over lunch."

CHAPTER V

BERNSTEIN STUDIED THE MENU with considerable care and ordered half a dozen Blue Points and a filet mignon. "No potatoes," he said, patting his miniature, hardly discernible paunch. "You have to watch yourself when you get to my age."

He lit a cigarette. The doctors were taking all the fun out of that, too, he thought resentfully. You could fool yourself with those filter tips, but it still left the nagging fear at the back of your mind. There were too many things to worry about these days; he was getting old, he couldn't take it any more. But the first martini cheered him up a little. He said, "I think we did pretty well this morning, all things considered." When Marshall said nothing, he went on, "You should be satisfied anyway, you got everything you asked for."

"I suppose so."

Bernstein mused for a moment. "It's a bad situation—a real crisis—but right now I feel optimistic. Something tells me we're going to lick it."

"It does?"

"Yes indeed. A few days ago I wouldn't have thought it possible. When your brother came into my office last week and told me the story—believe me, Chris, I'll never forget it. I thought to myself, 'There goes the company, there goes everything we've all lived and worked for all these years!' " He shook his head at the memory. "I just couldn't see a way out. Then I pulled myself together and I said to myself, 'We've got to fight this thing somehow.'"

Marshall looked at him with mild interest. It occurred to him that Bernstein was really quite a stupid man. To some extent it was concealed in the trappings of power. And there was always a tendency to assume, as Jeff had done, that because he held a position of such enormous authority he *must* have ability, even if it was not obvious on the surface, since if he had not, the implications were too appalling to contemplate. If a man without real capacity could reach the top by chance and then remain there by virtue of an amiable personality, a talent for minor personal intrigues, and the sheer inertia intrinsic to the structure of any large organization, then there was no use going on, the whole competitive system was a joke.

"So you fought it," he said.

Bernstein raised a hand. "With your help," he said handsomely. "It's due to you that we've managed to sit down together and find a solution to this problem. God knows what might have happened if one of our competitors had got onto this before you did. It was indeed fortunate for us that it was one of our own men, somebody with loyalty to the company." He was rather like a general making a speech before conferring a decoration. He said solemnly, "Your father would have been proud of you, Chris."

"You forget," said Marshall, "that the swindle was his idea in the first place."

Bernstein frowned. "I wouldn't call it a swindle exactly. Besides which," he continued, regaining confidence, "that was some time ago. Who can tell?—there may have been circumstances—— I don't think," he said, "that we have a right to set ourselves up in judgment. What I do know for sure is that if he'd been alive today he would have approved what you did a hundred per cent. I'm confident of that. And when all is said and done, I knew him better than most people."

"I guess so."

"He always thought very highly of you, Chris—better than you thought of him. It was a great grief to him that he couldn't build you up in the business as he wanted to."

The oysters were good, thought Marshall, if one refrained from dipping them in that revolting cocktail sauce. A little pepper and a squeeze of lemon . . . But he was growing a little impatient. He had not been invited to lunch purely as a social exercise. When was the old man going to get to the point?

"I'll be quite honest," said Bernstein, "and say that at one time I doubted his opinion of you. It didn't seem to me that you were cut out for the game at all. But it's always been my philosophy to admit when I make a mistake. I've made quite a few in my time," he admitted handsomely. "I know now that I made one with you."

With regret Marshall speared the last oyster and popped it into his mouth. He let it slide down his throat; an elusive tang of sea and surf lingered on the surface of his pharynx. So Jeff was right, he thought, Bernstein was going to offer him the International. Partly to silence him, but perhaps also to some extent because he had proved himself, shown that he could play the game with the best of them when necessity arose. For the first time they respected him. There was satisfaction in that—and even greater satisfaction in the thought that he did not need their respect, that he was prepared to throw their rewards back at them. That was something they would never succeed in understanding. "At one stage," he said, "you told me you didn't like my attitude."

"Well, that's true," admitted Bernstein without malice. "It did seem to me at the time that you were crowding me a little. But that's not so important. In business we fling around a few hard words now and then and it's all taken as part of the game. When the deal's over we shake hands and forget about it. Believe me," he said with some feeling, "I wouldn't be where I am today if I was a man who took offense too readily."

He paused while the waiter brought the next course and then went on.

"No, what *is* important is that in a difficult situation you showed drive and responsibility and a grasp of realities. You've realized that in administration it isn't possible to spend your life with your head in the air—you've got to grapple with facts—pleasant or unpleasant. That makes you just the kind of man we're looking for."

Marshall said nothing. It was coming now; this was the end of the build-up. Bernstein leaned toward him confidentially.

"But I didn't bring you here," he said, "to throw bouquets at you. I brought you here to offer you a job."

"Yes?" He gave a faint smile. He remembered that this was how it had begun, with his being offered a job. But he had moved a long way since April. He remembered his interview with Kingham ("How would you like to go to Europe, Chris? The job's made for you. What we need is someone with background—it could lead anywhere"). Well, that was true enough, it had led both himself and Kingham into positions which neither of them would have conceived possible a few months ago.

Bernstein looked at him benevolently, a dapper, custom-tailored fairy godmother. "How would you like to be general manager in India?" he said.

"India!"

Marshall was stunned. The contrast between expectation and reality had rendered him almost speechless. He was so taken aback that for the moment he felt no emotion except astonishment. Presently the first reaction would die down and give place to something more positive. He waited, wondering what it would be. At heart, was he angry—or simply amused?

Bernstein regarded him closely, searching for some clue to his state of mind. "It's a wonderful opportunity, Chris. Believe me, things are moving out there. In fact, if anybody were to ask me where I think the biggest possibilities for business expansion are right now, I'd answer without hesitation—the Far East. . . ."

He warmed to his theme. Professional pride was involved—this was a job of selling, and he had always flattered himself that he could sell a bill of goods as well as the next man. Gradually, as he spoke, Marshall's mood defined itself. He was not amused—far from it. He recognized that for some time now he had been deluding himself. Once again he had fallen a victim to flattery; he had allowed himself to think that they looked upon him differently, that they respected him, that everything was changed. But nothing was changed. Once they had wanted to get rid of him because they thought he was no use to them. Now the reason was different—

he was dangerous. But the methods, the cheap, contemptuous tricks were the same.

Bernstein continued, bland and optimistic as a travel poster, "You'll be right out there on your own. Have a chance to pick your own staff, work out some of your own ideas. I promise you," he assured, feeling around for the reason for Marshall's obvious lack of enthusiasm, "that there won't be any unnecessary interference from New York. Flack has definitely agreed——"

"Flack?"

"Yes." Bernstein smiled amiably. "He's going to take over the International."

There was a silence. Bernstein's smile became replaced by a look of concern; it was becoming apparent to him that he had lost his grip on his audience. From Marshall's mind all thought of the plans he had made before this meeting had completely disappeared. He could not even be bothered to decide whether Bernstein had offered him the Indian job seriously or merely as a way of trying to provoke him into resignation. Everything was obscured by the vision of Flack, the colorless, flat-voiced, frog-faced nonentity Flack, in charge of the International. Had he worked and suffered, cheated, threatened, betrayed—for this?

He shook his head. "No," he said.

Bernstein looked up at him sharply. "What do you mean—no?" His smile had disappeared, to be replaced by the expression of a man who has been tried almost to breaking point. His lips were tight, his eyes narrowed. He replaced the fork on his plate with a clatter. "Chris, I warn you, you can go too far. I've stood a lot from you because I understood how you felt——"

"You stood it because you had to. All you care about is your own safety and your own convenience." Why, he thought, why in God's name had Bernstein chosen Flack? Did he owe him something, for support once given at a critical time, a judicious silence when speech might have caused embarrassment? Did he like him? It hardly seemed possible. Was his very dullness attractive? There had been a note of fear in Bernstein's voice when he spoke of Kingham, a perceptible relief at the thought of getting rid of him. Kingham had grown strong in the last few years, strong enough to threaten the men who sat above him. It might be by no means a disaster to have him removed and replaced by a safe, dull, aging man who owed his advancement to Bernstein himself. . . . "You know as well as I do," said Marshall, "that Flack isn't the man."

"I disagree. In my opinion he's an excellent man. But in any case, this isn't your affair. It's for me to make the appointment——"

"Why don't you stop pretending you don't have to listen to me?" said Marshall impatiently. "I tell you Flack isn't the man."

Bernstein breathed deeply. "I suppose now," he said with heavy sarcasm, "you're going to tell me who is?"

Marshall was silent for a moment. Then, as if he were being washed forward on a tide he had no power to stem, he said, "I am."

Bernstein gave a scornful, uncertain laugh. "You're crazy," he said.

"Why?"

"You haven't the experience, for one thing——"

"I have as much experience as some bull-witted lawyer you only pulled in because you needed somebody to talk you out of a spot." Marshall could hear his own voice rising in volume. He was tired of fighting. It was necessary to finish it for good and all. "I know you want to be rid of me and I know why. But you can forget it. You're stuck with me."

"Do you think I'm going to let you dictate to me what appointments I make——"

"You're going to do it," he said. "I tell you, you're going to do it." His father had had this same habit of repeating statements to emphasize his determination. "Otherwise I'll bring you down. I may not have meant it before, but I do now. Don't think I wouldn't."

He was almost shouting now. People at nearby tables had stopped their conversation to look at him. One of the waiters was whispering to the maître d'hôtel, who was looking anxiously at Bernstein. Was the young man drunk? his eyes asked. Was it necessary to interfere? But Bernstein was unaware of him. Tired, frightened, resentful, impotent, his face pale with anxiety, wrinkled with the memory of forty years of struggling toward the light, he looked helplessly at Marshall. Marshall stood up and dropped his napkin onto his plateful of congealing, unregarded food. "Look around you," he said. With a wave of his hand he took in the smart restaurant, the scurrying waiters, the whole world of the prosperous and powerful and well fed. "Think of what you've got and what you had to do to get it. You could lose it all tomorrow—to please Flack——"

"It's nothing to do with pleasing Flack," he said weakly. "It's a matter of principle."

"You want to be a martyr to your principles?"

Bernstein squeezed his fingers together. "But I've actually spoken to Flack. I promised him——"

"Tell him you changed your mind. Tell him," said Marshall mercilessly, "that you made another mistake."

CHAPTER VI

He paid off his taxi at the hotel. The doorman helped him out of the cab; the girl at the cigarette counter smiled at him as she always did when he crossed the lobby to the elevator. Everything was as usual. Nobody looked at him with any special interest. It seemed strange to him that he should have passed through such an emotional upheaval and yet bear no signs of it on his face. He felt obscurely insulted by their lack of perception. His companions in the crowded elevator pushed against him listlessly; the operator intoned, with the flat indifference of a croupier at a gambling table, the numbers of the floors. In this city, he thought, everyone had his own worries—an ulcer, a drop in the stock market, a wife he couldn't trust . . . He passed by thousands of them every day and never noticed a thing. Why should they notice anything unusual about him?

He got out at the eighteenth floor and unlocked the door of his suite. Jane might be waiting for him—he had not been able to say when he would be returning. As soon as he opened the door he saw her. She was sitting on the sofa with her shoes off and her legs tucked beneath her, reading the paper. Discarded sections of the *Herald Tribune* lay strewn on the carpet beside her. In the middle of the room was a table with the remains of lunch.

Throwing his hat into a corner, he went to an armchair on the other side of the table and sat there for a moment in silence. Any elation he had felt following his victory over Bernstein had completely gone. All that remained was confusion and shame. It was as if in the course of some drunken escapade he had performed actions which he found impossible to explain. He had no confidence in his ability to handle this present situation. It was more, he felt, than could be reasonably expected. He needed time to think, to calm down; he needed a rest, a week at a sanatorium under sedatives. He said, "I'm glad you got something to eat."

She looked at him anxiously and walked over to him. "Darling, what's the trouble? You look terrible." At least, he thought, somebody was able to recognize it. She sat on the floor by his feet and took hold of his hand. "Darling—darling, what happened?"

"It's a mess," he said. "Everything's a mess."

"The meeting?"

He nodded.

"Did it go wrong?"

"No." He laughed shortly. "It went fine. I was terrific. I kicked them around. You should be proud of me. Everyone should be proud of me." He stopped for a moment and then said desperately, "But I don't know what I could have done. He *made* me do it. He practically forced it on me."

"Bernstein?"

"Yes." For the first time since he had entered the room he actually looked her in the face. "You saw me before I went, didn't you? I wasn't looking for trouble. I was prepared to be reasonable. I don't enjoy banging the table and threatening and pushing around old men who are scared for their skins. I never was like that, and I can't have changed so much. I'm not *such* a bastard, am I?" He demanded painfully, "Do you think I'm a bastard?"

"Of course not." She squeezed his hand. "Now please—tell me what it's all about."

"It's just that people won't leave you alone. You start off with the best of intentions, but for some reason they have to try to put something over on you, and that gets you mad and——" He stopped suddenly, trying to rearrange his thoughts. Then he said, "Bernstein's a fool—do you know that? The boss of the corporation, and he's a fool."

"What did he do?"

"He tried to play the same game as Kingham. After the meeting was over he took me out to lunch. He bought me a few drinks and told me what a wonderful guy I was and how he was so impressed by what I'd done that he'd saved a beautiful new important job for me"—he paused and then concluded with venom—"running a branch office in Calcutta."

There was a silence. She looked up at him in perplexity. Eventually she said, "Was that all?"

"All! Can't you see what he was trying to do?"

"Of course. But, in any case, you were going to resign——"

"You mean," he said, "that you can't see the difference? You mean that refusing the International and refusing the opportunity of being shunted into some garbage can in the Indian Ocean are the same thing to you?" He added hopelessly, "If that's how you see it, there's no point in going on."

"I can see the difference."

She was going to say something further, but she stopped herself. She wanted to say that the difference shouldn't matter, it was purely a matter of pride and prestige, that it had no essential importance. But this was something there was no use in explaining. To him, when the moment came, it *had* importance—and that was that. There was nothing more to be said about it. It occurred to her that this was the moment she had known must come eventually: the time when everything that mattered had been said, the point of no return.

"What did you do?" she asked.

He did not answer her directly. "What I want you to believe," he said earnestly, "is that when I told you the other night that I was going to quit, I meant it sincerely. And I meant it this morning too—right up to the point where he tried to sell me this job in India. I knew then that he'd never even considered me for the International. And so——" He hesitated.

"So you took it," she said. "Because he wouldn't offer it to you, you took it. Is that right?"

"Yes." He was relaxed now. The story was over. Whatever the result, there was nothing further he could do. "I suppose," he said vaguely, "it may be only temporary——"

"Don't fool yourself." Her voice was gentle. "You won't let it go. You wanted it all the time."

He shook his head violently. "No, you're wrong there. I never wanted it."

"You wanted to win."

"So did you."

"Yes, I won't deny it." She spoke with resignation. "It seems that once you start, you have to take it all the way."

As soon as she had said it, it surprised her that she had not realized this before. They were at the natural end-point of a process which she had herself initiated. She had said to him at the beginning that anything was better than to live out his life in futility and defeat. She had not expected or hoped for this result, but she knew now that it was the only result possible. Her reservations had been unreal, a childish desire to eat her cake and have it at the same time. She had driven him to action. She must accept what action had made of him. Love, if it meant anything, was a surrender without conditions.

She looked at him and saw on his face a bewilderment close to despair. It was as if he was not aware of what had happened to him. He said: "Are you going to leave me?"

It was important that he too should have no reservations. She said seriously: "You really want me to stay?"

"You know I do." Eagerly he went on: "We could be happy together. I'm sure of it. After all, we have so much——" Perhaps, she thought, we have too much—we should be so much safer with less. But safety was too much to ask for. He went on: "You might not like it over here as well as England just at first, but——"

"Places aren't important."

"You'd soon settle down, I'm sure. And I'll do everything I can." He paused and then said unhappily: "I know that what I did today must have been a shock to you. But now it's all over, I promise——"

"Please don't promise," she said. "Don't promise anything." When you took a man, you took him as he was, not as he hoped to be. It was not possible to guarantee the future. His sense of bewilderment would pass—and what then? Would he regard the events of today as a victory—or as a defeat? How much would he understand, for how long would he remember? In the act of conquering, he had gone down before his enemies, Kingham, Bernstein, the Old Man—it was their world he had accepted. And now that he had accepted it, he was bound by its rules. With Kingham disposed of, the path was clear in front of him. Jeff was a nonentity, Bernstein was growing old. She realized now that it had always been inevitable. He had not wanted it consciously any more than she had, but in the last instance what either of them wanted was of little consequence. You could not get out while you were ahead of the game, because the game never finished. Each move led to another; there was no point at which you could relax without sacrificing what you had already gained. Men, like nations, acquired power almost accidentally, to fill a vacuum, to establish order and justice, to protect their interests. Afterward they felt a little ashamed and tried to justify themselves. With their hands on their hearts they protested that power was not of their seeking, it meant nothing to them personally but worry and overwork, that only a sense of responsibility prevented them from handing over to others at the earliest possible opportunity. . . . Nobody believed them. They did not even know whether to believe themselves. Lonely, envied, hated, they were fortunate to find a person here or there, a friend, a wife, a mistress, to understand their isolation and comfort them against the measureless hostility of the world.

She took him gently by the hand. She would not leave him now.